Love, Pucks, and Other Stories

Rush Hockey #4

Elise Faber

LOVE, PUCKS, AND OTHER STORIES
BY ELISE FABER

Newsletter sign-up

LOVE, PUCKS, AND OTHER STORIES
Copyright © 2023 Elise Faber
Print ISBN-13: 978-1-63749-091-4
Ebook ISBN-13:978-1-63749-090-7

Rush Hockey

Big Puck Energy
Filthy Puckboy
So Pucking Over It
Love, Pucks, and Other Stories
All's Fair in Pucks and War

PROLOGUE

BILLIE ROSE

My town was in ashes.

Monroe's Bar, with its wide green columns and huge plate glass windows and old wooden bar sticky from years of use, had been reduced to a skeleton. All that remained was the foundation, the footprint of a place that I'd grown up walking by.

Skipping along the sidewalk that ran in front of it.

Skipping along the sidewalk that ran the full length of Main Street.

Skipping along all the places that were familiar and safe and *mine*. This was my happiness, my childhood, my *life*.

Then I'd grown up.

And I'd made memories *inside* of Monroe's.

Laughter filling my ears as I leaned against that sticky wooden bar top.

My first taste of beer—and thinking it was disgusting but drinking it anyway because my dad had wanted to share it with me on my twenty-first. And yeah, I lived in a small town and there wasn't much to do except play hockey and watch hockey and drink and get high and make out on the Ridge—but my dad had talked about sharing a beer with me at Monroe's from the time I'd become familiar with what a beer was.

I hadn't wanted to take that away from him.

Not when I wasn't what he wanted.

Not when I could never be what he wanted.

Billy.

My older brother.

Who'd died before he was two years old. So young and yet still a tiny human I felt like I knew because the memories he'd left behind were vast.

How he'd giggled when my dad blew raspberries on his belly. How he hadn't slept more than two hours at a time for the first six months and then one night he'd gone to bed and slept for a full ten, freaking out my parents when they, too, had woken after finally getting a full night's sleep after all those months. How Billy had always kicked off one sock—just one—and how it was always the right sock.

How, just after he'd turned one, he'd had a seizure—intense, long, and frightening.

And then how he'd had more.

So many more.

That the doctors hadn't been able to find the cure for or the cause of, and then, one day...

He hadn't woken up.

I'd been in utero then, my mom nearly seven months along. Initially, I'd been a joyous surprise. A sibling for Billy. A surprise addition to the large family they'd always wanted.

Then I'd become a burden—a parasite that made her sick and tired when she needed to care for Billy or go to his appointments. Something that had taken attention and focus away from her son, who she'd known wouldn't be on Earth much longer.

Something that had then become been a painful reminder of all she'd lost.

Then I'd been born...

My parents loved me—I had no doubt about that.

But they were also sad I was there, and Billy wasn't. I had no doubt about that either.

So...I'd saved the beer for Monroe's and my dad, giving him the memory he craved, even if it wasn't with the child he'd wanted it to be, with the *son* he'd wanted it to be with.

And it was fucking *awful*.

The beer (and maybe also the bittersweet knowledge I held in my heart that I wasn't what he wanted).

I'd still choked it down anyway, had smiled and told my dad that I loved it, loved spending that time with him. Just like I still choked them down when we met up weekly for a cold draft, listening silently as he rattled off all the things I needed to do.

Because—like I said—I knew I was loved, and I loved them just as much.

I just wasn't...

Enough.

"No," I whispered. "Billie. *Enough.*"

Of the thoughts, of the memories, of the fact that I was staring at a place that had been a hefty chunk of the backbone of River's Bend, and it was just...gone.

Turned to ash by a fire that had torn through my town.

Same as Haggarty's, the other bar on the opposite end of downtown. Another chunk of that backbone. And Sip and Purl —the wine bar-slash-yarn-and-fabric-store where I'd taken knitting classes. Just a mayor supporting her town's small business even though I'd hated every moment of those lessons.

Clearly, I wasn't cut out for knitting.

Not unless it was to use the needles to stab someone.

Say a certain annoying hockey player who lived to annoy me.

That thought—stabby, stabby—brought a smile to my face

even though smoke was still in the air, and heat seemed to resonate off the wood and charred buildings. But it faded just as quickly as the thought did.

Because even the roads had been scorched.

The *roads*.

Which meant that—*fuck*—rebuilding would be...

The biggest project I'd ever undertaken.

The *worst* project I'd ever undertaken.

So, yeah, there wasn't much to smile about.

I just kept moving, seeing—but not really allowing myself to fully process—that Wag's Pet Store was gone.

I'd just bought my niece's puppy, Spock, a pretty collar from there. Taking way too long to make my selection from the racks and racks of collars. Bailey, my niece—but more like best friend since she was only two years younger than me—had loved it.

Niece. Best friend. Only two years younger.

How all of that went together was a long story—*really* long —but the important thing was that we were close.

Close enough that Wag's had been added onto my regular rotation—and not just because of the pretty collars, but also because they'd baked and decorated beautiful cookies for dogs.

And now, all that remained of Wag's was concrete and spikes of rebar.

A sharp bolt of pain ricocheted through my insides.

Right.

Enough.

I needed to go.

To find somewhere to breathe and process and—

My eyes stung. The world went blurry.

"Not the time, Donovan," I whispered, fully aware I was talking about myself in the third person. But better that than breaking down, than allowing the sobs that clung to my lungs, that squeezed the air out of me with each and every glimpse of the damage, to escape.

I *had* to stay strong.

I *had* to be what the town needed.

Even if the Civic Center, with its historic buildings and where I'd spent the last six years working my ass off for the town, was gone.

Even if the grocery store—not a chain one, but a small supermarket that had been owned by the Brown family since the Gold Rush days—was gone.

Even if all the restaurants—the diner, the pizza place, the Greek gyro stand that had just been opened by a young couple who'd recently moved to town, Luna's Italian Eatery, the deli, and the Chinese restaurant—were gone.

My history.

My work.

My *life.*

Gone.

Which was why the sobs I'd been holding in for the last days —ever since Bailey had called and activated the phone tree, reporting the fire—had to stay held. Why I'd used every bit of my focus to make sure each and every resident—human, furry, feathered, or otherwise—got out safely.

It hadn't been enough.

I'd failed.

People had died.

And for two hellish days, I'd thought my niece, Bailey, had died with them.

Bailey, who'd been through a lot. Too much—and not just having to outrun a fire on horseback with a dog and steer in tow.

She'd survived. Then *and* now. Survived too *fucking* much.

And...I hadn't been what she needed either.

One of the damned sobs choking me escaped, making a wretched, awful sound that revealed too much. Sucking in a breath, trying to shove them down, lock the emotions away, I dropped my gaze to my feet, hurrying down the charred wooden boardwalk. I needed to find somewhere that wasn't burned, wasn't ash, wasn't *destroyed*.

But the fire clung to the air, to my lungs, my hair. There was soot on my cheeks, making it hard to breathe, and the world looked alien, dystopian, *wrecked*.

And eerily quiet.

My busy, happy town was gone.

Gone.

Tears blurred my vision, choked me, threatened to escape the cage of my lashes.

Fuck.

"Fuck."

Because I knew there was no holding in the sobs. They were too big, too overwhelming, too—

I needed to get in my car.

I needed to get away.

I needed a few moments to just...cry with no one seeing. Needed time to—

"*Oof!*"

Warm hands came to my shoulders, steadied me as I bounced off a big, strong chest (a big, strong chest that was part of a big, strong body...that was, incidentally, part of a big, strong man).

A man I recognized even through the blurred, watery lenses of my tears.

Because he was a man I *hated*.

Joel Marshall.

Sexy, smart, funny, kind...to everyone but me.

To *me,* he was an asshole.

I heard it then—that assholeness—in the lazy drawl of his voice. Felt it in the way he quickly set me away from him, as though he couldn't stand to be within five feet of me, as though I was so disgusting that my body touching his was enough to send him running for the toilet.

"Slow down there, harpy." A caustic order that sliced as deeply as the disgust.

Because...yup. *Harpy.*

That was me.

The unwanted daughter.

The annoying, bitchy woman who filled men with disgust.

The *harpy* who—

All at once, the last of my control of those sobs splintered.

They erupted out of me, tears pouring down my cheeks, my breath hitching, my body bending in half as I shattered into pieces and completely lost it.

In front of the man I hated.

ONE

JOEL

Warm, sexy woman pressed against me.

My arms tightened, drawing her closer, feeling her ass brush my cock. My naked cock. And, hell yeah, *all* of me was naked.

Happy place.

As in *my* happy place.

And my favorite way to wake up, even if my mind was still foggy from sleep and it was still dark outside, the faint gleam of dawn barely penetrating the windows.

Penetrating.

Yeah, *that* was my happy place too.

Lips curving, I buried my face in her hair, thrusting my hips forward, hoping the movement would wake her. Her breathing was even, slow and steady despite the gentle rocking of her pelvis that rubbed her ass against my dick. As though she wanted more, even while she was sleeping.

Well, I'd be happy to give it to her.

A morning fuck? Okay, *that* was my happy place.

Slick, hot pussy.

Warm, lush curves.

Soft, silken skin.

Woman.

Her cries of pleasure in my ears, her pussy convulsing around my dick, starting my day with an orgasm that cleared away the dredges of sleep and—

"Mmm," she moaned softly, her body arching against mine as I ran my palm over her stomach, sliding it down and then up, testing, discovering.

She was naked too.

Yes. *Yes.*

Up.

Up first.

I ran my hand along her side, up to cup a breast that over-filled my palm, immediately feeling her nipple bead against my skin.

Her breath hitched, body startling.

"You with me, love?" I murmured.

"Mmm," she moaned again, my fingers pinching lightly, rolling deliberately, but not giving me the words I needed.

It might be the butt crack of dawn, a hangover clinging to my mind, making my head hurt and my brain not want to function, but I wasn't so lost as to not need the words.

"That's not telling me you're with me, love," I said.

Her body stilled.

I plucked at her nipple. "You awake, baby?"

A shudder, her hips jerking, ass pressing, but quiet words that cleared a bit more of the fog in my mind. "I'm with you."

Thank fuck.

I flipped her to her back, slammed my mouth down on hers.

Fuck morning breath. I needed to kiss this woman, to feel her mouth on mine, to know if it matched the ass pressed against me. Then I needed to kiss her other places, make sure I tasted every inch of the silky skin covering her curves since I couldn't see them in the dark room.

That was something I had a vague recollection of doing the night before, recollections that were blunted, if the throb in my head and the taste in the back of my mouth were indicators, by copious amounts of tequila.

Not an issue.

I'd remedy that by kissing every inch of her again.

Immediately.

Her tongue tangled with mine, her moans drifted in my throat, her legs parting, wrapping around my hips, cradling my body in the apex of her thighs.

Fuck.

That was good.

That sent any memories skittering, my mind focusing on the then and there, on the woman beneath me in my bed.

The dark meant I couldn't see much of her, just the faint glow of her hair, turned silver in the dim light, a glimpse of pale, naked skin, of breasts and curves and—

Her arms curled around me when I bent, trailed my tongue along her throat, tasting her skin, all sweet and tart and *woman*, making it so that I didn't have a chance to take in more than that glimpse of her, of those curves and pale skin, her light hair before her fingers were weaving into *my* hair, drawing me closer, wrapping her legs around me, brushing that wet pussy against my cock.

Hot.

Slick.

Fuck, I didn't want to lose that.

She was small, almost tiny, and when she was pressed against me like this, that wet pussy, the soft curves, my mouth on her skin, I didn't want to move. I wanted to keep tasting her, keep feeling her. I just...

Wanted to taste all the other parts of her too.

Fucking decisions, man.

Her fingers tensed in my hair, a slight downward draw that told me enough.

Told me she wanted my mouth on other parts of her body as well.

Told me she wanted me to get to work.

I grinned, nipped at her throat.

Luckily, this was my favorite type of work. Aside from hockey, that was.

So...I got to work. Trailing my tongue along her throat, losing her pussy for the greater good as I slid down, her legs falling away as my body shifted, as I dropped my head and sucked one of her nipples deep.

Her breath caught, a moan tumbling from her lips, fingers tightening, body rocking.

Turned on. A lot.

With very little.

Then again, I was the same.

My dick was throbbing, demanding I slide through the slick folds of her pussy, thrust inside and do it deep and hard and *repeatedly*.

But I needed to taste her first.

So, I suckled at her breast, drew on her nipple, kept at it when those fingers tightened in my hair, and then gave her other breast the same treatment, loving the soft sounds that slid up and out of her throat, the way her body moved beneath mine.

She reached between us, fingertips just brushing the top of his cock.

Right.

Enough.

I released her breast, moved down with deliberation, tasting my way across her ribcage, her stomach, gripping one thigh and then the other, spreading them wider.

I wanted to look my fill, to see plump pink lips, glistening folds, a pussy that was calling for my mouth, my cock.

But it was dark.

So, I had to get my feel by touch.

Hot and slick when my hands drifted up, fingers brushing the edge of her cunt. She was wet. She was *dripping*.

And I'd hardly even touched her yet.

That morning, anyway. Flashes of blond curls and curves for days, of naked skin slick with sweat as I pushed home, of pale pink lips and a smattering of freckles on a dainty nose I'd kissed as we both tried to catch our breath. The images pinged through my mind, there and gone in an instant, a swirling mess of color and memories from the night before that left me with a feeling of disquiet...and satisfaction in a way I'd never had before.

I tried to grab on to them.

Because disquiet was...concerning.

But then she shifted, her hips bucking, a needy, desperate sound filling the air, and the disquiet disappeared.

I'd already spread her thighs, positioned my body between them, so that movement of her hips meant her pussy came against my mouth, brushing against my lips, giving me a taste that meant I had no hope of thinking, of processing, or trying to hone those memories into focus. My body was reacting to that taste, to the scent of her—floral and sweet and tart.

I slid my tongue into her swollen pussy.

And I ate her.

Not thinking.

Not processing.

Just listening to her body, to the soft hitches of her breathing and the moans that came in increasing frequency. Listening to how she touched me, her fingers coming back to my hair, gripping tighter, holding me to her.

Nearly bursting out of her skin when I sucked on her clit.

Yeah.

That was what I was talking about.

I kept sucking as I slid a finger inside, feeling her pussy ripple, hearing the way her moans changed, feeling the sweat beginning to bead on her skin, and knowing she was close.

I'd made her come before.

Enough times that we'd fallen asleep exhausted only hours before.

So, I knew she just needed—

I ran a finger through that dripping pussy, used the slickness of her desire to ease the way as I found the taut rosebud between her ass cheeks, pressed in, and felt her come apart around me.

"Joel!"

Her body was still shaking, her pussy still clenching around my finger, but my name on her tongue had that disquiet roaring to the forefront of my mind.

Turning to dread.

Please, God, *no.*

I slid my fingers free, reached up, and turned on the light.

"Fuck," I whispered as it fully illuminated the woman in my bed.

The pussy I'd just been inside of was...

Billie Rose's.

Two

BILLIE ROSE

I'd thought he'd known it was me.

Last night, we'd...

Well, every moment from the night before was emblazoned in my mind, even after the bottle of tequila.

I knew I wouldn't ever forget the way he'd held me as I'd cried, his gentle touch as he'd bundled me into his car. I wouldn't forget how he'd taken me to the apartment he was staying in, since his house was one of the ones lost, and how he'd shepherded me in through his front door.

All while I'd been losing my shit.

But even as I'd begun to get it together, embarrassment heavy in every cell that *he'd* seen me that way, that he'd witnessed me break down, he'd been...

Nice.

Kind.

Treated me like he treated everyone else.

And then he'd brought out the tequila...

I bit the inside of my cheek, hard enough to taste blood.

When I'd woken up to him curled around me, that big body holding me, touching me, *kissing* me, I'd thought he'd remembered, knew who he was in bed with.

Would remember.

Thought that maybe he wouldn't come to regret fucking me.

His expression told me otherwise.

He was already regretting this and I was still in his goddamned bed.

Humiliation crawled over every inch of my body, choking me, heating my skin in a way that *killed*.

I wanted to die.

Just have the floor open up and drop me down into the seventh circle of hell.

"Harpy?" he asked, disbelief and remorse on his face, in his eyes, lacing his tone, in every tense inch of the body I'd spent hours exploring.

Memorizing him. Committing each moment of our time together to memory.

Because it had been so good, so unexpected. Because...I knew it wouldn't last.

And, God, why did it sting so much that I wasn't *honey* or *baby* or *love* any longer?

Instead, I was *harpy*.

The annoying, aggravating woman who wasn't wanted.

The *harpy* who made Joel's life a living hell.

I'd been living in a dream since last night. For a couple of hours, I'd been a woman this sexy, smart, kind man wanted. I'd been the woman *Joel* wanted. I'd been *baby* and *honey* and *love* and a woman who'd made him go soft, who'd made him hold me gently and fill my ears with sweet words.

That was gone. I saw it in the hard already inching into his expression, in his hands dropping to my hips and clenching.

Firmly.

Not gentle. Not soft.

Just...*harpy*.

Pain rippled through me, making my cheeks burn, my eyes sting, the sobs beginning to clog up my chest again.

I'd had a couple of hours.

That was typical.

Because then it always came down to *this*—I waved a mental hand at the disbelief on his face. I knew from experience that soon enough the disbelief would become disgust.

So, I did what I could.

I grabbed tight to my spine and yanked it firmly in place.

Protect your flank, Billie girl.

Words Gran had told me more than once, usually over spoonfuls of cookie dough while I told her about my troubles.

I'd become an expert at that even before I'd been on the receiving end of that advice, a fucking *professional* at it.

Because my dad was my dad.

Because men were men.

So...I put those skills to work. Then *and* now.

"Thanks for the orgasm," I said lightly, brushing my hair out of my face and spying a hair tie on my wrist.

Perfect.

I swept my locks up, letting my gaze go unfocused, wanting to avoid his eyes, his face. Something I failed at because he startled when I spoke and I instinctively looked back at him, and, yup, *there* was the disgust.

My lungs squeezed.

Tight.

Fuck.

But I held on to my spine and stayed calm and steady, forcing my tone to remain light as I made an offer I knew he wouldn't take me up on, but one that would save me from this *feeling*. Lips turning up, I jerked my head down toward his waist. "Need one in return before I get the hell out of here?"

He recoiled, lips pressing flat, nose wrinkling.

Ouch.

I mean, I'd known what the answer was going to be, but...the truth always stung.

"Right then," I said, my lungs convulsing. I shoved him back, not missing the fact that he didn't hesitate to put distance between us, even though he outweighed me by at least a hundred pounds. I couldn't move him on my own.

Not unless he *wanted* to be moved.

Another feeling to bury.

Another night to forget.

I used the brief window of time of me crawling out of Joel's bed to spot my clothes. Shirt in the corner of the room, jeans crumpled on the floor right next to the mattress, socks and shoes scattered nearby, my bra a few feet away.

No underwear, but I'd worry about that in a minute.

First, I grabbed my shirt and yanked it over my head. Then, not spotting my underwear in the five seconds I allowed myself to look for it, I yanked my jeans up over my bare ass, went to work on my socks and shoes.

Thirty seconds later I was dressed.

I didn't have my car.

Fuck.

"Harp—"

I flinched, and *God,* I hated that I flinched. Hated what that revealed.

"You gotta get dressed, Lothario," I said lightly. "I need a ride home."

He pushed off the mattress and his face did something I couldn't read, flickered with emotions I couldn't distinguish. "What are you doing, harpy?"

In that moment?

Dying a slow death as panic and hurt stabbed repeatedly at my insides?

That wasn't the answer I was going to give him.

Protect your flank.

Yeah, I was working on that, Gran.

I bent, fixed my shoelace, mostly so I could avoid looking at him. "That"—I waved a hand at the bed, at the mussed covers—"happened. It was...an *experience.*" More pieces of spine being tugged in place, held together with Scotch tape and pipe cleaners. "But now I need to get back to work."

"Harpy—"

This time I was shored up enough to prevent the flinch.

"No worries, Joel," I interrupted. "We had a night. It was fun. But it's done now." I shrugged. "So, what I really need is a ride."

His brows came up. "It's done?"

Abso-fucking-lutely.

"Yup." I lifted and dropped my shoulders, affecting casual, even as it was killing me slowly inside. "Now I need that ride."

"A ride," he muttered, tossing the sheets back, revealing...

Good God.

Revealing too much.

I'd kissed and licked *all* of that and it had been glorious and—

Fuck.

"A ride?" he asked again, in a tone I didn't get.

He almost sounded pissed, but then again, I was asking for a ride at the butt crack of dawn, and he'd woken thinking he was going to get an orgasm from a woman he liked.

And instead, he'd gotten me.

"Yup," I said again, retying the other shoe, just for good measure.

"A *ride?*"

Fuck it, I'd walk.

"Never mind. I've got it covered." I brushed by him and hauled ass into the hall. I had a vague recollection of leaving my purse in the kitchen. I'd start walking, then call in a favor for a ride. God knew that one of the good things about living and breathing for River's Bend meant I knew pretty much everyone in town, in the surrounding towns, and in the surrounding, *surrounding* towns.

I was good at my job.

I made it a point to know everything I could.

Which was why I knew the fire hadn't torn through Grizzly Valley. The winds had turned, and the firefighters had enough time to get a line up to protect the town. The best part? Grizzly Valley was relatively close to River's Bend. Close enough that they were housing a large portion of our evacuees—including the Rush Hockey players in this recently completed block of apartments.

And in the gymnasium at the local middle school.

That was more of a temporary holding facility for those with pets until they found accommodations that allowed animals, or for those who didn't want to be placed somewhere, hoping they would pop back home like the fire hadn't happened, *or* for those who just needed a place to wait until relatives came up to get them.

But all that being said, the gym wasn't far.

I could walk there, get a ride home myself.

Done.

Easy.

Protect your flank.

Exactly.

"Harpy," Joel said, snagging my arm as I wrapped my fingers around the strap of my purse, the one that *was* in the kitchen.

I tugged free of his hand, ignoring the fact that he was still naked, ignoring the fact that I was still *wanting*, and slung it over my opposite shoulder so that the strap laid diagonally across my chest. A breath, steeling myself. Then I spied my jacket on the couch.

Good.

I'd need that too.

I used that as an excuse to put more distance between us and scooped it up, intending to execute the whole purse-for-jacket swap when I got the fuck out of here.

Already my mind was snapping into focus, the pieces of armor and spine locking into place. I needed to implement my exit, and I needed to do it in a way that wouldn't reveal I was bleeding all over my insides.

"Billie Rose."

I froze.

Because, *God*, that might have been the first time he'd ever said my name.

And it devastated me.

Clink. Clink. Clink.

More rapid armor gathering, more frantic protecting.

I needed an exit.

And, fortunately, the universe gave me one.

Joel's phone rang from the bedroom.

"You should get that," I said when he didn't immediately move.

"No." He stepped closer, and his expression was one that I couldn't read. "We need to talk—"

Okay. Right. Time to go.

No talking.

No prolonging this.

I understood *exactly* what was happening here.

The call cut off, then immediately started up again. "You really should get that."

He ignored me, stepped even closer, having to stoop a great deal to meet my eyes. I wished he hadn't bent, hadn't met my gaze. I could live another ten lifetimes without having to see that. "This shouldn't have happened," he said, the words soft, but no less eviscerating.

My armor rattled, threatened to fall to the floor under the force of that blow.

I held tight to it, anyway.

"What shouldn't have happened?" I asked dryly, watching his brows slam down, his eyes close off. "You fucking me? Or me fucking you?" A careless shrug. "Can't go back and erase it." I flashed a grin. "But it was decent and got my mind off the stress of the fire for a little while, so that's a thing. Now, I've got shit to do—" I turned to the door, reached for the knob.

His hand came to my forearm, squeezing just tightly enough that I remembered him holding me in bed, fiercely powerful, his strength barely banked as he'd fucked me hard and deep, seemingly a hairsbreadth away from losing the last vestiges of his control.

It had been exhilarating, all that intensity.

But...it wasn't for me.

I'd just thought that, for a minute, it could be.

His cell began ringing a third time.

"That sounds important," I said, nodding toward the hall, toward the ringing phone and doing it by leaning into a tactic that was sure to get him to back off, "but then again, you'll probably keep ignoring it."

His eyes narrowed.

"Because you're good at hockey"—I shrugged again—"but we both know you're better at ignoring your responsibilities."

Fury in those eyes.

"God," he muttered, dropping his hand. "I can't believe I was inside *that*."

Another blow to my armor, but as I'd prepared for it, my armor stayed in place.

"Buh-bye now," I said snarkily, giving him a finger wave.

Then I wrenched the knob.

And got the fuck out.

THREE

JOEL

"I'm sorry," Bailey whispered, not moving, probably because Axel, one of my best friends and former teammates, was sleeping next to her.

He looked like he'd had all of five minutes of rest in the last two months.

Dark circles beneath dark circles, pale ass skin—pallid even for a hockey player. Stubble on his face, hair a mess, clothes wrinkled. But he was asleep next to the woman he loved, the one who'd he'd thought was lost and spent the last days searching for.

They'd *all* spent the last days looking for Bailey.

Lost as the fire had come for the town, her warning enough that most of the River's Bend had been evacuated safely.

Except for the ranches on the far side of town.

Where Bailey had lived.

And now, where none of her neighbors did.

River's Bend had been destroyed, but the only fatalities had been from the stretch of ranches on the far side of town.

Bailey's neighbors.

So...hope hadn't been high.

But, somehow, she'd survived, and she was banged up—ribs, leg, lungs, and various scrapes, bumps, bruises, and burns.

But she was *alive.*

"I didn't want to panic you," she continued whispering, "but he's"—a nod to her man, holding her gently around her middle like the precious object she was—"barely closed his eyes since they'd found me, and I need to make sure he goes."

I knew Bailey had been found—Axel had called me and I'd let the rest of the guys looking for her know.

But I also knew because of Billie Rose—she'd told me as much in between her bouts of tears.

Tears that were fresh in my mind.

Mostly because they'd come before the tequila-hazed memories.

When I held her and her pain over the town being destroyed and losing those ranchers had collided with relief that Bailey was alive and whole and—

And she'd lost it.

In my arms.

Fuck.

"It's okay," I said, focusing on Bailey and not the mess I'd made with the mayor. I moved close, gently ran my thumb over Bailey's cheek. She wasn't mine, but she'd grown on me. Smart, sassy, tough, she'd been through more than her fair share, but she'd come out with a big heart and a quick smile.

She was perfect for Axel.

"I called four times," she whispered. "That was overkill."

I had to admit that when I'd seen Axel's name on the screen as those missed calls, I'd been fucking worried, especially knowing that Bailey had been in the hospital recovering from everything.

And the blow about responsibilities that Billie had laid on me before she'd left had struck again.

Only harder.

Because my friend's woman was in the hospital and Axel had called four times.

But then I'd called back, and Bailey had picked up.

She was okay. She needed my help.

She—

Was biting her lip and looking uncertain.

"It's fine," I assured her. "I was worried about you, but you're good and so, it's all good."

She didn't release that lip, not for a long moment. "And do you...agree with me?"

Agree with her conspiring with the doctors to be released early from the hospital so that Axel could play in game seven of the Stanley Cup Finals? Fuck no. If Bailey was my woman and I'd come as close to losing her as Axel had, I'd want her in the hospital for a few extra days, just for good measure. But, at the same time, Axel was my friend, and he'd worked his ass off to make it in the NHL, to make it to the playoffs, to even *be* in a position to play in a game where winning it meant he'd get to heft the Cup.

That, alone, was *huge*.

That shit didn't come often, even for the best of the best pro players.

I got why she didn't want Axel to miss it.

"He's not going to be happy about it," I told her something she probably already knew.

"Yeah," she whispered, "but I need him to do this. I need him to not look back and have regrets."

I got that.

Which was why I was about to agree to talk my friend off the ledge he'd be perched on in a few minutes. He was absolutely going to lose his shit because his woman with bruised ribs and a broken leg and burns and cuts and scrapes wanted to drive four hours with all that and watch her man play in a fucking *hockey* game.

I rubbed my forehead, sighed.

Fucking hell.

It wasn't even up for discussion.

I was going to do it.

"You break the news," I murmured. "I've got your back and I'll make sure the other guys do too." Because she'd confessed to having called in other reinforcements as well.

See? Bailey was smart.

"You're the best, honey," she whispered, reaching for my hand. "You've had my back more times than I can count, and I don't know how I'll thank—"

"Shh," I whispered, squeezing her fingers gently. "It's nothing."

And it wasn't.

It was for my friends.

For Axel.

For *her*.

Yeah, I'd have their backs.

But also, much like Billie had laid out a few hours before, I had some making up to do. I'd been on the wrong track and Axel had helped steer me right, helped me get my head together. Not to mention, if it was one of *my* sisters who'd gone through the shit Bailey had, I'd want someone steady and stable there for her.

So, really, it was nothing.

I'd watched out for her when Axel was out of town with the Gold. I'd answered a phone call. And now I'd make sure my friend held it together, so he wasn't eighty and gray, that pretty face of his lined with wrinkles, and looking back with regrets.

"It's all good," I said, squeezing her hand again. "I promise."

"Stop touching my woman," Axel rumbled.

I glanced over Bailey's shoulder, saw that his eyes were

open—and bloodshot—the little bit of sleep he'd gotten clearly not enough to erase the exhaustion weighing him down.

How he'd play in a pro game, I had no idea.

But I agreed that he needed to have the chance.

So, when I saw movement in the doorway, saw Ryan and a few of the other guys walking in, I knew it was time for Bailey to press her hand.

I glanced back at her, held those soulful brown eyes, and asked, "You ready to lay it on him, sweetheart?"

A determined nod. "Will you get the doctor? She knows, too."

Axel frowned, rubbed a hand over his face. "What are you two talking about?"

"Joel?" There went that lip again, pressed between Bailey's teeth.

"No problem, sweetheart." I touched her cheek again, whispered, "You got this."

Axel sat up, sleep disappearing from his eyes as they instead grew concerned. "What the fuck, buttercup?"

I stepped away, headed for the door to flag down the doctor before Axel could growl at me for touching his woman again.

When I got there, Ryan lifted his brows in question.

"Get ready for it," I muttered, popping my head out into the hall and meeting the doctor's eyes.

As though she'd been waiting for the signal—and she probably *had* been considering all the machinations Bailey had put in place—the doctor immediately headed for the room.

"For what?" Ryan asked.

Bailey answered for me. "I'm going to that game, honey."

And then—no surprise—Axel lost his shit.

And kept losing it when the doctor gave her approval and the guys, including me, had Bailey's back.

And kept losing it even as I moved close and tried (and

failed) to talk him down from the edge, as Bailey held firm and the doctor left to fill in discharge paperwork.

He kept losing it until Billie Rose walked into the room, still in the clothes from the night before, only this time they were even more wrinkled and dirty and she had soot on her cheeks and in her hair, as though she'd been combing through a building's remains looking for a priceless family artifact—

Hell, knowing her, she probably *had* been.

Probably found it, too.

Billie Rose didn't let her appearance faze her. Then again *nothing* fazed her, not waking up naked with a man she hated, not her niece surviving a harrowing experience and calling her in for backup, not her town burning down.

She was still as calm and collected as ever.

"Why's big, hot, and hockey glowering?" she asked the room at large.

"I'm being discharged," Bailey told her.

A smile. "That's a good thing."

"She thinks she's going to Game Seven tonight," Axel gritted out.

Billie's gaze swung toward Axel's, holding it. Then she glanced back at Bailey, and they seemed to have a silent conversation as I came to realize that I'd seen at least one moment when Billie Rose had been fazed.

Last night.

In my arms, crying and letting it out, showing a vulnerable side I'd never expected. Then under the tequila we'd both begun drinking, a wild side.

Because now I was fully awake.

Had been for hours.

Those tequila-hazed memories had shifted, grown more in focus.

I remembered the buzz of the alcohol. The way it had flushed her cheeks and softened her eyes.

For a moment there, I'd liked her, and she'd liked me.

I'd kissed her, or maybe she'd kissed me, or maybe we'd just kissed each other.

Which had led to other things.

Lots of other things that had been...

Incredible.

With *Billie Rose.*

With the fucking *harpy.*

Fuck.

Billie Rose, with wrinkled clothes and soot and tired eyes, finished that silent conversation with Bailey, strode purposefully to her niece's bedside, then lifted her brows and turned her gaze to Axel's.

"So, are you taking her? Or am I?"

Rage on Axel's face.

A muscle twitching in his cheek.

But it was Billie Rose speaking, and she had a fucking magical ability to get what she wanted—even if what she wanted was for big, stubborn hockey players to give in about something as important as their woman's safety.

Because after a long, angry silence, Axel snapped out, "*I'm fucking taking her.*"

And it was after that acquiescence that I looked at Billie Rose.

Really looked at her.

For the first time ever.

FOUR

BILLIE ROSE

I took a small sip of my beer, resisted the urge to gag, and kept my focus on the game playing in the background, projected on the white wall by a borrowed laptop.

I was back in the gymnasium, though this time I'd driven instead of walked.

Luckily, no one had questioned my need for a ride early that morning. Mostly because I'd faked it until I made it, not giving excuses or explaining myself. Just securing that ride. And seriously, feigning confidence was a useful skill to have in my repertoire—something I'd learned more than once over the years.

Being the youngest mayor in River's Bend's history had once been a terrifying prospect, but I'd learned I could handle it... mostly by pretending I knew what I was doing.

So, fucking a man who'd blown my mind and then walking out of his apartment while my proverbial internal wounds left a heavy blood trail behind me? No problem.

I was good at pretending I was fine.

At pretending like those hurts—big or small, deep or superficial—were no big deal. I'd learned that eventually my heart and mind would get on board with the program.

That was something I employed that evening—watching a game that had fear coiling through my insides (because the last time I'd been watching a hockey game, had watched the *Gold* play, a fire had roared in and destroyed my town). No worries *that* evening, though. All was good. I'd sit with my beer, cheer at all the right moments, smile and laugh and bury that fear.

My people needed it.

Everyone around me hissed out a breath as one of our guys —that being a player from the San Francisco Gold—was crushed against the boards.

I couldn't see his number, but I thought his name was Coop. I watched as he bounced off the glass and collapsed to the ice, hard enough that I found myself hissing too.

Not that it seemed to slow him down.

A second later, he was back on his skates, gloved hand adjusting his helmet, and then was off, hauling ass back into his end of the ice.

"They'll get it."

I jerked, nearly spilling my beer all over my lap as Joel sank down next to me onto the cot I was using as a chair. "What?" I asked dumbly.

"They'll get it," he said again, tipping his beer in the direction of the game. "They're good, mostly healthy, and Bailey's there—so they're extra motivated."

"Oh," I whispered, picking at the edge of the label on my bottle. "It'd be good if they did. Otherwise, Bailey will always feel guilty."

A shrug. "No reason to."

I snorted, rolled my eyes. "Feelings don't follow reason."

He lifted his own beer up to his lips. "That's true enough, harpy."

And thus ended the most civil conversation I had ever had with Joel.

Back to *harpy*.

Luckily, I was armored up, and I'd braced from the moment I'd heard his voice. No flinching this time, especially not under the bright lights inside the gym.

"Still," he said after a moment, and I glanced over at him again, saw his gaze was still glued to the game projected on the wall. "They'll get it."

Right.

I hoped so.

I really did.

But...feelings didn't follow reason.

So, I deliberately ignored the line of his jaw—strong and sharp and covered with a beard that had raised gooseflesh on my skin as he'd kissed his way down my torso. I deliberately ignored the way my middle clenched with the memory of him, ignored my pussy getting wet, my fingers itching to stroke that hair-covered jaw.

I ignored all that and just watched the game, picking at the label on my beer until no adhesive remained on the brown glass.

"Gonna drink that?"

I blinked, realized the game had gone to commercial without really processing anything further except that it was still tied and likely heading into overtime.

"What?" I blurted.

"You gonna drink your beer?" Joel asked. "Or are you just going to pick at the label and let it go to waste?"

My nape prickled.

First of all, I hated beer. *Still* hated it, even after all the beers I'd drank at Monroe's and Haggarty's, choking them down with my dad, my friends. But because of those public beers, everyone thought I liked it.

So, I often found one stuck in my hand.

My townspeople thinking they were taking care of me.

So, I drank the beer.

Because it came from love, and it was their way and—

"Never seen you this quiet before, harp."

Slice.

"I drove eight hours today." A shrug. "I'm tired."

That wasn't a lie. I'd followed Axel and Bailey down, dropping a load of medical supplies and clothes off at Axel's apartment so Bailey would be comfortable, making sure she made it to the arena. From there, I'd handed her off to several members of the Gold back-office staff who would babysit her because Axel had to be at the arena early to prepare for the game and he'd wanted Bailey to rest for as long as possible.

He'd still hovered (coming up as soon as he'd gotten word she was there) and continued to buzz around like a worried little bee as I'd gotten Bailey settled on a couch in a plush suite, stress lining that pretty puckboy face until Bailey had grabbed him by the ears and laid a kiss on him that had me averting my gaze. When they'd broken apart, she'd whispered soft words and I'd wanted to plug my ears.

Jealous, much?

Yup.

But the end result was that Axel had settled. Somewhat.

So, Bailey had sent him on his way, and I'd stayed until a woman named Mandy had begun her babysitting duties. Not leaving until I'd seen that Bailey was comfortable and ready for the game.

Then...even though every protective instinct was sparking in my belly, I'd made my goodbyes. My niece was healing and in good hands.

But also, she was smart.

She'd been distracted with everything that had gone down, so she hadn't seen how fucked up I was. Still, if I spent more time around her, I knew she would. My armor was good, but it didn't mean it could withstand her scrutiny. Not with how raw I was feeling.

Not with how well she knew me.

So, I'd driven home—

Or, well, not *home* since that was fucking ash, but I'd driven to the gymnasium, made it in time to watch the second period.

"Yeah, I know you did," Joel said, yanking me back into the present.

I glanced over at him, saw his gaze had gone back to the game when, wondering how the hell he'd known what I was up to before mentally shrugging. River's Bend was gone, but the gossip tree was intact, and he'd been in the hospital room earlier. He had to know I wouldn't leave Bailey to fend for herself.

"Though," Joel said, "it's weird that Axel didn't get you a ticket for the game—or at least, a pass to watch in the box."

I'd had offers of both.

To stay and watch—either in the owner's box since the game was sold out, or with Bailey back in the Family Suite.

But, as previously mentioned, I'd needed to escape scrutiny.

Plus, this was Bailey's moment.

I wasn't going to horn in on it.

"Too much to do here," I told Joel, bringing my bottle up to my lips and pointedly drinking from it.

A mistake since it was now even worse than normal.

Warm and flat.

Ugh.

Gross.

Smothering the shudder that threatened to escape, I forced myself to swallow the sip. Then to continue sipping deliberately. Mostly because the sooner that I'd finished the warm, nasty beer, the sooner I could get something else to wash down the awful, lingering taste.

"Seems like everything is done here."

My head whipped toward him. "You're kidding, right?"

God, this was just the beginning. There was *so* much to do I didn't even know where to start, and *I* was supposed to be the one with a plan. *I* was supposed to be the one who always knew the proper course of action. But I was running on a loss and for fuck's sake, the fire was still burning, and there was smoke still in the air, making it feel like nighttime no matter what hour of the day. Adding on to that, my people were scattered on the wind, and most of the town had burned to the ground.

It would take months—*years*—for life to return to normal.

If that was even possible.

Because I had the sneaking suspicion it would *never* return to normal. Not completely, anyway.

A narrow-eyed glare. "Don't love the sarcasm, harpy."

Slice.

I took another swig of beer, choked it down without gagging, and dropped the bottle to my thigh. Then I pointed out the obvious. "If you don't love it, then you don't have to sit here and listen to me."

Silence.

For long enough that I turned and looked at him.

He was staring at me.

Watching me.

"Right," he muttered.

And that was all he said before he stood up and walked away.

Slice.

FIVE

JOEL

I was in bed, in the apartment the team had arranged for me, knowing I was lucky as hell to have an actual bed and not a cot in the gymnasium.

I'd tried to refuse, wanting to give it to someone else who might need it more.

But that had just ended up creating more chaos, more stress.

For the team, for the people organizing accommodations.

So, I'd shut the fuck up, let them do their job, and moved into the apartment.

I had nothing. I'd lost every piece of clothing, my expensive suits, the new couch and TV I'd just bought. All the furniture that had cost a fucking fortune since I'd only recently moved into my house.

A forever place because I'd accepted that I wasn't ever going to be an NHLer. My place was in the minors.

I might pop up for a game or two, but I wasn't a lifer.

I wouldn't make my career in the big leagues.

And I'd decided to finally accept that. I'd decided that I liked

River's Bend and that was where I wanted to put down my roots.

Which was why I'd finally bought my place.

My *place*.

It was gorgeous.

Big. Spacious. With plenty of rooms for my crazy ass family.

And...all of it was gone now.

Sighing, I shoved that line of thinking away.

Nothing I could do about it. And I was luckier than most. I had insurance. I had funds to set up another place in the coming days to weeks.

I had a bed and a full fridge and clothes in the closet of this apartment thanks to the team (I'd be wearing Rush and Gold-emblazoned clothing for the foreseeable future—even down to my underwear).

Lucky.

So, it was time to shut up.

Unfortunately, my *brain* wouldn't cooperate.

It was back in that school gymnasium, watching Billie Rose, trying to understand why she looked different, *seemed* different.

And not able to figure it out.

I wasn't book smart.

I hadn't gone to college, had only gotten my GED a couple of years ago. I knew how to shoot pucks and hit opposing players.

I'd lived carefully, saved a shit-ton—I hadn't needed to be smart for that, my parents had taught me well and I wasn't one of those idiots who'd needed to blow my first paycheck on a dumbass sports car I wouldn't be able to fit into anyway.

Newsflash, I was tall. I was big.

I didn't enjoy getting claustrophobia just by sitting in my car.

I'd kept my clunker until it had died, and then I'd bought something practical.

So...not book smart.

But life smart—again, thanks to my parents.

Who'd finally just stopped texting me—tag teaming me with worry and excitement. Worry because the fire was still burning. Excitement because Axel had won a Cup.

He'd won a *Cup.*

Which meant that I'd texted my former teammate—and gotten a reply from Bailey, pictures of my friend living it up, living his dream.

But it was late, and I should go to sleep. Fuck knew I hadn't had enough of that lately.

Only...my mind kept drifting.

Back to Billie Rose.

She'd sat next to me earlier that night, herself and yet not, drinking a beer I got the distinct impression she didn't want. Her eyes on the game being broadcast on the wall, seemingly concentrating, even as I'd sensed she was a million miles away.

She hadn't seemed that far when she'd looked at me, when her blue eyes had pierced straight through me.

They always did that.

Acted like laser beams whose primary focus was to blast their way right through my soul.

And expose each and every one of my copious faults along the way.

Copious.

"Right," I muttered, slamming on the mental brakes.

Sleep.

No more thoughts of the troublesome Billie Rose.

No more texting.

Sleep.

I flicked a finger along my screen, turned my cell to Do Not Disturb, and then I went the fuck to sleep.

Unfortunately, while I did it, I dreamed of a certain blond-haired, blue-eyed *harpy.*

———

The sun was up.

I was standing with a cup of coffee, staring out my window, not enjoying the view, mostly because it was obscured by smoke.

I couldn't see the mountains.

Nor the Gold Rush era buildings.

Because all I *could* see was Billie Rose, her arms laden with bags, walking down the street in front of his apartment at her typical pace.

That meaning she was in a hurry.

The fucking woman was *always* in a fucking hurry.

Even carrying a shit ton of supplies.

What, had she raided every single Costco from here to San Francisco?

It sure as hell looked like it.

"Fuck," I muttered, plunking my mug down onto the counter, moving to the door and shoving my feet into shoes.

Then I was pounding down the stairs, hitting the concrete walk.

Hustling after the woman who was the bane of my existence.

And no, I wasn't looking at *my* actions too closely.

Because that would bring too much fucking enlightenment, and I didn't need that bullshit in my brain right now.

"What the fuck are you doing, harpy?" I called as I watched her juggle bags and an open roll of toilet paper and...apparently about seven hundred pairs of socks.

She jerked, dropping one of those seven hundred sock couplets, and glared at me over her shoulder. "I don't have time for your particular brand of bullshit this morning," she snapped, bending and retrieving the package of socks and tucking it under her arm along with the six hundred and ninety-nine others.

"Ah," I drawled. "There she is. My sweet, sweet harpy."

And she was.

The cantankerous mayor who always had business to see to. The woman who was more crotchety old man than soft, sweet, and female.

Clearly, I'd wasted my time the night before worrying about her, about the many faces of Billie Rose and that beer she didn't seem to like, about the tequila and the orgasms and the sexy, curvy body, the tears and the concern for her people and the shadows in her eyes as she watched a hockey game seemingly without taking in a minute of it.

She tossed her head, curls bouncing, and clutching the load she was carrying even tighter, took off down the street.

Clearly, she was fine.

Why wouldn't she be? She was Billie Rose.

Her town burned down. Yeah, she had a breakdown—but only one from what I'd seen. Only one under extreme circumstances, one that was intense, and I just happened to be there for it. But it was over and now she was back to kicking ass and taking names.

Back to the *mayor.*

"The *harpy.*"

"Hilarious," she muttered, moving faster.

"So." A beat. "Where ya going?" I asked, unable to return to my apartment.

Not when I could walk beside her and push her buttons.

Her shoulders hitched up. Then dropped on an audible sigh, her gaze still pointed forward. "The gym."

I glanced back to where her little SUV was parked (not remotely close to the school at the end of the street). "There a reason you're not parking closer?" I paused. "Say, like in the school's parking lot?"

A cold look shot my way, a clear glimpse of disdain, of that disapproving mayor. "It's not like there's a lot of street parking."

That was true enough. This town, Grizzly Valley, had taken the brunt of evacuees.

Still, the parking lot at the school was large and reserved for those from River's Bend.

She answered my next question before I could ask it. "Bailey and the Gold cavalry have set up a supply drive and that parking lot is going to be full of delivery trucks soon enough."

Truckloads of supplies.

And her arms were full of bags.

This woman was confounding.

"So is there a reason you're carrying shit when trucks are en route to deliver supplies?"

A pause, her legs still moving at a rapid clip. "Trucks were full," she clipped out. "Some of the overflow made it into my car."

I looked back at the SUV again, closer this time, seeing it with a new light—or a lack of one. As in, it was a fucking miracle that any light could make it through the windows because it was so full of shit.

"You drove up here like that?" I asked, not missing that my tone was icy.

Deadly.

Protective.

I ignored all that.

And Billie Rose ignored *me*.

And...kept walking down that damn sidewalk.

And...I lost my mind.

Six

BILLIE ROSE

"*You drove up here with your car like that?*"

It wasn't a simple question. Nor the first time he'd asked it.

Nope. On the second round, it had become almost a roar.

One that had my feet sliding to a stop, my gaze unerringly going to a face I'd sat on, *come* on. I registered that it was contorted in fury—not an uncommon reaction for me to induce in Joel, but the fury on his face in this moment was...*deeper.*

Rawer.

Okay. Yikes.

Deliberately ignoring that, ignoring the way it coiled deep in my stomach, I started moving again.

Only, he caught my arm, threatening to dislodge the packs of socks, sending the rolls of toilet paper teetering. Considering the package was open, I had to perform acrobatic maneuvers in order to keep the rolls from toppling to the ground. "What are you—?"

He tried to snatch the packages from me then, but I stepped

back, gripped the bags and bundles tighter, stepped away from him. "I'm a perfectly capable adult, Joel," I snapped. "Which means I can carry my own shit and I can drive with a full carload."

"Without mirrors?" he asked, his voice pure ice.

I'd been moving away from him again, but his cold question almost had me missing a step. I recovered, though.

Mostly because he added, "No denial forthcoming, harpy?"

Ugh.

I fucking *hated* hockey players.

And I fucking hated Joel Marshall in particular.

"Forthcoming is an awfully big word for a hockey player," I muttered.

A growl. "Hilarious."

"I know I am," I told him, straightening my shoulders, hating this interaction with every fiber of my being.

"Could you even see out of the rearview?" he asked, quietly this time, albeit just as frostily.

Okay, so truth?

I hadn't been able to see out of the rearview.

But I'd had my side mirrors, and I'd driven these roads a million times in my life. Hyperbole? Yes. But only slightly. Because I'd made my way to and from San Francisco from the moment I could drive. To see Bailey. To get into trouble in the city. To run from the disappointment of my parents and avoid the specter of my older brother who'd done everything possible to infuriate my mom and dad.

So, not a million times.

But close.

I didn't need my rearview, even with the closed roads and equipment blocking the highway and the smoke and the burned cars on the shoulder.

I hardly even needed my side mirrors.

There weren't many people heading up into the mountains.

Away.

Everyone wanted to get away.

But there was no escape for me, not here, not now.

Not ever.

Fingers on my arm again. A big body close. "Harpy—"

I flinched.

God *damn*, I knew I flinched.

And I knew he'd seen it because he inhaled sharply, because his fingers convulsed on my biceps, because he...gentled.

His voice, his hold, the aura surrounding him that was choking me with his anger, raising my hackles—it always did that. Smothered, overpowered, obstructed. *Influenced*.

Me.

I hated it.

I hated him.

Except...I didn't.

"Billie Rose," he began in that gentle tone and I sucked in a breath through my nose, got a whiff of spice and man and...

Yeah, I hated Joel Marshall.

Especially, when his thumb brushed lightly over the skin of my forearm and made me shiver. Made me want him, all over again.

Yeah, that wasn't going to happen.

Couldn't happen.

I'd already revealed too much. He'd *seen* too much. Fuck, he'd been *inside* me, had kissed that very spot on my arm on his way down my body. Before he'd spread my legs and tongue fucked me the first time.

So, yeah, that shiver, that need, that *yearning* couldn't happen.

"If you want to make yourself useful," I said, taking a deliberate step away from him, "the car is full and unlocked."

He'd moved with me, that damned thumb still brushing my

skin, his fingers wrapped around my arm, his body remaining close, his voice gentle. "Sweetheart, you know—"

I *knew* I didn't want to hear the rest of that sentence.

Jerking away from him, I managed to put a few feet between us. "Go back to your coffee, Joel," I snapped, having smelled the bitter beverage on his breath.

Because—fuck me—he was close enough for that, too.

Because—fuck *me*—I wanted to taste it on his lips, his tongue.

"Or do something helpful for once," I added when he looked like he was going to retort back, icing my words, knowing I'd entered full Bitch Mode, and embracing it. "I know that's a stretch for someone like you who doesn't *do* responsibility, but—"

His jaw flexed, eyes flashing with hurt, and I didn't get a chance to finish the barb because he spun on his heel and walked away from me.

But he didn't walk toward his apartment.

He walked to my little SUV, opened the trunk, and loaded himself up.

Then he strode by me, silent, his gaze averted...and his arms full of bags.

———

My triceps and biceps burned. My back was on fire. My eyes were gritty.

It was hours later. Well into the following morning and I thought that I'd maybe had an hour of rest, collectively.

But we'd needed to get the borrowed trucks back to the Bay Area, so they couldn't sit in the parking lot for days on end. They'd needed to be unloaded and sent on their collective ways. We'd done that and as the hours had gone by, I'd dispersed a good portion of the supplies to the other evacuation centers, the hotels and motels, the apartments and Airbnbs where my people were staying. More housing had come through, so I'd spent some time organizing that and making sure the information went to my assistant so she could continue getting people out of this fucking gymnasium.

It was noisy. There wasn't any privacy. Dogs were barking and kids were alternating between stunned and crying.

There was food and showers and entertainment, the best that we could arrange.

Fresh air and a safe space.

But it was a stopgap.

I needed to get my people into temporary housing.

And then I needed to get my town rebuilt and my people back home.

But first, I had to sort the last of these boxes, get them packed into volunteers' cars, and send them off to their proper places.

Then I needed...to find something to do to, *anything* to do that would take me away from the memories. If I just stayed busy, I would be okay. I could stop thinking and—

"You need to take a break."

I froze.

Fucking Joel Marshall.

He didn't like me. He'd made that clear.

So why wouldn't he leave me alone?

"I'm fine," I snapped, glaring up at him, not wanting to care that he was clearly exhausted too—his hair askew, his short, scruffy beard gone crazy. His skin was pale, and his eyes were bloodshot. He looked...like I felt.

And I knew it was because of my words earlier.

I'd seen his face, his eyes.

I'd wounded him.

I didn't care. I *didn't*.

Anyway, I didn't have time to care about Joel and his

precious feelings. I had shit to do. Starting with finishing this sorting.

Clenching my jaw, I forced myself to remember that as I reached for a box from the stack in front of me.

"*I said* you need—" He snagged my arm, and *God* I did not want to feel that touch in my very soul, in the flutters of my stomach, in the goose bumps on my skin, and the pulse thudding in my veins.

I jumped back. "And *I* said I'm fine. I need to sort these supplies and get them over to the other shelter." I stopped *just reaching* for the box and put my mouth where my money was, yanking a one of the cardboard cubes out of the stack. Of course, I didn't really consider that I'd grabbed one from the middle and sent the others teetering.

And in my subsequent effort to stymie a collapse, I nearly ended up on my ass.

And, because the universe hated me?

Joel caught me.

Warm hands, a big, strong body. My pussy immediately knowing what it wanted (and for the record, that was his cock thrusting inside me, stretching me wide and doing it again and again and *again).*

Joel, though, didn't feel the same way.

I knew it because he set me away from him almost as quickly as he'd caught me.

I knew it because he was...like he'd been that morning.

He was the *expression* he'd worn on his face that morning, seeing me, realizing who was in his bed.

The disappointment.

The disgust.

"You're about to collapse," he snapped, slamming a hand onto the boxes so they didn't topple over. "The black circles beneath your eyes have their own fucking black circles."

I glared at him, stepped back when he tried to take *my* box from me.

Joel just sighed and his tone gentled—and I hated that it gentled...because I *loved* that it gentled. "You need to lie down for an hour and then can get back to it. You won't do anyone any good if you burn out, sweetheart."

Sweetheart.

Yeah, I couldn't deal with the whiplash of harpy to sweetheart.

My temper snapped, and I dropped the box. It hit the wooden floor of the gym with a *thump*. "I'm not your sweetheart," I growled, jabbing a finger into his chest.

Joel snagged my wrist, those fucking fingers wrapping around it, searing into my skin. "Okay, *sweetheart*, so I'll go back to harpy."

Slice.

Yeah, fuck, I couldn't do this.

I tugged, even as I knew it was pointless because I wouldn't be able to get him to release me. Not if he didn't want to. "Let me go."

Joel didn't. Of course, he didn't.

And...I wanted...

No.

I slammed the doors on that want, let my fury fly instead.

It was the only way to get some distance.

"Ugh!" I growled, and, fuck, kill me now, but I actually stomped my foot. Like a toddler having a temper tantrum. Or maybe...like a woman on the edge.

Because I *was* a woman on the edge.

Because I didn't know if I wanted to punch him...or kiss him.

I was leaning toward—

"Billie."

I jumped, glanced over...and saw Bailey and Axel standing there.

With shit-eating grins on their faces.

My shoulders slumped.

Fuck. My. Life.

Seven

Joel

I watched Bailey and Billie sitting on the edge of a cot talking, their expressions serious, and wondered why I gave a fuck that she was exhausted and pushing herself well beyond the breaking point.

Awake for days at a time.

Driving to San Francisco and back twice in as many days.

Not stopping for hours—not to eat or sit down for a few minutes.

But she'd made certain everyone *else* in the gym had food and had a few minutes with her. She'd doled out hugs and hand squeezes and kisses to temples and cheeks and forehead.

She hadn't even stopped while on the phone.

She'd just slipped in an earbud and taken the calls, all while chopping food for the food station and sorting boxes that had come off the truck.

I'd known Billie Rose was scarily efficient.

Hell, I'd seen her spreadsheets—yup, that was a *plural*.

But watching her in action was...impressive. And that was...conflicting.

Because I *shouldn't* notice that. I'd never bothered to before. She was loud and bossy and opinionated...and now I knew what she sounded like when she came.

She didn't want that. And neither did I. Our personalities didn't mesh.

I just...didn't want her to kill herself rebuilding the town.

"She'll be more likely to rest if you do it yourself," Axel said, wrenching my focus from Billie and the exhaustion written into the way she held her body to my former teammate.

Who looked way too fucking smug.

Christ.

I opened my mouth.

His brows came up, stubbornness and smugness in equal measure on that pretty fucking face. "You know it's true."

I also *hated* that it was true.

"No," I muttered, not willing to admit to Axel that he was right. Not when he wore that fucking cat-ate-the-canary smirk—one I wanted to punch off his pretty face. "She would probably take the opportunity to stay up for another twelve hours," I said, still muttering.

Axel nodded across the gym, didn't comment on my muttering, just said, "Bailey's got her."

We watched the women continue to talk, and even from the distance, I could see Billie's eyes drooping.

Bailey *did* have her.

She'd be out in no time.

"Right," I muttered. "So, help me move those boxes."

Axel didn't argue, thank fuck, since I had enough bullshit in my head.

He just trailed me across the gym, and we moved boxes.

And did so following Billie Rose's previous instructions—medical supplies to the first aid station, food to the meal prep area, clothing hung up on the proper racks, and on and on it went, but we got it done so the stubborn fucking mayor wouldn't have to worry about that when she woke up.

Because she *was* asleep. Finally.

Bailey had tucked a blanket around her, and the mayor hadn't moved.

Fucking *finally*.

"Here."

I glanced down at the plate Axel shoved in my hand and my stomach rumbled.

"Come on."

I followed him to the bleachers that were half pulled out and we climbed to the top, and as I sat next to my former teammate, my *friend*, it all hit me. I forgot about Billie Rose and my twisted worry. I sure as shit forgot about my plate and hungry stomach. Though, I knew the latter wouldn't be for long. Mostly because I fucking *loved* Costco muffins. They were huge and calorie-laden and delicious. So, scarfing that down would definitely be on the agenda. But right then, my friend, my *friend*—

"Fuck, man," I said. "You won the Cup."

Axel grinned. "Yeah, we did."

"How's it feel?"

Axel sighed, settled back against the bleachers, and seemed to consider that. "It feels..." He shoved a chunk of the muffin into his mouth, chewed and swallowed. "I guess it still feels surreal and strange and not real, you know?"

I didn't really know, considering I hadn't won a Cup myself, but I nodded like I got it before my gaze drifted out onto the floor again, toward a certain pair of women, one sitting with her casted leg propped up, the other—the one with blond curls—sprawled out on the cot next to her.

Still out. Thank God.

"You had quite a span of experiences this year."

Billie rolled, dragging the blanket with her and I held my

breath, expecting her to wake up, knowing it was too soon, that she hadn't rested enough.

"Maybe it'll sink in at some point," Axel said, and I blinked, tore my gaze away. Again. "But right now—especially with all of this"—he waved a hand at the gym, at the people, the cots, at the fact that we were in this shelter in the first place—"it hasn't quite settled that deep."

Meanwhile, I'd fucked the mayor.

Cool.

I took a bite of the muffin, spoke through the chocolate deliciousness. "I feel that."

And then Axel got sappy on me.

But, for once, I couldn't give him shit.

Not when his words struck deep.

"I almost lost her," he whispered. "And I would have lost *everything*. None of it would have meant anything. The win. The goal. The Cup. It would have all been just...nothing."

Fuck.

I didn't want to feel that. Didn't want to acknowledge how that settled in my belly, especially with blond curls in my periphery. But I wasn't kidding when I said Axel had gone through a breadth of experiences.

Town fuck-up to NHLer. Finding the woman he loved and almost losing her. Dealing with his crazy ex and hers and then figuring it all out. Beginning to live his dream and then almost losing it.

Losing *her*.

But his life wasn't *my* life.

And just because Billie Rose and I had found a half-second of peace between us (mainly by fucking each other senseless—because orgasms were definitely the way to get her to chill the fuck out), that didn't mean I was on the same path as him. I was just feeling sappy and nostalgic because of all my friend had been through.

It was my friend who I should be focusing on, considering he'd been through that fucking whirlwind.

I dropped my hand onto his knee, squeezed tightly. "She's your person."

"Yeah," he agreed.

The quiet fell between us again.

Axel slanted a knowing glance toward me. "And I'm starting to think that Billie Rose is—"

For fuck's sake.

"Don't," I snapped.

"She's smart, driven, *and* local."

For fuck's sake.

"*Don't*," I repeated.

Axel ignored me. Because of course he did. "And you're protective of her, and she pushes your buttons. Plus, she has a great ass and—"

I dropped my plate onto the bleacher, shoved his shoulder. "Cut it out, fuckhead."

"—and," he said, going on like I hadn't even spoken, "there are sparks for days, man." A beat. "So much so that you can't keep your eyes off her, even when she's sleeping."

Fuck.

I *was* watching her again, staring at her, holding my breath through every twitch, every rise of her chest. I tore my eyes away from the cots in the corner of the room—and it was harder than I wanted it to be, though I *did* manage—and glared at my friend.

Former friend.

Who just grinned at my glare and shoved the rest of his muffin into his mouth.

"Just saying."

The idiot sprayed crumbs all over me.

Not to mention it sounded like jush shayling.

I repeat. *Idiot.*

Unfortunately, I was starting to think that the idiot was right.

Maybe that was why when, after we ate our muffins, after Bailey and Axel went over to talk to one of Bailey's friends, Desiree, I found myself winding my way through the cots.

To Billie Rose's cot.

I sank onto the bed next to her, played creepy fucker and watched her sleep, watched her breathe slow and steady, all the while hoping that the rest would erase some of the lines on her face, disperse the fatigue and sadness in her eyes.

And calling myself an idiot for staying next to her, staring at her, risking waking her up.

Risking having to talk to her.

The woman who I hated and was starting to like...in equal measure.

"Fuck," I muttered.

But I didn't move.

Instead, I stayed there, playing creeper, and eventually giving into the fatigue.

Lying down on that adjacent cot and watching her.

Until sleep claimed *me*.

EIGHT

BILLIE ROSE

One second, I was out.
    The next, I was awake and alert.
    Like always.
And even without opening my eyes, I instantly knew where I was.

Like always.

The gym. God, I knew I would never forget the feeling of the mesh digging into my hip, leaving my leg full of pins and needles. My shoulders ached. My neck throbbed. Some of that was because this was one of the few times that I'd slept in the last days. The rest was because the cots weren't comfortable.

They got us off the floor.

They were better than nothing.

But I'd never enjoyed camping, and I was too damned old for the post-fire version of it now.

I wouldn't be sleeping anywhere else, though. Not in the apartments. Not in the houses or on the couches offered.

Not until everyone had a place to go.

You didn't mind sleeping in Joel's bed though, did you?

Cool. Thanks, conscience. *Just* what I needed. To be reminded of not only my breakdown but that night and all I'd felt and all he *hadn't* felt.

"Fuck," I whispered, allowing my lids to peel open, bracing myself against the bright lights overhead.

But they'd been dimmed, and the buzz of conversation had died down.

Like it was late.

Like I'd slept for hours and hours.

And considering how stiff my body was, that seemed likely.

Groaning softly, I shifted on the cot, stretching my toes, discovering that some lovely soul had removed my shoes. Socks and jeans and a tee and a hoodie. My preferred uniform, even though I'd had a closet full of business—blouses and skirts and suits and heels.

All gone now.

I wouldn't cry about *that* loss—though I might cry about having to shop for new work clothes.

River's Bend wasn't all about the fancy. It was a small town that appreciated authenticity with very little fuss. But my goal had been to make it a city where schools and streets and community events were funded, where we had nice parks and a solid police force and an awesome library with lots of books and new computers and classes for seniors and kids. A great place to raise a family. Somewhere kids could walk home, and teens could hang out.

Good restaurants and a nightlife that meant the street didn't roll up at nine, but that wasn't so raging it kept the entire neighborhood up.

When I'd somehow found myself in the role of mayor—a role I'd never really wanted, but one I should have known I would never be able to escape—I'd known River's Bend had good bones.

I'd loved my childhood.

But we, as a town, had problems.

And not enough funding to fix them.

So, I'd done my part. I'd secured the contract with the Rush during my first term, raised money to refurbish the local rink, make it a home for a minor league hockey team. That money meant we'd also improved the infrastructure surrounding that part of town, and because the team was good and there wasn't a lot of professional hockey in the area, the games had drawn visitors from the surrounding cities and towns. This meant extra income for River's Bend that had allowed for a revamp our downtown, something that had drawn new businesses and raised property values.

A success all around. Until the Rush had begun carousing and making trouble and the City Council—in a moment of short-sighted idiocy—had threatened to pull their contract.

I'd had to take them in hand, take Axel and Joel and the others to task.

But I was Billie Rose. I'd managed.

Unfortunately, it had put me in the crosshairs of one Joel Marshall.

"Stop," I whispered.

I'd been mayor for eight years.

River's Bend was finally where I wanted it to be.

Or—I felt my eyes begin to burn—it *had* been.

Because, right along with my heels and suits, all of my hard work in town had been reduced to ash.

The ceiling overhead went watery, and I blinked that bullshit right away.

Enough thinking and moping and wishing.

I needed to keep moving forward.

Starting with getting my ass out of this cot.

Rolling to the side, I pushed up to sitting—

And froze.

Joel was next to me. On the next cot over. Close enough for me to see the slight scar just in front of his ear.

From a puck? A stick? A—my heart convulsed—skate blade?

I wouldn't know.

Not now. Not ever.

That should be the motto of my life.

Not now, Billie Rose, I'm busy.

Which meant, in Mom Speak, not ever.

Not now, Billie Rose. I'm not looking for anything serious.

Which meant, in Man Speak, not ever—at least not for me.

I jerked my eyes away from that scar. This wasn't the time. I wouldn't find out the story behind that scar and I didn't *want* to. I had enough on my plate, and I didn't even like Joel Marshall, magical dick or not.

He was a troublemaker.

A pain in my ass.

And he thought I was disgusting.

So...there we go.

A trifecta of hurt and a man I needed to stop thinking about.

Work. *Work.*

That was what I needed to focus on. The town needed me and, frankly, *I* needed to get lost in it.

So, moving as silently as I could, I carefully folded the blanket, grabbed my shoes, tiptoed through the cots, and slipped out the side door.

The night was cool and there was a breeze in the air.

Not strong enough to whip the flames of the huge blaze the firefighters were just beginning to get under control—last I heard, it was thirty percent contained. But there was enough movement in the air so that I didn't get a full inhale of smoke standing and breathing under that night sky.

It was still otherworldly, the moon and stars obscured.

But...maybe a beginning, a crawl forward, a slow, inching return to normal.

"Not now," I whispered to remind myself of where I stood, slipping my shoes on, straightening my sweatshirt. "Not ever."

Then I went back to what I did best.

I went to work.

And I forgot about hockey players and orgasms and a glimmer of hope that had died a slow, painful death with just a single glance.

———

I clicked off the video call, the last of many of them from that day. Media had become an important part of my life, mostly because insurance companies were assholes, and the public had a short memory, and I needed River's Bend to stay in the news.

That meant interviews and podcasts and blasting social media.

It meant meeting with the governor and fire chiefs and infrastructure experts.

It meant long as days in makeup and suits and doing my hair, wrestling my curls into some semblance of control.

Sighing, I stretched my shoulders and pushed up to my feet. My desk in this makeshift office wasn't nearly as nice as the one that had burned to ash nearly a month before, but it *was* a space to spread out.

And it had a door.

Go me.

Privacy for all those interviews and podcasts and Zoom calls.

Did I sleep on the couch shoved against one wall and surrounded by boxes and boxes of files?

Yes.

But was it a whole lot better than the gymnasium at the middle school?

Absolutely.

It wasn't spacious, but it *was* air-conditioned against this summer heat, and it *was* in River's Bend.

Progress.

I could definitely do without it being next the ice rink. But, considering the rink was one of the few buildings in town that hadn't burned to the ground, I got what I got. The bonus was that it had a huge parking lot so that trailers could be brought in to create temporary offices for city workers, along with short-term headquarters for police and fire.

Plus, we'd done some serious work in the last weeks which meant that we'd moved from gas-powered generators to running on the newly repaired electrical grid.

More progress.

Same as with the investigation into the cause of the fire—they suspected arson.

Reading between the lines? Someone had burned my fucking town down.

My town.

A thought that sent rage through me.

For now, though, my rage had to wait. I still had work to do, but at least my video calls were through for the day. I could take off my makeup and sneak in a quick shower then settle into my files for the rest of the night. Except, even as I was grabbing my makeup remover wipes from my desk drawer and imagining how silky smooth the new pajamas Bailey had bought for me would feel against my freshly cleaned skin, there was a knock on the door.

I moaned, dropped my head back, staring up at the boxed-in fluorescent lights, taking a beat. Then I blew out a breath and straightened, calling, "Come in!"

The door creaked open, and my dad poked his head in. "Hey, BR."

Fuck.

NINE

JOEL

It was strange as fuck, going to practice in a town full of skeletons.

The rink itself was okay and though there were some smoke stains on the exterior of the arena and the trees lining the far end of the parking lot where burnt, what I could see of the inside looked exactly the same. Minus the ice, of course, which had needed to be remade (no power, no cold...no *ice*).

Metal rattled as I yanked open one of the outer doors that were flanked by large windows on either side of the entrance. It was a familiar clatter—the handle jiggling on the open and banging against the surrounding metal frame on the closing swing. But as I stepped into the huge lobby area dotted with benches where people could lace up their rental skates when the facility was open to the public, I was home. Straight ahead there were wide plates of glass showing one of the two rinks—the more public-facing one—and to the right, a metal railing and ticket booth that separated the lobby from inner entrance to where we played and practiced.

The Rush logo was at center ice on this rink.

Bleachers filled one side of the arena, and boards with ads from businesses that no longer existed, topped with flexible and clear Plexiglass surrounded our playing surface. Banners from past titles the team had won hung above the rink and a large scoreboard took up most of the far wall, another Rush logo emblazoned above the home team's section.

Behind the teams' benches were two doors that looked innocuous but had keycard readers on them.

Our entrance to the locker rooms from the rink—one for the Rush, one for whoever we were playing, and never the two shall meet. That was how shit-talking escalated to drama to fighting actually breaking out, and that shit should stay on the ice.

No point in wasting punch-throwing where coaches and teammates couldn't see it.

Fighting had a place in hockey—to send a message, to ramp up a team's energy when we weren't playing to our potential, to protect a player who was being targeted. Of course, there were other reasons too, but those were the biggies.

Putting aside fisticuffs and how to prevent them, there were similar keycard readers at the separate team entrances on the outside of the building, so I could have gone that way.

But I'd needed to see...*this*.

To see if it felt the same.

Newsflash...it didn't.

Mostly because the rink was empty of employees and the public. Even when we were on the ice practicing, there were always people around. Some watching us, others not caring what we were up to—employees walking through and doing their business, kids coming for skating lessons and their own hockey practice or games.

The rink was its own universe, always teeming with activities and people, and...it was home.

But no one was coming to free skate a month after a fire ripped through their town or worrying about winning their rec game or whether the blades on their rental skates were sharp.

We still had practice, though.

Two and a half months off, and now it was time to get back to it.

The grind. The late nights and sore body. My lungs burning, feeling like they were going to explode. My legs throbbing, threatening to give out from all the conditioning it took to get ready for the season.

Weights and studying plays and systems. Working my ass off trying to get noticed.

And maybe making it to The Show for a game or two.

Then back down to the minors, back to this small arena and spending time on the bus, driving hours and hours for a tour of other small arenas. Playing for hundreds to thousands of fans instead of *twenty* thousand.

So many rungs up the ladder of my dream.

So close to the final one.

Just...not all the way there—at least not for me.

Axel had made it, though. He'd experienced his dream—*my* dream. And now he had a Cup to show for it. And a contract and a *life* living that dream.

If I wasn't so happy for the bastard, I'd hate him.

As it was, I knew I was lucky I'd made it this far.

I'd gotten into the hockey game late—growing up in California, it wasn't as natural of a sport for a young kid as something like soccer. But a friend had brought me to a pro game, and I'd gotten interested. And after one match of some street hockey, I had gotten the bug.

Nothing felt as good as getting the puck on my stick and firing it to a teammate. Nothing felt as good as stepping out onto the rink, the cold air on my skin, my skates crunching on the ice as I hauled ass into the defensive zone to protect my goalie and my teammates. Feeling free and powerful and—

Away from my sisters.

Who spent my childhood braiding my hair and painting my nails and generally trying to get me to cooperate with everything from Barbies to tea parties (but preferably Barbie tea parties).

I'd needed something that wasn't pink.

So, I'd shot my hundred pucks, morning and night, *every* morning and night, and I'd snuck out every bit of ice time I could manage—subbing and camps and skate and shoot—and eventually I'd graduated from in-house to travel hockey to juniors.

My sisters hadn't graduated from trying to braid my hair and paint my nails, though.

Hell, the last time I went home, I'd ended up with something called a Brazilian treatment and my toenails painted in an ombre of sunset colors.

Once an older brother, always an older brother.

But they weren't here now, and I'd seen them just a couple of weeks before—assuring them I was fine, that all was good, that I was still around for them to torture with blowouts and pedicures and holding purses while they shopped.

But...no one was here now.

I'd expected that, I supposed. I was early for practice—something I preferred, but I was *really* early today, having wanted to get a feel of what hockey would be like in River's Bend now, to get reacquainted without an audience.

Moving, I bypassed the metal railings, pushed into the arena, and inhaled.

Always that first smell of cold air, the crispness hitting my nose and mouth and lungs. Tightening the skin on my cheeks, cooling the tips of my ears.

Sometimes I stopped and savored it, but today I kept moving.

It was *too* quiet.

I punched in the code behind our bench, let myself into the back, and made my way down to the locker room. Empty with the lights off, but ready for us. Jerseys hanging, bags of equipment in front of our stalls.

We weren't spoiled like the NHL guys and had to carry our own shit to and from the bus. But we did get a *little* spoiled when we were at home.

Namely in the form of our gear magically appearing in the locker room.

My teammates hadn't magically appeared though, and I found that, for once, I didn't want to be first in the locker room, didn't want to be alone in the space. So, I decided I wasn't going to be. I walked out into the hall and then I didn't stop walking.

Not until I'd made it to the fresh air.

No smoke.

Clean and quiet and...a conversation to my right—

No. A *lecture.*

"And that's why do you don't do that, BR," a male voice was saying. "You need to learn to..."

I should turn and walk away, ignore the oppressive air inside and get ready for practice. Especially since cars were pulling into the lot and I wouldn't be alone in there for much longer.

But...I was a nosy bastard.

And the lecture seemed to be gaining steam, not losing it.

I sidled around the corner, took in the two people talking (or one lecturing and one listening, her eyes downcast, her blond hair sleek and shining).

Not curled.

I blinked.

Not *curled.*

Blond curls straightened out; their wildness contained. Bright blue eyes. Curves for days clad in business casual.

Except for her feet. Those were in slippers.

Fuzzy pink penguins.

Her head was down, as though she was studying the adorable faces on them.

"Do you hear me?" the man, older, a bit portly, and definitely domineering, asked.

Billie Rose—*Billie Rose!*—nodded meekly.

I felt anger begin to boil deep in my belly. I hadn't talked to the woman in a month, but the Billie Rose I knew didn't meekly nod and stare at her feet while someone lectured her.

She did the lecturing.

She did the ball busting.

She—

"Joel, you gorgeous bastard! How the fuck are you?"

Billie Rose—*Billie Rose!*—looked up.

Straight from her feet...right to where I was spying.

TEN

BILLIE ROSE

I jerked, saw that—to my horror—Joel was standing just ten feet away, well within earshot, expression guilty as he turned to greet a teammate.

A face I didn't recognize, which was a rarity.

I knew pretty much everyone in River's Bend.

But the Rush's roster changed regularly—players going up to the NHL, down to the ECHL, being traded to another team —and sometimes I was a few days behind pairing a face with a name.

Worse—and this was another rarity—I'd forgotten they had practice this evening.

The first of the season, and it was a good thing. It meant that the town was getting back to normal.

Cleanup was commencing. Rebuilding would begin soon.

I knew the team coming back was important.

A sign of their solidarity because they wouldn't be making as much money as they could somewhere else, where there was a town full of people to buy tickets and attend games and pay for food and beer. River's Bend was scattered in the wind.

I would make sure my people had a place to get back to, would find that safety and security of River's Bend again.

But it would take time.

And I knew that because of that, the Rush coffers wouldn't be as well off as when the entire town seemed to gather at their home games, cheering on the team.

We'd finally made peace with each other—the town, the team, the players, the population—and the peace and camaraderie we'd created...had gone up in flames.

We'd get it back.

We *get* it back.

"BR," my dad snapped, "I asked if you could hear me?"

I'd lost my cool—just slightly—during one of the many interviews I'd done in the last couple of days. Mainly because for the last *month*, I'd dealt with a barrage of stupid questions after a barrage of stupid fucking interviews. Yes, the town needed the press—we needed the donations and the focus and the attention to make sure River's Bend got back to how it used to be.

But being in the press so much meant that *I* was in the press.

Not the town.

Me.

And *that* meant the press wasn't always positive.

And *that* meant the reception to *me* wasn't always positive.

The questions got dumb, and the interviewers today thought it'd be more interesting to push me and accuse me of seeking attention.

I *was*, of course. Just not for me.

"*BR*."

Jumping, I glanced up at my dad.

Who was giving me his quintessential *Dad* look. His superpower was embracing the three D's—disappointment, disapproval, and discontent.

"I heard you, Dad," I said, deliberately not looking to the right, to the two men—big and strong and so much taller than me, both attractive and athletic, (and only one whose name I knew...coincidentally that being the one who I'd fucked). "Now, I'm glad you stopped by, but I have more work to do."

Something else I said that earned another Dad Look.

He didn't like to be dismissed, and I wasn't even being sly about it.

His mouth opened, and I watched the protest form in his eyes, travel to his tongue, ready to dance out his lips.

Luckily, though, his phone rang.

Yes!

An escape route.

I rose on tiptoe, kissed his cheek. "I'll let you get that."

"BR—"

It rang again and I backed up. "I'll call you and Mom tomorrow, okay?"

Then I didn't wait for an answer—and I sure as shit didn't look toward where Joel and his teammate were still talking, smiles huge, shit-giving clearly in progress.

Fucking hockey players.

And seriously, Joel was big, bigger than any of the other guys on the team that I'd met, but the guy next to him was *huge.*

I was short—most of the team was at least head and shoulders taller than I was (hell, most of humanity was)—but this dude was *huge,* and his voice was deep, and his hair was long and bushy and crazy.

Wild.

He gave me full-on *wild* vibes.

Great.

I'd finally gotten the bad boys of the Rush tamed, and now this giant one was here, and I had a feeling he was going to fuck things up and cause trouble and just genuinely make a nuisance of himself.

How did I know this?

Because he had that twinkle in his eye.

Because his rumbly, deep voice went silken when I started to move past him—ignoring Joel because that was best for my sanity (something that had been easy to do over the last month because I hadn't seen him since I'd left him sleeping on that cot in the gym).

"Hey, princess," the big, big man murmured. "Nice slippers."

I turned, raised my brows (and in order to give the giant my signature Mayor Look, I did that looking way, *way* up). "Cute," I muttered.

A wide grin. "I know." He winked, ran a hand down his torso. "And we could be cute together."

Laughter bubbled up in my chest, but I didn't let it loose.

I knew instinctively that if I gave this man an inch, he'd take a goddamned mile.

"Or," I said, "I can continue to be cute by myself and you can continue being"—I waved a hand from his toes on upward and started to take off—"whatever it is that giants are."

This was my critical error.

Because it gave him an opening.

"Just saying I'm giant *everywhere*."

Shit.

The laughter in my chest exploded.

The big man laughed too, his face lit up with amusement, his smile framed by that big, bushy beard.

Joel didn't. He was scowling, his body angled as though he was going to stand between us, *move* between us. "Cool it, Fox," he muttered, shoving his teammate back. "This is Billie Rose, the mayor of River's Bend."

Fox—and seriously, what the fuck kind of name was Fox?—didn't cool it.

He smirked, tugged at a strand of my hair, the curls straightened and tamed for once. "I like a challenge, princess."

I smiled up at him sweetly. "Call me *princess* one more time and I'll shove this *cute* slipper"—I lifted my foot in question—"where you won't appreciate the pointy little beak."

That smirk didn't go away. "Maybe I'd *like* the pointy little beak, princess."

Swear to God. Fucking *hockey* players.

They just blew right by any barriers I tried to erect. Meanwhile, I slid one arch glance to anyone else and they immediately got in line.

That didn't mean I backed down—and it didn't mean I disliked the verbal sparring.

In fact, after the lecture, the disappointment settling over me like a weighted blanket, compressing my lungs, and making me feel far too fucking claustrophobic—after all of that, bantering with Fox was like breathing free.

No smoke.

No fire.

Just...me.

"Sure, playboy," I drawled. "Next thing, you'll tell me you want me to give you a pedicure and buy you your own pair."

"And, *princess*, maybe I'll bring the nail polish." He clicked his tongue, lifted one of his giant feet. "I think my toes would look good in the Rush colors."

Joel retched—and fuck me if he didn't look sexy even while he was doing *that*.

One month.

I'd missed him.

I was pathetic, lusting after a man who didn't like me.

But, more importantly, I needed to get the hell out of here before my dad finished up his phone call.

"Or maybe it might give me a chance to see those feet

beneath those slippers"—Fox brought his fingers up to his lips and chef kissed—"I'd bet they're gorgeous."

Sure. Mine were more like Hobbit-feet—as wide as they were long and with hairy toes that I had to shave.

Yup. I was a catch.

That was probably why Joel had looked at me like—

Right. I needed to end this.

I'd had enough lectures for the day.

I'd had enough feeling like shit for the day.

And I'd definitely had enough of being in the proximity of hockey players.

Of *Joel*.

"Don't you have a practice to go to?" I asked pointedly.

Fox sidled closer. "Want to watch, princess?" A coy flutter of his eyelashes as he leaned in and tugged at my hair again, his tone so silky that it was ridiculous...and he knew it, if that twinkle in his eyes was any indication. "I'll have you know that I'm *really* good with my stick."

"Dude," Joel muttered.

I didn't get offended with the blatant innuendo, and I certainly wasn't upset. Instead...

I was amused.

So much so that I laughed again, twice in as many minutes, and...it felt damned good because I hadn't done enough of that in the last weeks. Definitely not without a bitter edge to it, without it feeling forced or painful. This laughter that Fox had given me was natural and after too much time spent stressing and worrying and too many tears leaking from my eyes late at night, on that lumpy ass couch, it felt great.

This was...*me*.

It was laughing in the face of a man who thought his shit didn't stink, who was beyond confident and that bearing bled into each and every cell in his body, and who also didn't give a damn that his lines were cheesy.

Because he liked that he'd made me laugh, even at his own expense.

"There she is," Fox murmured, tugging at my hair again.

"What?" I batted at his hand, knocking it away, and stepped back.

"Nothing," he said. Then, just as abruptly as he'd taken over the conversation with his ridiculous nicknames and terrible flirting, he left it, turning and walking away.

Fox was a strange, strange man.

My gaze flicked to the side.

Up and to the side.

To Joel.

Because...I was a glutton for punishment.

His face was thunderous and beautiful and—

Time to go.

Time to go.

Spinning on my heel, I started to hightail it for the trailer. Work. My couch. Forget that there were hockey players—a certain hockey player—within shouting distance.

A hand on my arm, staying me.

"Harpy."

Pain through my middle, that nickname slicing deep.

I closed my eyes, closed out the burnt trees in the distance, the proof that all I'd worked for was gone, closed out the man at my back.

Then I opened them again, huffed out a silent sigh, summoned my mayor-ness, and turned back to Joel, tugging myself free of his grip at the same time.

"Something I can help you with?"

Eleven

Joel

"**S**omething I can help you with?"

Yup.

That was seriously what she led with.

A question spoken in an icy, businesslike tone after she'd just flirted with Fox.

Now there wasn't any fire in her eyes.

No spark to make me want to bicker with her, to push her buttons, just to see how her eyes changed.

Darkening to cobalt with sparks of bronze when she was furious (something I saw a lot from her).

Almost as pale blue as the sky on a hot summer day when she was like this—cold and frosty and distant.

Settling somewhere in between—a baby blue shot through with veins of gold—when she was hanging with her friends in Monroe's, nursing a beer.

I wanted the baby blue, the veins of gold.

To sit next to her without any hackles lifting, without bickering.

Just her and me and—

I stopped that line of thinking right in its tracks and switched to another one.

"Who's that?" I asked, doing it while not engaging with all her frosty business, nodding to the older man talking loudly on his cell phone—barking out questions and making it clear he wasn't happy with the answers he was receiving from whoever was on the other end.

She jerked her head to the right but didn't actually look where I nodded.

But she also didn't pretend to not know who I was talking about.

Probably because she wasn't stupid, and she knew that there was only one other person I *could* be talking about, considering Fox had gone inside and the parking lot was empty of everyone but the man, the mayor, and me.

In typical Billie Rose fashion, she wasn't fazed by my inquiry, and in even more typical Billie Rose fashion, she didn't fuck around with an answer.

She just...gave me one, even as it shocked the shit out of me.

"My dad."

Two words, but what crossed through her eyes told me a wealth of information.

And it wasn't pleasant.

And seriously—*that* guy was her dad? Calling her BR and lecturing her in parking lots and snapping out orders on the phone. Okay, well, that last part was pure Billie Rose, but the rest of it—

Well, it was cold and hard, and she *could* be a hard ass when she needed to fight for her people, but it came from a place of love and caring.

I'd allowed myself to learn *that* much about her.

It was something I shouldn't know, definitely something I shouldn't want to know more about.

But I was standing in front of her asking questions, anyway.

I stepped closer, resisted the urge to do what Fox had done—tug on one of those straightened locks. "You two don't get along?"

More emotions crossing through her blue eyes—bronze to gold, cobalt to sky. "You're going to be late for practice," she murmured, ignoring my question.

I was still ridiculously early, but I gave her that play, anyway. "Or, let me guess, more *importantly*, you have lots of work to do," I teased, inhaling, and not getting smoke for change. Getting flowers and woman and—

A rueful smile that sent a pulse straight to my cock.

It wasn't defensive. It was one I'd seen her shoot toward Bailey and Axel—soft and a little sweet, as though she couldn't help herself but to work all hours of the day.

An overachiever.

Never stopping.

Never taking a break.

All work and no play.

But before I'd tasted her, touched her, held her close and wiped her tears, I didn't let myself think about those characteristics being something that were appealing, that I might want to see more of, that I might want to get creative in all the ways I could to tempt her to *stop* working and to start—

Enough.

Because that night was...well, it didn't matter. It wouldn't go anywhere. It *couldn't*.

I knew it months ago, and I still knew it now, even after the night we spent together. It was an unchangeable fact and why I'd spent all my time focusing on how abrasive and annoying and unwanted Billie Rose's workaholic tendencies were, on pushing her buttons instead of pinning her to the wall and fucking her until she didn't even want to *think* about opening up her laptop.

But now I'd tasted her and touched her and held her close and wiped her tears and—

Nothing.

Now it would be nothing. It *meant* nothing.

So why couldn't I turn the fuck around and walk into the rink, get dressed, warm up, and get lost in practice? Why couldn't I forget about this woman? Get on with my life and go back to how I was before the fire?

Because of the fucking *look* in her eyes.

Because the flames had torn through River's Bend.

But they'd also torn through me and everything I thought was important in my life.

"Yeah," she mumbled, chagrined smile fading, her voice growing soft. "I've got work to do." A beat, the walls coming up. "And you have practice."

Don't plunge my hand into that silken hair.

Don't pull her close and see if she kissed just as good without the tequila.

Don't strip her naked and spread her legs and—

I stepped back.

She didn't miss that, the deliberate distance I put between us. I saw that in her eyes too.

"Practice," she whispered.

My throat was suddenly tight, so I nodded, rasped out, "Practice."

And...for the first time ever, I didn't want to go play hockey.

But I went anyway.

———

A sharp smack to my shin guards had me blinking, focusing on my teammate.

"What's up with you?" Ryan asked.

I scooped up a puck and volleyed it across the ice right on

cue, not wanting the drill to break down even though I was zoning out, even though I'd done this particular exercise with half of these guys at least a hundred times.

It wasn't bad, but it *was* basic. A good way to knock the cobwebs off and for Coach to see where we were coming in from the off season.

But all that basicness meant there was plenty of room for my mind to wander.

To blond curls and a pussy that tasted like honey.

My dick twitched.

Which didn't feel great, considering I was currently wearing a cup.

Not good.

Very *not* good.

"Nothing's up with me," I told Ryan.

Whose expression told me he didn't buy that. Not for a fucking second.

That was the problem with Ryan.

He was smart, too damned smart—and not just in a book way. Though he was that, too. Which was really fucking annoying. We shot pucks and hit things. We shouldn't be pretty boys with a "pristine jawline" and an IQ that put him close to Mensa levels.

The first was a verbatim quote direct from a puck bunny's mouth. I wasn't sure if she didn't know what *pristine* meant, or if I was just too much of a dumb jock to understand what a *pristine jawline* meant (I didn't have an IQ that brought me anywhere close to Mensa levels). The second was straight from the hockey player's mouth himself.

Ryan had gone to a certain Ivy League school that had produced presidents and CEOs. He was the one player on the Rush with a four-year degree.

The fancy degree wasn't why he was a class act, though.

It *was* why he was still on the team, older than a typical

rookie (though I suspected he wouldn't be in the minors for long). A late start, but his college hockey years had helped develop his game (why I suspected he wouldn't be on the Rush for much longer).

He was a class act because he didn't fuck around—not with the team, not with women and booze and getting into trouble.

He kept his head down and he worked hard, and he was loyal to his girlfriend.

He was also boring as hell.

Which was why his girlfriend had dumped him.

Something we'd been dancing around since he'd dropped the bomb about the breakup the last time he and I had hung out with Axel. He was acting all together and cool and collected... but I'd also seen the ring he'd been planning on giving his girl.

So, there couldn't be a whole lot of cool and collected and all together under that calm veneer.

I'd get it out of him, eventually.

And it would probably involve alcohol.

Which was certainly the same tactic he was going to use on me.

Which was *why* I gave him what I gave him.

I shot a puck, turned to him, and said, "I fucked the mayor."

TWELVE

BILLIE ROSE

I sat on the steps of the trailer, staring up at the sky, finding a blip of peace in the stars.

Small.

I was a minor cog in the wheel of humanity, a tiny piece of the universe, one part in a tapestry of—

And *that* was enough self-reflection and spirituality for the day.

Enough self-reflection and spirituality for the week. The month. My *lifetime*.

I had a to do list that was a mile long, a pile of notebooks, my trusty brand of pens and highlighters I used to organize my thoughts and plan my day. This was me communing under the moon, giving to the universe.

With spreadsheets and color coding.

We couldn't all dance naked or meditate.

Some of us needed to *organize*.

So, my laptop was open, my planner was in my lap, and I'd taken my moment to appreciate the glimmering stars and light that had traveled millions and millions of miles just to reach my eyes. Now—I clicked my pen—it was time to sort my shit for the next day.

Something I set about doing like the planning badass I was.

Something that left the stairs of the trailer covered with supplies—punches and stickers and washi tape and scissors.

Something that had filled the tops of the two—yes, *two*—camping tables tucked close, one with my laptop and one loaded with my extra planners and the pens and more washi tape and stickers and punches.

A.K.A. the Keys to the Kingdom.

Media schedule. Rebuilding tasks. Insurance claims and city and state contracts. A contacts list with a rotating timetable, so I reached out to all of my people on the regular. And a master schedule that put it all together.

That was in my lap, and I was reviewing my obligations for the next day when I heard it.

Them.

Footsteps.

Crap. For all my mental smirking about communing at the moon, there was a reason I was out of the trailer and working this late at night (why I did this *every* night). It was my slice of peace and quiet. It was getting me out from my office and that lumpy couch and doing it after everyone else went home.

So, I'd *have* that peace and quiet.

Footsteps meant that was going to disappear.

I couldn't pack up and rush inside, not with my music playing softly and my camp lantern illuminating my planners, my laptop shining brightly.

I had to grit my teeth and stick it out.

My superpower.

Stickers, spreadsheets, and sticking it out.

Cute.

My mental spiraling meant that the footsteps came closer,

echoing across the empty parking lot, growing louder and louder until I knew they were right in front of me.

I looked up.

Wished immediately that I'd brought out earbuds so I could pretend not to hear him. Wished I'd never emerged from my working cave to do my communing (planning) under the moon.

"Hi, harpy," Joel said softly.

A quiet jab through my midsection.

"Hi," I replied and went back to planning.

Joel didn't seem bothered when I glanced back down at my lap, summarily dismissing him. In fact, he just stood there and said, "Practice went well. Thanks for asking."

I didn't give him a dismissal this time.

I just straight up ignored him—something that was pretty fucking difficult to do when he was shoving one of the camping tables down to the side and sinking down onto the steps next to me.

Steps that barely fit my own ass.

Steps that meant he was now pressed against me from shoulder to thigh.

"Glitter, huh?" He reached over me, ran a big, *thick* finger over the strip of washi tape I'd put along the border of tomorrow's page.

Bright and cheery. A fresh, positive start.

Something that made me smile when I looked at it.

Something I didn't want to explain to Joel Marshall. No matter how good he smelled.

I snapped my planner shut, probably wrinkling the page I'd been working on and cringing inwardly. I still didn't open to check, though. I'd jump into recovery mode once I got him to back off, salvage anything that was damaged.

But step one was to get him to leave.

"What do you want, Marshall?"

He was quiet for a heartbeat, and I braced for him to lash out at me. He'd never failed to match my snark with *his* snark.

Today he didn't, though.

He just asked, "How many nights have you worked this late out here?"

A question I didn't want to answer.

Because it had been pretty much every night since I'd managed to get the trailers here. Hell, I'd worked this late regularly before the fire. After, my job as mayor had consumed me— the need to get as much done for my people during every waking hour as I could. And there were a lot of waking hours because I'd barely slept.

Still barely slept.

I wasn't sure I'd made it through an entire sleep cycle without nightmares.

Not since I'd fallen asleep in powerful arms, cuddled against a big, solid body that had given me several orgasms.

Joel took my silence as my answer and I didn't know what conclusions he drew, but I knew he *did* draw them based on the emotions swirling through his green eyes. "What time do you head home?" he asked softly.

Something else I wasn't going to answer.

No one knew that my couch, my office, was home.

Though, it probably wouldn't be a surprise. It wasn't like I kept my workaholic tendencies secret.

I wanted to look away from him, to find the stars in the sky again, study the perfect roundness of the moon shining so brightly overhead. I wanted to focus on the sticks of burnt trees in the distance, the faint brightness from the rink lights gleaming, diffusing through the large plate glass windows out onto the asphalt of the parking lot around the corner of the building. I wanted to look anywhere except for Joel and his green eyes— irises a deep green like the scalloped leaves of an oak tree in summer. Before they'd dried out and turned golden.

Though there were specks of gold in Joel's eyes, too.

I'd noticed them when he'd slid his cock inside me, when his lids had gone half-mast and he'd watched me take him, studied my face like it was the most complex puzzle on the planet, one if he only solved would cure cancer and resolve world hunger.

All that studying had paid off.

Because he'd watched me closely enough to know every single thing he did to me.

Which stroke was better, which tempo, how hard or gentle, when to switch angles. Fucking me had been that puzzle. Getting me to orgasm the answer.

Something he'd done more than once.

Tonight, though, I saw that gold and I knew it wasn't because he wanted to fuck me—he'd made that clear while I'd laid in his bed the morning after we'd fucked, his disgust illuminated in the light of a single bedside lamp.

So, I figured the glinting specks in his eyes were him happy hockey was back, and I just happened to be a warm body he could share that joy with.

Joel lived for the sport.

I knew that. Had seen it plenty of times in his tenure with the Rush.

Just like I knew he was sitting next to me in that moment because I was convenient and there and in his...emotional splash zone.

He'd leave.

He'd do it soon enough—sooner, probably, if I actively inflicted myself on him.

Then I could get back to my washi tape and my planning and my communing beneath the moon and stars.

I clicked my pen, slid my foot in so I could rest it on the bottom step, and fixed him in place with my trademark Mayor Look.

"How does the roster look this season?"

THIRTEEN

JOEL

I studied her, wondered why I'd never noticed the fragility in her before.

On the surface, she seemed like her normal self.

Beneath that? Something incredibly delicate.

How the fuck had I missed that?

Probably because she always seemed huge, larger than life. Untouchable and unstoppable.

Except when I'd held her in my arms as she'd cried.

Except...when I'd looked up at her face, the taste of her still on my tongue, the proof of her desire, her orgasm drying on my beard, and stared into her wide blue eyes.

Cobalt then, though not from fury.

Pleasure.

Warmed through by pleasure I'd given her from my mouth, my lips, my tongue.

Her brows lifted, and I realized I hadn't answered her question. Hadn't really heard it, honestly. I was trying to figure out the puzzle of this woman who I watched weathering a flurry of questions on a national morning show and then had sat on this trailer's steps, carefully sticking some glittery tape shit to the top of a page. And dotted a bulleted list of items she clearly meant to tackle with bright pink butterfly stickers.

Pink butterflies and gold glitter.

So not Billie Rose.

Except...it was.

Because there wasn't anyone else out here sticking on butterflies and rolling out glitter tape.

Just Billie Rose.

I filed it away, another piece of that puzzle.

"The roster is good," I told her, winding back through my mind, focusing on what she'd asked. "Though I have the feeling our entire first line won't be around for long." She blinked, tilted her head. "They're solid. Smart. Strong. Well-developed game. They'll be up on the Gold in no time, space on their lineup permitting."

The Gold were solid.

The Gold had just won a Cup.

Some guys had retired, so there were a few spaces open, but a team that had won the biggest prize there was to win didn't play smart by shaking things up, at least not in a major way. A few players would have their chance, but I suspected that the Gold's roster wasn't going to be dramatically different this season.

"Right," she murmured, and I didn't miss the gentle way she ran a finger over the plastic disc things that were holding her planner together, as though it were a pet she was stroking. "Well, that's good for the Gold to have a lot of returning players. Though not as good for you guys to have less opportunity to play there."

I shrugged. "It is what it is." Then I took advantage of the way her body had relaxed slightly against mine. "What time do you go home, Rosie?"

She jerked, gaze darting to mine.

Cobalt.

Warm gold sparks.

Not pleasure. Not fury.

Something else. Something deeper.

Then her eyes slid away, and the pieces clicked. The aversion. Why she wouldn't answer. What it meant and how it fit in with the other puzzle pieces I knew of her.

That hit, collided through my mind, and the next moment I was on my feet, yanking open the trailer door, moving inside, my big ass feet stomping down the narrow hallway.

Shut. Shut. Shut. Shut. Shut.

Two rows of doors closed—and I tried one—locked. Presumably all of them locked.

Except one...whose door was open, and light was spilling out into a cone on the linoleum floor.

"Joel." Billie voice from behind me. "What the fuck?"

Then softer footsteps following me.

I was already at the door to her temporary office (a place I hadn't been to, but one I immediately recognized as hers).

Her scent—sweet, floral, tart—in the air.

Her jacket hung on the back of her desk chair...pushed back from a desk that was covered in file folders and stacks of papers. Cords for her laptop. A wide monitor. A ring light. A cup crammed full of pens.

Boxes shoved against the wall, hardly leaving enough space for a person to move between the chair and desk.

A narrow file cabinet topped with a television to the left.

A loveseat that would barely fit one of his butt cheeks, let alone his entire body filled the opposite wall, a fleece blanket crumpled on the cushions, a pillow—not one of those square throw ones my mom had a million of on her much-bigger couch. It was full-sized with a plain white pillowcase.

And that was when I saw it.

When it was confirmed.

She was sleeping *here*.

And that was when…I lost my shit.

"What—"

I spun and gripped her shoulders, dragging her toward me and forcing her to look at me. "What the fuck are you doing?"

Her eyes went wide, and they were still that deep cobalt.

Only without a lick of pleasure in those blue depths.

This was *all* fury.

"Get your fucking hands off me." Cold. Clipped out words. Ice in her eyes, frosty flecks of blue in her irises.

"Tell me," I gritted, "that you're not fucking sleeping on this couch."

A flicker in her eyes—fury giving way to chagrin. Before her chin came up and she tried to step back.

I tightened my hold. "Tell me."

She glared at me. "Where I sleep is none of your fucking business."

"That's not you telling me you are not *sleeping on this fucking couch!*"

Yes, I was yelling.

No, I wasn't a yeller. I didn't like it.

My parents were good folks. They loved us kids, and I didn't have a moment in my childhood where I didn't know I was loved. But they weren't always patient. Two parents. Both working intense jobs. Four kids. All busy with extracurriculars and friends and eating them out of house and home and fighting on the regular (mostly about the nail polish I'd found on my hockey pucks or Delilah borrowing Avery's sweater or Kira forgetting to do an assignment until nine-thirty the night before it was due and getting it done thus required rummaging through everyone's—well, my sisters'—stash of craft supplies).

This meant our house was full of love and plenty of chaos.

This also meant that sometimes my parents lost their cool and there was yelling.

I didn't like this, nor the way it made my sisters jump and cower and immediately get in line, nor how it settled like a snake coiled, ready to strike, in my belly.

So, I made it a point to not yell unless it was on the ice and it was specifically regarding hockey—

"Get your fucking head up!"

"Give me the fucking puck!"

"Yeah! Yeah! Yeah! Let's fucking move!"

But I didn't yell much otherwise—and I definitely didn't yell at women. Even if the woman in question was infuriating...and sleeping on a fucking *couch.*

Billie didn't respond to my yelling how I had as a kid, nor how my sisters had. She didn't jump and cower. Didn't wilt under the force of my unprovoked anger. Her shoulders straightened, eyes flashing cobalt and bronze—from fury this time—and then, just as quickly, I watched the steel bind itself to her spine, saw the ice descend.

Buried.

Beneath a frosty tone.

"I'll repeat," she clipped, "that where I sleep is none of your fucking *business.*"

It wasn't.

But I found I wanted it to be.

And *that* slammed me hard into the mental boards in my mind, cracking my head against the glass, rattling my brain around my skull like I'd just taken a ridiculously hard hit.

But I was a hockey player.

I got hit all the time. I just shook off the impact, mentally straightened my helmet and skated on down the ice.

"No," I agreed. "It's none of my business." A beat. "You're going to tell me, anyway."

Her eyes flashed brighter, and she opened her mouth, no doubt to tell me—rightfully—to go fuck myself.

I engaged evasive maneuvers, striding to the desk, picking up a tube with more rolls of that glitter tape stuff—except these ones were printed with cartoon cats on a background of blue that almost matched her eyes. "Where do you get these, anyway?"

Silence.

I spun back to face her, relieved to see confusion had broken through fury. "I-uh...what?"

I held up the roll. "This stuff."

Her brows dragged together. "Washi tape?"

"Wash—who?"

Suddenly, she was hesitant in a way that wasn't the Billie Rose I knew. She stepped forward and tugged the tube of rolls from my hand, opening one end and shaking out one of the colored wheels. "Washi tape," she said, peeling the end back and tearing off a short piece.

She handed it to me, and I took it, feeling the strange stickiness.

"Fancy tape that sticks to paper but is removable without ruining it," she whispered on a shrug. "I get it with all of my other planner stuff. Online or at craft stores or"—a nod to the tube—"at very special Etsy stores."

That was a lot of information I hadn't heard before, but because I had sisters and they had their own addictions to things —though not washi tape—I could process and assess with the best of them. And file it away for future use.

Or, at least, I knew what Etsy was.

"You like stickers and shit too, huh?"

Her nose wrinkled slightly at the addition of *shit*. "I like planning," she said. "It's a hobby, and it helps me focus, especially when I want to be done staring at screens." A tilt toward the monitor on her desk. "What I do isn't not fancy or perfect like some of those YouTubers, and a lot of my stuff got burned in the fire, including some of my favorites." A breath. "But I had some supplies in my backpack and during a down moment, I hit up the craft store to stock up enough to get me through."

I watched in fascination as her cheeks flushed.

Stepped closer.

Allowed myself to touch one of those curls that had been straightened out.

It looked nice, felt better, but I liked the curls better. "This is pretty, baby."

She blinked.

"Your hair straight." I released the lock. "But I like your curls better."

Another blink.

"They're like coiled silk."

She bit her lip. "I don't understand you."

"Me neither."

I stepped closer. Inhaled.

Sweet and floral and tart.

And...I gave in.

FOURTEEN

BILLIE ROSE

He was close.

And I was babbling.

About my nerdy planning hobby.

He couldn't possibly have the least bit of interest in my preference for letter-sized planners over A5 (my to-do list was long, and my writing was big, so I needed the extra room). He didn't even know what washi tape was, and he certainly didn't seem like the type of guy who'd like stickers.

And...I shouldn't care if he was or wasn't.

I just...didn't want him to think I was dumb.

That something I *loved* was dumb.

Which was the only explanation I could come up with for why I kept blathering on like an idiot.

"This is pretty, baby."

I blinked, thinking at first, he was talking about my supplies, which *were* pretty.

Then he kept talking. "Your hair straight, but I like your curls better."

I swallowed hard, locked my knees.

"They're like coiled silk."

Coiled silk. *Coiled.* Silk. What the fuck was this man doing? "I don't understand you."

"Me neither."

But he didn't back away or leave. In fact, he seemed to lean closer, to inhale.

And I kept blathering.

"I know it wasn't critical, and it took time away from my duties…" I cleared my throat, gaze dropping away from his, focusing on his throat, and—fuck—why did the man have to be sexy everywhere, including that throat? That stretch of skin and corded muscle just called for a woman to shove her face in and hold on.

His arms would wrap around her, around the woman he wanted close, and the world would fall away.

And everything would be all right.

She would be enough.

Not overwhelmed constantly. Not feeling like she was constantly alone, and the world was on her shoulders. Not ever doing enough, never *giving* enough.

She would be me and I—

Was not *her.*

I released a breath. "Anyway, it doesn't take much time and my pages are bright and colorful and that makes me happy." I shrugged, cleared my throat again. "So, yeah, I like planners and stickers and washi tape and cute little paper clips and—"

"Harpy," he said gently.

Stiffness in my shoulders, my jaw flexing.

Well, I'd wanted to stop blabbering on about stickers and washi tape. Congrats. That nickname poured cold water on my rambling tongue, stoppered up the talk about planning.

I wasn't the woman he wanted, the one who'd cuddle close and press her face to his throat.

It wasn't like I was tall enough to reach, anyway.

Joel didn't like me. That was okay. He didn't have to. He was —as much as it pained me to say—a good guy.

Just...not with me.

Which wasn't fair, I knew. It wasn't like I expected everyone to like me. I had plenty of people on my shit list.

The difficulty came from the fact that I *wanted* everyone to like me.

It was a character flaw.

And I wanted the good guy who was Joel—who looked after my niece in her time of need and had gotten his shit together and become a valued member of River's Bend—to like me.

To be as gentle and kind with me as he was with Bailey, with Dessie, with the other women in our circle.

So, when he showed me a glimpse of gentle, I died a little bit inside.

From happiness.

From...knowing it wouldn't last long.

Because it *never* lasted long. Not for me.

"You're allowed to take a minute for yourself," he said giving me that gentle, *gentle* tone. "Even more than one."

Safe and gentle and warm.

I inhaled, shook it off.

"They're just stickers," I said, setting the roll down and turning away from him.

"Rosie."

Sweet Christ. That blasted through me like a bullet ricocheting through my insides.

"And washi tape," I blabbered. "And premium paper. And stencils. And—"

Fuck, Donovan. Shut up!

Shutting up would be good. *Really* good.

But I found I couldn't.

"And I'm left-handed," I said, "so most planners don't work

well for me. The rings and coils get in the way, so when I found this one"—I quickly stepped back, grabbed one of the note-books from the brand I preferred—"I was in love. I can take the pages out and put them back in. And don't get me started on pens. I have so many different kinds and—"

"What time do you go home, sweetheart?"

Rosie. Sweetheart.

Not harpy. Going in for the kill by keeping me off-kilter.

I couldn't take it—the gentle, the questions, the concern. *Rosie.*

I inhaled, exhaled, buried the yearning, the pain.

Then I did something stupid.

I went to the couch and grabbed my jacket, the one I'd set on the bag of clothes I'd bought after all of mine had burned up. The bag I purposely kept covered so that no one knew I was living out of a duffle bag.

But I didn't have time to worry about that.

I was too busy being stupid.

I shrugged into my jacket, bent over my desk, and grabbed my backpack, hauling the packed canvas—full of pens and stickers and washi and more notebooks and backup chargers and a dozen other items I *might* need—over the top of my desk. I clutched it to me like it was a life preserver and I needed it to survive the sinking of the Titanic.

Then I marched to the door of my office.

And marched along the hall.

And I marched down the trailer's stairs.

I jammed supplies into my backpack before quickly yanking the zippers closed, ignoring their protesting groans.

My keys were—luckily—in my jacket pocket, so I tugged them out and kept marching.

Around the corner of the rink and to my car, tossing, "Lock that door for me," over my shoulder to the big, hulking hockey player who'd followed in my wake of marching and jamming.

I relaxed—slightly—after I heard the lock *click* and the trailer's door slam closed.

But not completely, because there was a beat of quiet and then footsteps trailed me across the lot. My own personal big, hulking hockey player shadow.

Perfect.

I wasn't going to let myself stop being stupid. Nope. In typical Billie Rose fashion, I was going to see this through to the end.

My lights flashed as I bleeped my locks and I yanked open the passenger side door, dumping my backpack onto the seat. Then I rounded the hood and moved to the driver's side door. More yanking commenced, along with more dumping—though this time it was dumping my ass into the seat before I strapped myself and jabbed at the button to start up the ignition.

Only then did I allow myself to connect eyes with the big, hulking hockey player.

"*This* is the time I go home."

Then I slammed the door, peeled out of the parking lot, and took off down the road.

Driving into the night and doing it pretending that I was driving home.

But instead...I was driving into the abyss.

Fifteen

Joel

I watched her drive off, and I knew I had a decision to make—

Get in my car and follow her into the dark of the night, make certain that wherever the stubborn woman stopped, it would be a safe place.

Because it sure as shit wouldn't be where she was staying.

Because I was absolutely fucking positive she was sleeping on that damned couch in her office.

So, I had a choice.

And I made that choice, walking back to the trailer, tugging open the door I'd pretended to lock earlier, and heading down the hall to her office.

I flicked out the light, crammed myself through the narrow opening between her desk and the row of filing cabinets along the wall—something that was hard to do with my big ass hockey body, especially in the dark.

But I did it.

Then I parked my ass in the mayor's chair.
And...
I waited.

Sixteen

Billie Rose

I'd sat in the back of my little SUV, the trunk open, leaning against the seat while I finished my planning, working until I worried I was going to drain my battery too far because I was using the overhead lights to see while, at the same time, playing my planning playlist over my car's speakers.

"Men," I muttered, closing my planner and carefully stowing it in my backpack. Not cramming it like before and bending the pages.

But I didn't sit in that, in all that Joel made me feel. I just pushed it down, fought with the zipper on my backpack, and dropped it back into the passenger's seat. Though, I *did* pause to buckle it in so I wouldn't have my car beeping at me the whole way back to the trailer, thinking that there was an unbelted person sitting in the seat.

A girl had *one* backpack crammed to the brim with every single office supply she might need, and her car rebelled against her.

Geez.

Smirking, and feeling better because I knew exactly what was going to be on my agenda for the following day—yay for planning!—I rounded the hood, took one more look at my silent town, and made the same vow that I made every single time I did when I saw the bare bones of my childhood, my dreams, my future.

"I'll get you back."

Then I swung into a wide turn and drove back to the rink.

Parked.

Grabbed my stuff, moved across the lot and to the trailer. Unlocked the door, tugged it open. Walked down the hall to my office.

Flicked on the light and—

Screamed.

Joel stood up, my desk chair crashing into the file cabinets behind it.

Then he was right there—right *there*—his hands coming to my jaw, cupping it lightly, tilting my head back so that I was staring straight into his deep green eyes.

"Such a beautiful liar."

Soft. Silky. Gentle.

Devastating.

But as I was absorbing the blow of those words, his head was descending, his lips were finding mine, and he was kissing me.

Sober.

Aware.

He was kissing *me.*

He was groaning against my lips, tugging my body close—

No. Tugging my backpack from my shoulders, dropping it with a *thud* to the trailer floor, and *then* tugging me closer, slamming my body to his so fiercely that all the breath squeezed out of my lungs.

He absorbed that gust of air, didn't break the kiss, just held me fast.

And kissed me.

Oh, how he kissed me.

His tongue stroking along the seam of my lips, gliding inside, dancing with mine. Heat blossomed in my middle, sparking into flames of need as quickly as the blaze that had razed my town. Except this time, *I* was razed.

"Rosie, baby," he groaned, breaking the kiss, nipping at the corner of my mouth, fingers gripping my hips and dragging me even more firmly against him. "God, sweetheart. This *mouth.*" His tongue flicked out, tasted me again, a long, drawing kiss that melted my brain and my knees and my heart. Then he was breaking the kiss again, trailing his mouth along the underside of my jaw, down my throat.

Teeth pressing in, deeply enough that the sting had me coming into rapid focus, had me remembering where I was, whose mouth had been on mine, was flush against my throat.

And I stiffened.

But only for a second.

Because then Joel inhaled. Deeply. And groaned. "This skin. Fuck." His teeth released me, and his tongue slid out, slowly, relishing in my skin, my taste, my *smell.* "I've dreamed about it. I've jerked off to it. I want to come *on* it instead of in the shower or in a fucking sock like a damned teenager. I want to kiss every inch of it. I want to bite and stroke"—his palm slid down, covered my ass—"and spank until I watch it turn pink." Another inhale. "And then I want to soothe that sting with my lips, my tongue."

My mind was spinning.

What the fuck was he saying?

What—

"Y-you've jerked off thinking about me?"

Now his head came out of my throat, came out of the *base* of my throat, where his lips had been nudging the material of my v-neck tee out of the way and using those lips and that tongue on the sensitive skin there, raising goose bumps on my flesh, stoking heat in my belly, my thighs pressing together, and fuck if I wasn't soaking.

And got even wetter when his mouth turned up, heat blazing amongst the emerald in his irises. "Fuck, yeah I have."

I froze.

My body was on fire, my panties were drenched, and I was frozen. Because I didn't know what in the fuck to do with *that*.

Joel had jerked off to me, to my body, my skin, my mouth, my *smell*.

But...he didn't like me.

Those were two facts that I wasn't able to sit in, to process, to focus and muddle through.

Because his mouth came back to mine, kissing the sense right out of me, and when he reached for the hem of my tee, I didn't stop him.

I wanted more. I *needed* it.

I was prepared this time for when it was over, for after we both got off and he changed, looked at me with the disappointment and disapproval.

So, I let him peel my shirt up and over my head. Then my sports bra.

I let him toss them both to the side, plant a hand in between my shoulder blades and bend toward my breast, beelining for my nipple.

Not starting with gentle licks and soft kisses. But remembering what I liked and giving it to me right away.

Suckling deeply.

Using his teeth.

Snapping the final leash on my control.

I drove my hands into his hair, held him to me, and thrust my breast into his mouth.

And as I'd experienced that night weeks ago, the man could take a hint...or a demand, anyway.

He sucked harder, used more teeth, and his hand came to my breast, squeezing tightly. Perfect. Almost as perfect as his other hand releasing my ass, squeezing between us, and shoving down into my sweats. Thank fuck I'd changed out of my work clothes and into my relax clothes. They meant he had access to me, to *all* of me.

And he took full advantage—spearing two fingers into my pussy, and they were thick and blunt, and he was spreading them *wide.*

My head dropped back. My knees threatened to give way.

A second later, I was on the couch. Well, my *back* was because my hips were being jerked up, his fingers slipping out, hand gripping the waistband of my sweats, his other joining it, lifting me, tugging my pants off, taking my shoes and my underwear off right along with them.

He left my socks on, but I didn't really process that fact—other than my feet weren't cold when they hit the cheap linoleum—because his mouth switched to my other breast.

That was good.

That was *great.*

That was—

He released my nipple and sat back, fully dressed to my fully naked.

And stared.

His nostrils flared as he inhaled sharply.

"Fucking beautiful."

Warm palms on my knees, pressing my legs wide.

A finger trailing up one thigh, sliding through my slick, *slick* pussy. "Fucking *beautiful.*"

I sat there, legs open, body on display, Joel so fucking gorgeous in front of me, and I was trembling. Needing him.

And he was kneeling between my legs.

Again.

Eyes hot.

Wanting me.

And I didn't know when that would change.

I just knew that I couldn't have him kneeling between my legs when he did.

SEVENTEEN

JOEL

Glistening folds.

Legs spread wide for me.

I leaned in, mouth watering. Needing to taste.

Desperate for it.

But then Billie was moving, legs closing and taking away all of that glorious pussy. Before I could complain, she was up, taking my hand, dragging me off my knees and pushing me into the couch. And then she was on top of me, yanking at my shirt. I lifted, jerking it over my head, tossing it in the same direction I'd thrown hers.

Her lips hitting mine.

Her kiss scorching through me, turning my insides to cinder.

Fingers in my hair, tugging back my head. Her body arching, offering up those glorious breasts for my mouth.

I listened to the silent request and got busy, cupping them, sucking one nipple while pinching the other between thumb and forefinger.

Not gently.

Not tentatively.

She didn't like that.

She wanted confident and more than a little rough.

Which was a good thing because that was exactly how I liked to give it.

But she only let me give it for a few minutes before she released my hair and pulled back enough to kiss along my jaw, to tug at my ear with her teeth. Down my throat, using her teeth there too. Down further, flicking her tongue over my nipples. More teeth. In a way that I liked.

Because I wasn't big on gentle or tentative either.

And because she used her teeth right.

Down along my stomach, shoving my legs open and crouching between them.

Reaching for the button on my jeans.

Before my next heartbeat, it was open, the sound of my zipper dragging down loud in a room absent of sounds except for her moans and both of our accelerated breathing.

"Harpy," I began as she yanked at the material covering my lower body, not missing the fact that she was tugging at both my jeans and my underwear, preparing.

To free my cock.

I liked that.

I *wanted* it.

I just...

We needed to slow this down a little.

But my warning did nothing. In fact, it seemed to propel her forward, to send her into a flurry of motion. Her nails grazed my skin as she tightened her fingers around the material of my jeans, my underwear and yanked.

Hard.

My hips lifted automatically, and like a fucking magical jack-in-the-box, my cock sprung free.

Turn the handle, rip the material away, and *pop*—

Went my dick.

"*Yes*," she murmured, almost reverently.

I opened my mouth to say...something meaningful, I swore.

But I didn't get that far because then she was letting go of my jeans and underwear, bending over me. Her mouth fastened over the head of my cock and—

"*Fuck!*"

My fingers tangling in those silken locks, my hips thrusting up, checking myself because she was little, and I was big and—

"*Oh fuck,*" I groaned, dropping my head onto the back of that damned couch, clenching probably too tightly, but not able to stop myself because Billie Rose had decided that she was going to give me a master class in blowjobs.

No. In *deep-throating*.

I'd thrust up, realized what I was doing, so I'd frozen.

But when I stopped, she gripped my hips, leaned in, swallowing me down until her nose brushed my pelvis.

Suction. Bobbing and using her tongue and my dick hitting the back of her throat.

Her lips stretched wide around my cock.

And just like that, I was close.

All of it was good, but seeing me filling her mouth to capacity like that...

"Rosie, baby."

Another warning. Another moment of me freezing.

Her mouth still around my cock, her eyes flicking up to lock with mine. Hazy and cobalt with lots and lots of bronze.

Fuck.

I was going to blow.

And then she released me. But she did it slow, drawing back millimeter by millimeter, circling my cock with her tongue, humming softly.

I thought she was going to heed my warning, pull back and let me take my turn on her body.

But she was Billie Rose.

I should have known she would never do what I would expect.

Her lips reached the head of my cock, her tongue flicked out, circling the sensitive spot, and then she gripped the base of my dick and swallowed me down.

Wet.

Hot.

Slick.

I needed her pussy.

That was my last thought before my control snapped.

I grabbed her shoulders, pulled her off me—and fuck if there wasn't a goddamned *pop*, she was so intent on sucking my dick. A heartbeat later, I tossed her back onto the couch and was bending to return the favor.

"No," she said, placing a foot on my chest, stilling me.

"I want to lick your cunt, baby."

Something came over her face then—there and gone before I could read it. "Later," she said, dropping her foot, spreading her legs wide, putting that pretty pussy on display for me. Then she lifted her hand, dragged one finger over her bottom lip, parting her mouth, showing me the glistening wet there too. She sucked her finger, flicked the tip of her pink tongue along it, drew it down the front of her throat, circling around one nipple, causing it to bead tightly. Then the other. Then... down, *down*. Over the slight round of her belly, straight through the close-cropped hair hiding the plump pink lips of her pussy.

Circling.

Pressing in.

Cobalt and bronze.

"I need your cock, honey." A beat. "Now."

And how could I deny her anything?

Anything.

I reached for my jeans, tugged my wallet free, and yanked out the condom I kept there.

A second later, it was open, and I was rolling it down my cock.

Then I was pressing into that pretty pussy, feeling the taut walls of her clenching tightly around my cock, sending me right *there*. Right to the edge.

Nearly *over* the edge.

So, I did what I had to.

I needed to get her to where I was, and I needed to do it quickly and I needed to do it *now*. I bottomed out, nearly contorted myself in half to get my mouth on her breasts. But I performed a miracle and was able to suck a nipple deep and hard, bracing my hand by her shoulder, using my teeth and tongue in exactly the way she liked it.

Her moans were fucking perfect.

Music to my ears. The sun breaking through the clouds on a cloudy day.

Mine.

Then her fingers were in my hair, tugging my head away from her, breaking the suction in a way that sent her eyelids to half-mast.

"Fuck me," she ordered.

"Baby."

Her pussy convulsed. Wet gathering around the base of my cock, making me wish the condom wasn't there, that I could feel all of that on me with no barriers.

"*Fuck me.*" Another order. "Now."

More orders. More Billie Rose. More of that mayor.

I didn't like that—and yet I did. It was part of her, even if I didn't want *only* that part, the demanding, brusque woman I hadn't been able to see beyond. I wanted the soft way she spoke of that glittery tape, the chagrined smile as she admitted to taking a couple of hours to shop for it.

I wanted *that* woman.

But...I also wanted this one.

The confident, taking no prisoners, knowing exactly what she wanted version of her. And better, I could give it to her.

In my way.

So, I fucked her.

My way.

Sliding out until just the tip of my cock was at her entrance, held just inside.

Then a slow, steady stroke back in.

Hard. More than a little rough.

But when she demanded faster, I stayed at the pace I wanted to give her. Mine. Mine. *Mine.*

And I kept the cobalt, the bronze. I also got sweat glistening on her brow, her throat, between her breasts. I got her nipples taut and reddened from my mouth. I got all that silken skin on display that I could trail my hand over.

So slow.

Hard.

A little rough.

But I also touched her the way I needed to—this woman sleeping on a couch in a trailer, overseeing her town.

I touched her slow and gentle.

Caressing. Building. *Sweet.*

Until she lost patience and, in typical Billie Rose fashion, sat up, straddling my waist, arms wrapping around my shoulders.

I grasped her throat, fingers wrapped around her velvety skin. "No."

But—also in typical Billie Rose fashion—she ignored me.

And started riding me.

Hard.

And...I couldn't deny it, couldn't deny *her.*

So, I let her fuck me.

Let her guide us both up and over the edge.

Eighteen

Billie Rose

I held completely still, my body reverberating from the aftershocks of pleasure, but my heart was racing like a rabbit's.

FUBAR.

Fucked up beyond all recognition.

This entire scenario.

My life. My heart.

My soul.

Just this afternoon, I'd gotten my weekly fatherly lecture. Then the shock of Joel hearing it. Then the shock of Joel intruding on my planning time. Then the shock of Joel intruding on my body—

Okay, the last wasn't fair.

I'd wanted that intrusion.

Needed it to blow off steam. Needed the orgasm like I'd needed to breathe.

And I'd managed to do it *my* way.

With him knowing that he was fucking me, that it was *only*

fucking, that it wasn't going to mean anything more than fucking.

But now he'd fallen asleep, his large body crammed into the couch, taking up way too much space. His big, strong arms wrapped around me; face buried in my throat. Beard tickling my skin. Breath puffing out, warm and a little damp. His smell— spicy and male—all in my nose.

I wanted him.

Wanted *it*.

This.

And it was something I *couldn't* have, couldn't allow myself to *want* to have.

Meanwhile, Joel was out like a baby who'd figured out his shit and was finally sleeping all the way through the night. And I was the newborn up at a two in the morning, wanting something, fussy and not understanding why.

Food. Diaper change. More sleep. Being held and rocked. *Gas.*

Nope.

Awake and ready to party for no fucking reason.

Or—in my case—awake, held in Joel's arms on my lumpy ass couch, and freaking the fuck out.

It was an effort to just breathe evenly, to not hyperventilate.

But I was used to making an effort.

So, I laid there for long minutes, steadying my breathing, coming up with a plan. I mentally tagged the locations of my clothes, my backpack, my shoes.

Then I waited for sleep to settle into him deeply, for his arms to relax around me.

To have an opportunity to escape.

It took a while, but it happened—his arm that had been wrapped against my chest, holding me flush to his big, warm body dropped away, falling to the worn material of the couch.

I took my chance, slipping away from him, and doing it in inches.

Until I was away from his body. And he didn't move.

Until I was on the floor, knees first. Then up to my feet. And he didn't move.

Until I was tiptoeing carefully, not shaking the floor any more than I had to. Underwear on. Shirt over my head. Sweats up my hips. I hadn't spotted my socks from the couch and standing, I turned away from Joel, my eyes trying not to drift to his naked body—the man was so fucking gorgeous that it wasn't fair—I *still* couldn't find my socks. So, I stopped trying.

I just grabbed my shoes, my backpack, my keys.

And I got the fuck out, closing my office door silently, flicking the lock, just in case someone came in early, eliminating the chance for someone to catch an eyeful of Joel. Then, still tiptoeing carefully, only this time doing it down the hall, out through the door, flicking that lock too.

Across the cold pavement, my bare feet frigid and jabbed with the occasional rock.

Sharp pokes of reality.

Of my stupidity.

Then I was back in my SUV, driving out of the lot. Carefully this time. Not tearing out and screeching my tires.

Not disrupting the night.

Not disrupting the man who...

Was my mental and emotion quagmire.

I drove down the silent and dark roads, noting the equipment, the lumber piled in numerous locations. The portable toilets and water tanks.

Getting infrastructure back in place.

Getting homes rebuilt.

Including—soon—Joel's.

And, fuck, just his name flashing through my mind felt like a stab wound.

"Get it together," I whispered, clenching the steering wheel, focusing on my destination and not the events of the day.

Down that way led madness.

I was Billie Rose. I was a badass. So...I got it together.

Breathed.

And drove.

Instead of downtown, I headed to the far side of River's Bend, past the remains of the ranches where the casualties—

No. Not just casualties.

That wasn't fair to Tom, Hank, and Eli.

That wasn't fair to the three men who'd lost their lives.

We'd called their house phones, their cell phones. Bailey had too. But they'd been out on the hills, drinking and shooting the shit and living their slice of quiet and peaceful.

They weren't much for tech, and we'd later discovered they hadn't even brought their phones. We'd found them in the remains of Tom's house, melted and tucked amongst the remains of a worn oak table I'd sat around more than once.

Eli and Tom and Hank had all sat there too, once Eli's wife had died and Tom's kids had moved out, getting grumpy Hank out of his house, away from the solitude caused by a lifetime of sadness—the details of which I'd never been able to get out of him.

But Tom and Eli had known or had known to leave well enough alone and not ask.

To just shut up, drink their beers, and talk about cows.

Three old guys who had bonded over life.

Three old guys who had died sitting on old logs, far from their vehicles, far from their phones and trucks and their escape routes. Maybe having drank too many beers, stopping them from attempting to get out, to run and flee, or perhaps deciding they'd lived long enough, and letting the flames come for them.

The only thing that made me feel better when I'd learned about where they died was being told by the fire marshal that they'd surely passed of smoke inhalation before the flames had burned their bodies.

I hoped for that.

Same as I hoped they'd been ready to face the sunset of life and not that they'd wanted to get out but couldn't because they were hammered.

No one would know.

A breath.

"And I can't keep wondering," I whispered, sending my thoughts toward the clouds, sending good wishes to the men who'd always been gruff, but who I'd loved.

Part of this town.

Part of my childhood.

Part of *me*.

I dropped my head back, resting it against my seat, breathing deeply. I clenched the steering wheel, blinked back tears.

Then I straightened, put the car in drive again, and kept driving.

To Gramps' ranch.

Bailey's ranch now.

I grew up here, but I'd never begrudged her having this place. For one, it had been in her mom's family. My family had some land on the far side of town, but they'd never been ranchers, and it wasn't in my heart either. I'd loved coming here, baking and cooking in the old kitchen with Gran, hearing Gramps tell old stories about what the town had been like when he'd grown up there (and I called them Gramps and Gran because every kid in River's Bend had been welcome at this place, and then every kid had subsequently called and known them as Gramps and Gran). For another, my niece—my *friend*—had spent her summers here, and she'd *lived* here at times growing up. Helping Gramps take care of the herd, riding horses, knowing and working on every inch of the property, the barn, the house.

It was Bailey's in a way that it would never be mine.

But it was mine too.

In a way that would never be Bailey's. Because of the time I'd spent with Gran.

Because the peace and acceptance I found here was—

Everything.

Now *and* then.

So, I turned off the ignition, reclined back in my chair, and closed my eyes.

For once, I didn't find peace that night.

But I did eventually find sleep.

And alertness, only a few hours later, when the sun rose early, glaringly bright through my windshield and highlighting the blackened hills.

Alertness that brought a new day.

A fresh start.

I turned on the ignition, drove carefully away from the ranch, and back into town.

To the rink, parking in the shade of one of the few surviving trees—my designated spot (or at least I'd made it that way), before heading for the trailer.

Unlocking the door and leaving it open.

Moving quietly down the hall, into my office.

Feeling relief (and *not* disappointment) when I found it empty.

Changing clothes. Assuming the role of mayor.

Sitting at my desk.

Setting out my planner, plugging in my laptop, and readying to start the day.

Then I saw the note propped up on my keyboard.

You can't run forever, harpy.

"Harpy," I whispered, crumpling the paper in my hand, shoving it into my trash can. "*Harpy.*"

I committed that word—and the slice through my middle—to memory.

Then I hit a key on my keyboard, started booting up my computer.

And as I waited for it to load, I gave in, dropping my head to my desk and allowing the tears to come.

Luckily, it was early so no one else was there, and no one would be there for a while. No one would hear me lose my shit, would walk in on me with reddened eyes and tears streaking down my cheeks.

Luckily, I had my makeup right there in my desk drawer...

And *luckily,* I was really good with concealer.

Nineteen

Joel

I hadn't seen the woman for a fucking month, and now she was standing two feet away from me.

And I couldn't do a damned thing about it.

She held the puck, gripping it with the same confidence as she'd gripped my cock weeks before, making the organ in question twitch in my fucking cup. Something that—newsflash—didn't feel good in the least.

Something that wasn't even in the *realm* of her fingers around my cock.

It was also something I couldn't do anything about.

She'd spent the last month playing teleporter or ghost or woman who was supremely good at avoiding things she didn't want to deal with.

Or *people* she didn't want to deal with.

Men she didn't want to deal with.

Me being at the top of that list.

Meanwhile, I'd been at the rink regularly, seeing that trailer parked into the corner of the lot and knowing she was probably still sleeping on that damned couch, though I never saw her car when I was there, never caught her when she was in.

It wouldn't surprise me if she'd gotten a copy of our schedule from Coach and added avoiding any events with the team to the long ass list of tasks she had in that planner of hers.

She couldn't avoid the event tonight, though.

Opening night.

The Rush arena was full. River's Bend was slowly getting back to normal. The first set of repairs had been completed on the houses that were the least damaged and people had moved home.

But not enough to fill the arena.

Nope. Instead, the townspeople of River's Bend had traveled from far and wide to support our team, to fill the stands.

It was enough to bring a tear to a hockey player's eye.

If only because the *one* person, the one *woman* I wanted to support me was deliberately avoiding my eyes as she held a puck in one hand and the microphone in another.

Red carpet had been rolled out.

TV crews were around, and cameramen were on the ice.

A lot of fuss for a minor league team.

Billie had made that happen. The grand return of hockey to a town that had been under siege by an insane fire caused climate change, that had suffered devastating loss from one end to the other. A town that was crawling its way back and one of the biggest steps of that resurrection was professional sports returning.

Income.

Status.

But also, a piece of River's Bend coming home.

And that was what she spoke of when the crowd quieted and she lifted the microphone to her lips. Confident body posture, easy and conversational tone. Funny, comforting. *Billie Rose.*

Also, short.

To the point.

Not losing their attention.

Just focusing them all on what was important and doing it looking absolutely beautiful.

Also, *Billie Rose.*

Then she passed the microphone to one of the media crew, stepped to the edge of the carpet and held up the puck like a pro, looked straight at the cameraman documenting the drop and ordered, "Smile, boys!"

I stopped trying to catch her eye—knew that she wasn't going to give it to me anyway—and turned, plastered a smile on my face.

Clicking ensued.

"Got it," the camera guy called.

"Ready?" Billie asked.

Not me. But my fucking opponent.

"Ready, Curls," Kurt said on a smirk.

She dropped the puck.

Kurt did the traditional thing, staying still and not trying to win the ceremonial drop, so I used my stick to scoop it up into my hand, glad to finally have the chance to get her to look at me, to touch her, to force her to *see* me.

But as I'd bent to grab the round disc of vulcanized rubber, Billie Rose had initiated evasive maneuvers.

A shield.

A shield I couldn't knock out of the way.

Because it was made up of tiny humans.

Three little kids—two girls, one boy—all in Rush jerseys.

All grinning at me expectantly.

I looked over their hands, was shocked as shit to see Billie's eyes, to feel that jolt, the one I always got when our gazes connected.

Cobalt irises. Pissed. Not pleasure.

Shields firmly in place.

I inhaled, shook my head slightly at her, letting her know I understood exactly what she game she was playing.

Then I bent so I was level with the kids, turned back to the cameraman, and called, "One more photo, yeah?"

Kurt joined me.

Billie Rose stepped away.

I smiled for the cameras, but all I could think was that the woman was a menace.

And that I'd been expertly played.

Again.

———

"Fuck, man," Fox said, tearing off the tight black undershirt he wore under his gear and sending it into the bin set aside for dirties that had been plunked in the middle of the locker room by the equipment staff.

It landed with a *thwump* that spoke to exactly how hard we'd played.

That spoke to the same feeling of adrenaline swirling in my belly, settling deep and filling us all with satisfaction.

Because as far as home openers went, this one was off the fucking charts.

Off the charts.

The arena only held just over three thousand people and, if I was being honest, before the fire, it was only completely sold out on evenings and weekends. Most of the working folks in River's Bend couldn't afford to take off time from work to watch a mid-week, daytime game.

And our schedule featured plenty of those.

Tonight, though, was a Friday.

Tonight, though, was the first big event in town in more than three months.

The town was coming back, and this evening had proved it.

There was a buzz in the air that had fed us, and our game was...on fucking point.

We'd demolished those fuckers.

And I'd loved every single second about it.

I hadn't cared that I was still waiting for my plans to be approved so the insurance company's contractor could start rebuilding my house. I hadn't cared that my friend, Axel, had found out some serious drama and that it had all nearly gone sour with him and Bailey before he'd gotten his head together. I hadn't cared that Billie Rose had left me naked and on that stupid fucking couch, waking up alone and with a goddamned crick in my neck.

And a boner only she could soothe.

Tonight, I hadn't thought about any of that.

I'd just played hockey and had done it well and if seeing a glimpse of blonde curls in the stands had given me a little extra strength and speed and motivation, then I wasn't focusing on that.

Instead, I grinned at Fox, sent my shirt sailing. "That was good," I said.

He grinned back. "Fucking *excellent.*"

No, *we'd* been good, but Fox, alone, had been excellent. Settled into his game in a way I knew that meant we'd soon be filling a hole in our roster because he'd be playing up a level.

I didn't tell him that.

If anything, hockey players were superstitious, and no way would I verbalize that to the man himself and risk jinxing anything. I'd think it. I'd share it with someone else if they asked who should be there.

But I wouldn't tell Fox that.

Logical? No.

But it was hockey player logic, and it worked in my brain, so it worked for me.

"I fucking *love* hockey!" Fox declared, arms out, spinning in a circle like a little kid seeing snow for the first time.

Idiot.

Although an idiot we'd all tolerate because he'd scored three goals that night and saved another.

We'd *tolerate*.

But we'd still give him shit.

Hence, the plethora of sock balls (made of dirty socks, no less) launched in Fox's direction.

"Bring it on, baby," Fox declared, arms still out, still spinning in that dumb little circle, the sock balls pelting him at regular intervals. "Bring. It. *On*."

They did, and the lunatic just smiled.

But he wasn't the only one.

We were all grinning.

Hockey was awesome.

Hockey was the greatest.

TWENTY

BILLIE ROSE

I grinned even though my reasons for grinning had been washed out by fatigue almost an hour before.

This was the first town event we'd had since the fire.

And everyone was there.

And they all needed the reassurance.

"I think you're done, honey," Bailey murmured, coming up behind me and looping her arm through mine.

"*I'm* done," I murmured back. "But they aren't," I added softly, turning so no one would hear while, at the same time, flicking my eyes to the group milling around, clearly ready to move in and discuss their necessary business with the mayor of River's Bend.

Things were moving quickly.

Lots of balls were in the air.

Lots of people needed me and my staff and *me*.

For reassurance or for technical questions or just for a soft word and a tight hug.

My job.

But...yeah, I was done.

I'd been done from the moment I'd walked onto that red carpet and saw Joel standing there, looking big and gorgeous and reminding me of how efficiently he used his strength.

Deftly.

A little rough.

But plenty of skill.

My pussy had gone on full alert, and that was something that I'd been trying to shut down.

But—this just in—my vibrators had nothing on Joel's cock and body and hands and lips and tongue. Which was something that wasn't fair in the least. Because I had *really* good vibrators. I'd even gone into the city to buy them after spending a long time making a careful perusal of a very expansive store.

I'd spent three hundred dollars on a vibrator—two months' supply of planning supplies—for a very expensive toy.

And it left me wanting.

In a way that was—

"Billie?"

I blinked, rubbed my forehead, and forced a smile, patting my niece on the hand. "Go rest that leg," I told her, nodding toward her recently broken femur. She'd been out of the cast for a bit now, but she was hitting physical therapy hard, and it was leaving her sore. "I'll be done soon. I promise."

Bailey smirked. "Don't make promises you can't keep."

"I'll wrap this up and rest soon. *I promise*," I added, cutting her off when she started to protest again.

She narrowed her eyes at me but didn't have a time to say anything further because I connected gazes with Axel and lifted my brows, and just like the good boyfriend he was, he took the nonverbal hint and hauled butt over to us.

I passed her off with a hug, kissed his cheek. "I'll see you guys soon," I told them. "I still need to come down and see your new house."

And meet the new people in Axel's life.

And give my approval since they were also going to be in Bailey's life.

Something that Axel clearly read because he grinned, shook his head slightly, and then nodded in affirmation.

They'd be around for my approval.

Bailey also knew me, so she read the undertone, tugging lightly at one of my curls. "Bring Dessie too. I can deal with both of you passing judgment at the same time."

Since I hadn't seen the other person in our trio of close friends (some said troublemakers) in weeks now, I nodded. "Done."

"Good." Bailey grinned. "And"—she held her cell up—"I'm calling you in an hour. You'd better be in bed by then."

I saluted. "Yes, ma'am."

Then I was hugging them both and murmuring my goodbyes and waving them away. A breath, stifling my sigh, and turning back to the people milling around in front of me.

I plastered on my smile.

And then I played mayor.

———

Later—much later—I inhaled the cold night air.

I held it deep in my lungs, waiting until they burned from the effort of not breathing.

Only then did I allow the air to escape. Through my nose and my mouth, using the large gust to release the stress of the last hours, the tension at having Joel nearby—on the ice, close enough for me to smell the spice of him, close enough to sense the heat of his body. To want.

No.

I'd wanted him even with distance between us—me tucked

safely into the stands and him on the other side of the rink, on the bench, focusing on his job.

I'd done that over the last weeks, ever since that night in the trailer.

But I'd been avoiding him, pretending that if I kept that distance, eventually I wouldn't want him. I'd even gone so far as to continue driving by Bailey's new house, pretending I hadn't been able to make our scheduled hangout because of a crisis in town.

All because I'd seen Joel's car in their driveway.

Because I couldn't be there with him.

Not feeling so vulnerable and raw.

I needed more time to stitch up the wound, solder down the edges of my shield. To feel untouchable. To *be* untouchable.

I'd thought I was there.

That tonight would be safe. The season underway. Joel playing hockey. Me playing mayor.

I'd thought I could do this.

Instead, I'd found that he was too close.

Too close to sending me to pieces, to tears, to sleepless nights and wanting something that wouldn't ever be.

Add in the fact that I'd been working late, sneaking around, still sleeping on the fucking couch, and I was exhausted and emotional and felt like I'd been put directly through the emotional ringer. Or an old-fashioned washing machine.

Rubbed fiercely against a plate of corrugated metal.

Dragged through its wheels, squeezed fiercely, all the moisture wrung out.

I was wrung out.

I was...so not in the mood to seeing my parents standing outside the trailer.

Waiting for me.

"BR!" my dad hollered when I'd slowed, debating whether

or not I could melt into the shadows, disappear until they'd gone home.

Home because my dad was making it happen.

They were rebuilding, and they'd begun with the bottom story. Specifically, one bedroom and one bathroom so they could live there while the construction crew finished the rest of the project. That sounded like an absolute nightmare to me, but my dad loved nothing more than being in the thick of things. So, micromanaging the rebuilding of his house from the inside out was perfect for him.

It was good, anyway, at least for the town. For people to be back living in River's Bend.

Even if it meant that I'd begun avoiding them *and* Joel at the trailer.

Another source of exhaustion.

"You sure you gave them enough time, BR?" my dad boomed.

I couldn't decide if *BR* was better or worse than *harpy*.

Worse, maybe. Because I'd been hearing it for longer.

"I stayed until the last person left, Dad," I said, pausing in front of them and holding in my wince. My feet were killing me because even though I'd changed into sneakers for the game, I'd spent the day in heels. And a pantsuit.

Ugh.

"Even the rink staff?" my dad pressed.

My shoulders tensed. "There was one guy left," I admitted, feeling like I was about to be sent to the principal's office. "But since he was on the ice resurfacer, so I couldn't talk to him."

The *not impressed* look appeared on my dad's face, and his verbal response was equally as unimpressed. "Hmm."

Right.

I couldn't do this tonight.

"Can I help you guys with something?" I asked brusquely.

Stay on target. Stay on target. "I have to go in and do a little work and then I need to get some shut eye."

My mom's voice was as distant as ever. "We just wanted to check in about tomorrow."

Tomorrow. *Fuck.* What was tomorrow? My planning had let me down. I didn't have anything scheduled with my parents.

At least I didn't think so.

Still, I didn't blink or look at her blankly or give that away. "What time are we meeting again?"

"Nine-thirty." Her throat worked, giving me the first glimmer of emotion. "At Billy's place."

It took everything in me to not react.

Fuck. *Tomorrow* was Billy's birthday.

I didn't know how I could have forgotten.

Not when we did this every year.

"I'll be there at nine-thirty," I told her gently. Be there to celebrate Billy's birthday as a family. Well, that *we* meaning me, my mom, and my dad. My brother, Jeff, didn't bother to show up. Bailey's dad was older, a product of my mom's first marriage.

But he was also an asshole, and a shitty father.

He'd borne about ten years of my dad—and I'm assuming my dad's hard press of responsibility—before he'd taken off. Whether he couldn't stand the pressure or that the burden had increased for Jeff *after* Billy had died and caused Jeff to take off, I didn't know.

All I *did* know was that my dad had been full-court press for as long as I could remember. And Jeff had been all about avoiding any responsibility for at least that same length of time.

I also didn't know if the pressure and the avoidance would still be there if Billy had lived.

Maybe.

Maybe not.

My dad was my dad.

But...my dad was also a product of his circumstances.

"Good, BR." My dad patted me roughly on my shoulder. "Don't be late."

I nodded.

I wasn't late.

Not ever.

Because of that full-court press from him, the responsibilities driven home and driven deep. Because my parents turned and walked away, leaving me at the trailer to work without a second thought, even though it was nearing midnight.

Bailey had called twice and texted three times, ordering me to bed.

My parents...

Billy's birthday was tomorrow.

That was it.

I sucked in a breath, released slowly.

Then I went inside the trailer, walked down the hall and into my office. Sitting in my chair, booting up my computer, too sad and exhausted deep inside to even bust out my planner.

I knew I wouldn't sleep.

But...I also wouldn't be late.

TWENTY-ONE

JOEL

The downtown area was starting to actually *look* like a downtown.

Some buildings complete.

Others in progress.

The houses on the surrounding streets in a similar situation.

A small town making its way back.

Because of the woman sitting in the large park. I'd spotted her curls from a block away, returning from the meeting with my contractor—the plans to rebuild had been approved, fucking *finally* —and knowing that I'd be settled again…in six to eight months.

I pulled over, parked in the lot that had formerly been shaded by old-growth oaks.

Talking to Billie, teasing her, verbally sparing with her would take my mind off the fact that it would be months before my house would be done and one-bedroom apartment living was my future for, at minimum, another year.

Billie wasn't sitting close to the lot, but she also wasn't

sitting all that far away. She should have heard the car and reacted, or at the very least heard the engine cut out, the door pop open.

She hadn't moved. Not one fucking muscle.

If she was listening to music, earbuds in, drowning out the world, we were going to have words.

River's Bend had been a safe place to live, to grow up, to walk and exist.

But the town still had crime.

Now, there were contractors and industrial crews all over. People coming in and out to work. People Billie didn't know.

People who could hurt her.

My temper spiked.

I shoved the little bag I'd been carrying around into my pocket, the bag I'd been wanting to give it to her for weeks now, *would* have given it to her if only the stubborn woman hadn't fucked around and gotten a damned gold medal in avoiding me and got out of my car, slamming the door.

Still no reaction.

"Fuck," I muttered, and moving quickly, I closed the distance between us, but when I got close to her, to her ass plunked on the small gray blanket positioned in the narrow strip of shade the freshly replanted trees threw—smaller now, their branches years away from providing the same type of comfort—I saw she wasn't wearing earbuds.

I frowned.

And dropped to the blanket next to her, my legs going to either side of hers, my arm wrapping around her middle.

She jumped, jerked in my hold.

"Easy, harpy," I murmured, leaning close, stopping just short of burying my face in those curls.

I could smell her shampoo from this distance and if I allowed myself to feel the silk of them against my face, I wouldn't want to stop there. I would need to feel the silk of her *everywhere*.

I wasn't sure if the mayor of River's Bend could get arrested in her own town.

But I was certain that *I* could be.

Worth it. Totally—

She squirmed, managed to gain an inch of distance between us. "Go away, Joel."

I'd been thinking about silk and hair and curls and naked skin and getting arrested for public indecency.

Her tone threw me completely.

Because...it wasn't Billie's.

It wasn't like that glimpse of vulnerable she'd given me before. Finally losing it after having held it together for an entire town—relief that Bailey was okay, grief at the loss of her people, anguish at the destruction of everything she'd worked hard for. This was...

Something completely different.

And...it was fucking terrifying.

I leaned around her back, got a good look at her face, her eyes, and my entire body seized.

She wasn't in there. Not really.

Her blue irises weren't a frosty sky blue and they sure as shit weren't cobalt and bronze.

They were...

Well, they could have been devoid of color.

Of emotion.

My heart convulsed, lungs going tight, every muscle in my body screaming that something was very, *very* wrong. "Who hurt you?"

She blinked, and I watched—fucking *watched*—the shield lock down.

"You know," she snapped, jerking out of my hold and spinning away from me, kneeling on the blanket with several feet between us. "Just because we fucked doesn't mean you're allowed to touch me anytime that you want."

I inhaled.

Because, first, that pissed me off.

And second, that *pissed me off*.

But I held my temper—because of the glimpse I'd gotten five seconds before.

That desolate landscape of her expression.

The vast loss of color everywhere my eyes could see.

Just because it was now covered by her playing porcupine, it didn't mean that pain wasn't still there.

Christ. When I'd first met Billie Rose, I couldn't stand her. She'd come across as an open book—annoying but beautiful, demanding and fiery and intense. Some of that had been appealing. Who didn't like a beautiful woman who was driven?

Not a real man, as far as I was concerned.

Confidence and capability were sexy.

So was Billie.

All of which meant that I'd spent a lot of time looking at her, thinking that, yeah, she was beautiful, but that she was too much fucking trouble.

I wanted my balls stroked. Not busted.

But...

This woman fighting tears on a burned street.

This woman wild and a little rough when she got naked.

This woman demonstrating her loyalty and tireless efforts as she stubbornly kicked ass at her job.

So, no, I wasn't going to let my temper get away from me in this moment—not when I'd gotten all those glimpses beneath her shield, not when I kept peeling back layers and with each newly exposed surface, I learned something else about her.

A breath to get my temper in check, and them, curiosity and concern in full-bore, I leaned back enough to tug the bag out of my pocket.

"Here," I said, thrusting the small brown bag at her.

That got a reaction, garnered me some color—only this time it was confusion.

"What is this?" she whispered.

I nodded at the bag. "Open it, sweetheart."

Another reaction quickly buried.

Then she narrowed her eyes. "I can't put a rush on your plans getting approved," she muttered, proving that she knew everything, including the fact that I'd been going around and around with the building department. "They're slammed and I'm not going to use my position—"

"Just got back from a meeting with my contractor," I said. "My plans were approved, and they'll start to rebuild in a week or two."

That had the fury sliding out of her like the wind had suddenly cut out, causing a boat's sails to abruptly lay flat.

"Oh." Her brows drew together. Then she glanced down at the bag sitting in her palm like it contained a live rattlesnake. "So, um, what's this?"

I shrugged, feeling the back of my neck heat, insecurity sweeping in. "I saw it." I cleared my throat. "And I thought of you." Another shrug.

The frown in her brows stayed in place. "Umm..."

I took her free hand, dragged it to the top of the bag. "Open it, baby."

"I—"

"*Open* it."

She pressed her lips together, sighed heavily, and then she opened the top of the bag, peered inside, and froze, going so still I could have almost confused her for a statue.

Her hand trembled as she reached into the bag, making the material crinkle, and I had the thought that this was deeper, heavier than I could have predicted. That this was something else altogether than what I'd expected.

Something *more.*

My throat was dry, but I didn't clear it, just sat in that discomfort.

Because she was having a moment.

Because she was slowly extracting the small cardboard box and setting it on her knee.

I took the bag from her, mostly so I could watch her study the small throwaway (or so I'd thought) present.

Then she blew out a breath, set the box of washi tape I'd bought for her on the blanket near her thigh. I'd seen the box in the window at a bookstore in Sacramento. It was Gold colors— black and gold (obvs), but there were also rolls printed with skates and sticks and one that looked like ice.

"Where did you get this?" she whispered, wide blue eyes hitting mine.

I gave into the urge and tugged at one of her curls. "Sacramento. I saw it in the window of a bookstore and thought of you."

"I-I—" She clamped her lips together, shoulders lifting on a deep inhale.

I'd thought of her.

I'd wanted her to use them and think of *me.*

Not go stiff three feet from me.

Not pull away from me, put even more distance between us, faster than I could stop her.

That breath she'd taken slid out in a hiss of air as she jumped to her feet.

"I can't," she whispered.

Then she was taking off across the park.

Walking away from me.

Again.

Twenty-Two

BILLIE ROSE

F uck.
    Fuck.
    I couldn't catch my breath.
I *couldn't.*

I was standing in the center of town fucking close to hyperventilating...over a fucking set of washi tape.

Sparkly black and gold. Themed with the Gold logo, but also rolls of generic hockey scenes—sticks, pucks, skates, ice.

Hockey-themed washi tape.

That *Joel* had bought me.

This big, strong hockey player had gone into a bookstore because he'd seen something in the window and thought of me.

Of *me.*

I could count on one hand how many times that had happened.

Okay, maybe two.

Bailey and Dessie were good friends.

But we didn't exchange gifts that way—mostly because

Bailey had been on the struggle bus for too fucking long and had refused help that wasn't me filling her fridge with food or basically forcing a gift on her. Dessie and I didn't want to add to that.

So, our gifts were time and teasing and the occasional wine night at one of our places.

And yeah, my mom was distant and my dad was intense, but my parents had still bought me things growing up—Christmas and birthday presents, books and food and technology.

But they hadn't bought me things like this.

Not seeing something they thought I would like and getting it for me...just because.

That Joel had?

It sent my pulse thundering in my veins, my heart pounding against my ribs. I couldn't catch my breath, my fingertips were numb.

The washi tape had cost eight dollars.

Eight.

But it might as well have cost eight *million*.

It meant that much.

And it *couldn't*.

Not today.

Not *ever*.

That truth had settled in my lungs, seized me tightly, sent me right along the path toward panic. Because I wanted it to.

And...I couldn't *breathe*.

Shit. *Shit*.

I just needed to get away—from Joel, from my feelings, from this day, from the last hours watching my parents grieve.

Billy's birthday.

The brutal reminder I was all they didn't want.

I'd run from Joel, sprinted away like a lunatic, and now I made it to the recently rebuilt bathrooms, erected next to the recently rebuilt playground, which had been put up next to the recently rebuilt soccer and baseball fields. I'd needed to make this space functional for the kids. School was back in session, and it was being conducted in lame ass portables, the school campuses nowhere near as nice as they'd once been. The kids needed a place to run and play and kick and hit some fucking balls around.

So, Central Park had been my priority—or it had been scratched to the top of my list of priorities, anyway.

A list that was a heavy weight and something that didn't exactly help me right then, no matter how hard I was trying to distract my mind. Not when my lungs felt like they were going to explode from the effort of trying to breathe.

But I couldn't catch my breath.

I stepped behind the building, crouched with my back resting against the pale, stuccoed exterior, hands clenching at my hair.

I wanted to tear it out.

I wanted the pain.

I wanted to forget.

Everything.

But mostly the fucking washi tape.

My breaths were short and staccato. I was too raw and vulnerable, and my gasps weren't bringing in enough air, but even as I was struggling to regain control, my mind was churning with tasks, with needs, with things that would draw on my time.

To do:

Get my shit together.

Breathe normally.

Don't pass out.

Ignore the fact that washi tape sent me into a panic attack.

Attend the rest of my meetings for the day.

Return phone calls. Emails. Do that podcast scheduled for dinnertime.

Work.

Plan the next day.

Sleep in my office.

And mostly importantly, ignore the fact that Joel buying me washi tape had sent me spiraling and that worse, he'd surely seen.

The list helped me focus, and I sucked in my first full breath in what felt like an eternity, loosening my grip on my hair, bracing my hand on my knees, preparing to stand.

When I felt it.

When I felt *him*.

That churning began again, low in my belly, gripping tight to my lungs.

I straightened fully and turned.

He was there, his face soft. "What was that baby?"

So, *so* many things.

A fucking nightmare and a dream and a lifetime of—

"Nothing," I said, lifting my chin, straightening my shoulders. "I just needed to take a walk."

He lifted his brows. "You needed to take a walk?"

"Yup."

Now I was going to take one back to my car and get the fuck out of here.

I brushed by him, but he caught my arm.

"A walk to the bathrooms?"

Right. That was weird. But I was nothing if not resourceful. I swung an arm out. "I needed to make sure everything was rebuilt correctly."

His mouth turned up. "And you did that checking by crouching on the ground and almost pulling your hair out?"

Damn.

The man had noticed.

Then again, he seemed to notice everything.

"I was"—here I faltered, taking a minuscule pause to sort my head (and come up with my excuse)—"making sure they back-filled the foundation correctly with the right material."

Turning away, I tugged at my arm.

He just turned me back toward him, those green eyes holding me in place. "*Backfilled* correctly?"

Thank God for copious planning and construction meetings.

I could bullshit this answer with very little effort.

"Yup," I said. "If they don't use the right substrate and it's not graded correctly, any water will drain toward instead of away from the foundation." I tugged again, succeeded in freeing myself. "We want these buildings to last a long time, so I need to make sure they're done right."

That was the truth.

It was also a lie.

"Bullshit," Joel muttered, stepping closer.

"It is *not,*" I said, unwilling to let it go. "I didn't give up two hours of my time learning about *substrates* just to—"

His hand came to my jaw, tilting my head up. "Shut up, sweetheart."

My mouth dropped open.

Then I got it together. "Did you just tell me to shut up?" My tone was dangerous.

He didn't give a fuck, his lips turning up when he murmured, "Yup."

Damn it, but my mouth dropped open again.

And, unfortunately for my sanity, he took advantage of that, moving into me, herding me back toward the building, walking me over that damned substrate, and pressing me into the stucco.

It was warm, heated from the sun.

But not as warm as him.

As hot as him.

"I need to get back to work," I whispered.

"That's the last thing you need to do," he grumbled. "Especially if it means that you're going to more meetings on *substrates*."

"They're budget meetings," I told him blithely, still whispering.

"Christ," he muttered. "It's worse."

My mouth wouldn't stop. "And a podcast and a meeting with the grant committee."

His lips curved further. "Fuck, baby, your job sucks."

"Later, though," I murmured. "I get to play with stickers and washi tape."

Washi tape. Jesus.

Nothing like circling us right back to why we were in this situation.

Then he was closer, somehow still moving into me, pressing in so that not even a millimeter separated us from thighs to chest.

He had a good chest.

But he had *great* thighs.

His palm cupped my jaw. "Which brings me back to wondering why *my* washi tape sent you off in a hurry to check out the *substrate.*"

This was not an inquiry I wanted to answer.

I still tried. "I'd forgotten I needed to check it."

"Liar." His fingers flexed on my jaw...and my scalp. Somehow, I'd missed that he'd boxed me in, and in doing so, he'd slid his other hand into my hair.

Positioning it as a barrier between my head and the stuccoed wall.

Fuck.

My lungs got tight again.

I needed to get out of here.

I opened my mouth, gathering snarky words with a dash of vitriol. They bubbled up in my belly, ready to shoot off my tongue, angry and unforgivable.

Joel's thumb pressed to my bottom lip.

Stifling the sentiments.

Stopping me before I did something unforgiveable and spoke that bitterness out loud.

His touch was like him—a little rough and completely inflaming. Not my temper this time, though. Nope. That had faded away the moment his skin hit mine. Instead, my body took over, remembering all the things *his* body had done to it and how all of them had been good.

Great.

Except for my heart.

I inhaled through my nose, holding that thought close, shrugging off the need and preparing my shield of sharp words again.

But then he spoke. "You never forget anything."

That was a problem.

It was *the* problem.

He knew me.

Which mean that there were too many things floating around in my head. Too many things about this man swirling there, putting me off my game.

Which was why I didn't see it coming.

I was entrenched in his palm on my jaw, in the strength and warmth of his body. I missed the meaning behind his thumb slipping from my bottom lip, dragging down my chin, pressing slightly into my throat.

I wanted his fingers wrapping tightly there, wanting them holding me in place as he pounded into me, as he fucked me hard and fast and exactly how he liked.

Taking over.

Taking care of me.

Just...taking me.

I was trying to push that thought away when his head dropped and his lips hit mine.

The kiss was...

How could one man's mouth undo me so completely?

All the strength just left my body, as though his kiss was pulling the losing straw in *Kerplunk*. The wrong plastic stick had been yanked from the tube and all the marbles were tumbling down.

I was tumbling down.

Resistance in pieces.

Body melting against his.

I didn't struggle when he banded an arm behind my back, his hand going to my ass, lifting, picking me up, wrapping my legs around his waist.

He groaned when our pelvises aligned, even with the fabric of our clothes between us.

Probably because he was fucking my mouth.

Yup.

Fucking it.

With his tongue. And mirroring those slow, powerful strokes with pumps of his hips, grinding against me, and shooting pleasure through my body.

I could come like this.

I could come in a public park after only a couple of minutes of this man grinding against me and his mouth and tongue fucking mine.

Christ.

Life wasn't fair.

Twenty-Three

JOEL

S he was with me.

Then she wasn't.

I was about to come in my pants like a fucking teenager.

And...I'd lost her.

I didn't realize it at first. She kissed me back, wove her fingers into the hair on my nape, tugged just on the right side of pain. Her thighs clenched around my waist, she ground back against me, matching my rhythm.

Then I felt the wet on my face.

What the fuck?

I pulled back from the glorious mouth, those lips that drove me fucking *crazy*, and saw that she was crying.

Lids closed, cheeks flushed, mouth swollen and red...and tears leaking out of the corners of her eyes.

"What the fuck?" I whispered.

Her eyes flew open and—

Hell.

The look in them eviscerated me.

Fuck. Fuck. *Fuck.*

"Did I hurt you?" I said quickly, leaning back, her hands sliding free of my hair. "Shit, sweetheart, was I too rough?"

"I-I'm fine." She cleared her throat, lifted her chin. "And, I'll be even more fine if you let me go so I can get back to work."

Bravado.

Billie Rose.

I was learning they were practically married.

Another fucking layer.

Filing that away to deal with later, I pointed out, "You're crying."

That frown deepened as she lifted a hand and touched her cheek. Her face changed as she glanced down at her fingers, rubbing them together, as though testing to see if the moisture was real.

She hadn't known she was crying.

What the *fuck?*

"I'm fine." She brushed roughly at her cheeks. "Put me down."

Yeah, that wasn't going to happen.

She couldn't run away from me when she was pinned between my body and the wall, her legs wrapped around my hips.

There were plenty of questions flowing through my mind, but I needed to ask the most important one.

"Did I hurt you?"

A beat. Her face doing something I couldn't quite read. "No."

I sucked in a breath, warned, "Sweetheart."

A spark of bronze in eyes darkening to cobalt, frustration making its appearance. "You didn't hurt me, you ridiculous man. Now put me down."

"No," I said, letting her ass go and using my now free hand

to stop her when she brushed roughly at her cheeks again. I slid my arm around her again and leaned back in, kissed her tears away, knowing as I tasted the salt of her pain on my tongue that I wasn't going to let to this lie.

I'd dicked around long enough.

I'd pretended to not feel what I was feeling for too fucking long.

It was time to act.

To press my hand.

I nipped at her earlobe. "Why the tears, harpy?"

Her fingers had gone back to my shoulders and my question had them digging in. In that moment, I thought it was because my tone had been all order. Thought she was pissed that I was demanding she answer me.

Only later I would understand her reaction, and the resulting regret from that understanding would sit heavy in my belly for a long, long time.

She dropped her legs, looked away from me. "Put me down," she whispered.

One of my hands was still in her hair, protecting her from hurting her head on the wall. The other returned to that lush ass of hers. I flexed both, pressed in even more tightly, letting her legs dangle in the air. "No."

A sharp inhale, nostrils flaring, eyes sparking. "*Put* me down."

I held her tighter. "Why did you run away when I gave you the tape?"

"Put me down."

My lips hit her jaw. "Why were you hyperventilating when I found you?"

"Put me down."

I touched my mouth to the spot just in front of her ear. "Why did our kiss make you cry?"

Her eyes closed. "Put me down."

A flick of my tongue. "Why have you been avoiding me?"

Tension in her shoulders, her frame. "Put me down."

"Why do you work so hard for every single person in this town, but not yourself?"

A tremor ran through her body. "Put me down."

I kept going. "Why were your eyes dead when I first came over?"

That did it.

Her lids flew open, and she went so, *so* still. "Don't say that," she whispered.

"Say what, sweetheart?"

Silence.

Long enough for me to hear the wind rustling through the leaves on the slender branches of the baby trees.

Long enough to hear cars in the distance.

Long enough to hear her breathing hitch and speed up and then slow again, matching the resolution that crept into her frame.

"Dead," she whispered.

I frowned. "What's that?"

"Don't say *dead.*"

I froze, understanding that this was important, this was us teetering on the crux of something. This could mean something more, something big.

I wanted to ask what she meant.

But I had the sense that if I pushed now, I'd crash and burn and this teetering close to something big would go end in disaster.

So, I waited.

And, after a long moment, she gave it to me.

"It's Billy's birthday."

I blinked. "It's your birthday?"

A shake of her head, her shoulders lifting and falling on a

breath. "No. Not Billie like me," she whispered. "No *ie*. Just... Billy with a *y*." A beat. "My brother."

I froze.

Because I *knew*. This wasn't going to be good.

And she confirmed it with her next words. "He's spent more birthdays in the ground than he did above it."

That ricocheted through me like a bullet.

"He's spent more birthdays in the ground than *I* have about it."

All the air seized in my lungs.

Fuck.

Fuck.

"And this year, my parents celebrated his birthday at a cemetery scrubbing the ash off my brother's headstone so that we could see his name again."

My hands convulsed. "Baby."

She shook her head, deliberately didn't look at me, and whispered, "So, don't say dead, okay?"

I forced out a silent breath, continued brushing her cheek lightly back and forth, back and forth, wanting her to turn her eyes back to mine, especially since I could see them swimming with tears, moisture glinting in the late afternoon sunshine. "Okay, sweetheart. I won't."

A shaky nod.

An even shakier breath.

"Thank you," she whispered.

And then we stood there, silent and not looking at each other. Until she shifted again.

This time, I let her go, let her slide down my body until her feet hit the ground.

We'd taken a giant leap forward, and even though from the outside it probably wouldn't seem like a lot, *I* knew it was huge.

She'd shared.

Had peeled back a layer, peeked out from behind that shield.

And she'd given me a tiny piece of Billie Rose.

I was greedy. I wanted her to drop the armor, let go of the layers. I wanted her to allow me to gather them all up and put her back together.

But I knew I needed to proceed carefully.

So, I cradled the piece she'd given into my care like the precious gifts they were, and I turned the subject back to lighter topics.

I hoped so anyway.

"So that wagyu tape?" I teased. "Did you cry because I picked the wrong type?"

Her body jolted and then—fucking *finally*—she looked up at me. "Wagyu tape. Really?"

I shrugged, fighting a grin.

A roll of her eyes.

I bopped her lightly on the nose. "So, was it wrong?"

Her lips turned up, but something soft settled in her face, and I held my breath when she reached up and touched my jaw, fingers stroking through my beard. "It wasn't wrong," she whispered.

"Oh," I whispered back. "Okay." A beat. "Too much hockey then? You've had enough of us in your vicinity?"

That soft settled deeper. "No." Still barely audible. "It was just the right amount of hockey." One corner of her mouth curved further, humor in those blue depths. "Especially since I'm a Gold fan."

"Ouch," I laughed, covering her hand with my own, pressing it lightly, not wanting her to stop touching me. "Them's fighting words."

Laughter and warmth.

So much better than ice and fury, sadness and death.

"Don't worry," she said lightly. "I have Rush colors too."

"Damn straight you do." I slid my fingers along the back of her hand, trailed them along the arm, discovering that she had a tiny tattoo on the inside of her forearm. Small and a faint gray. How had I not noticed that before?

I'd kissed my way across her naked body.

Though, I supposed, I'd kissed my way across all the fuck-able parts. I hadn't really focused on the others, hadn't made love to her. Not in the way I should have.

Something else I would feel guilty about later.

"What's this?" I murmured, brushing my fingertips along the fine, overlapping lines.

Her eyes flicked down, and she went quiet.

I worried I'd stepped on something painful again, something like Billy, knew that was the truth when her face went blank.

I waited to be shut down, to be snapped at.

Instead, her fingers pressed lightly against my jaw before she pulled back.

I let her go.

I had to, even though I hated it.

"Another time, yeah?"

My phone chimed.

She heard it, repeated, "Another time."

My cue.

This time I listened to it. I released her, stepped back, and watched her walk away from me.

A-fucking-gain.

Twenty-Four

BILLIE ROSE

"Tell me the truth," I said, three glasses into my own personal bottle of wine and enjoying every sip of it, "how are you *really* feeling?"

Bailey had weathered a curveball—one that had ended with her having a step kid and a baby mama in her life.

Both of whom were now living in my niece's house.

Bailey, meanwhile, wasn't doing what I would have been doing—chugging wine.

Instead, she looked...serene as she sipped at her beer and said, "I'm good, Billie."

My brows lifted.

"I'm *good*," she repeated. "I swear." Then she made a face and demonstrated how well she knew me. "Though, I know you won't believe that." A shrug, lips twitching. "You'll see. Eventually."

I would.

I *would* see.

And if that sounded like a threat, even in my own head, then it was.

I'd met Veronica (Axel's baby mama), and I loved the setup of Bailey's new house, loved how it gave her and Veronica space while also making it easy for Alex, Axel's five-year-old son, to all live together. Especially since Veronica was sick and would need help.

But Bailey was *mine,* so I was keeping my eye on Veronica.

"Hmm," I said by way of answer.

Bailey sipped her beer and sat back in the cozy armchair flanking the even cozier couch. "Don't *hmm* me."

"I'm your aunt," I decreed. "I can *hmm* you any time, day or night."

"Well," Bailey said, "it's evening and that's technically not day *or* night, so your *hmms* are not welcome here."

I didn't know if it was the wine or if that somehow that made logical sense.

Either way...it made sense.

So, I decided not to argue (or confirm).

Something, if given the smirk on my niece's face, she read.

Ugh.

She was a pain in my ass.

"Finish your bottle of wine," Bailey ordered. "We have plans and I need you at Billie-Rose-has-drank-an-entire-bottle-of-wine-by-herself mellow."

I was dutifully drinking from my glass when that processed.

Dropping it, I frowned, asked suspiciously, "Why do you want me to mellow?"

Guilt across Bailey's face. "Umm..."

Suddenly, I wasn't so buzzed.

I sat up. "*Bailey.*"

More guilt.

"Darling niece," I gritted out. "I'm warning you.'

"Umm—"

"I need you mellowed for"—Bailey nodded toward the door, a knock coming right on cue—"*that.*"

"What—" I began, turning toward the front of the house, seeing Axel clomping down the last couple of stairs and reaching for the handle.

Watching him open it to reveal...

Bailey sucked in a breath, as though she were bracing.

Dessie.

A choking sound that had my gaze whipping toward Bailey, who was being weird. My brows dragged together, and I widened my eyes, mentally asking her, *What the fuck?*

It was great Dessie was here.

She'd been nearly as busy as I was with rebuilding Monroe's and getting the business back on track again. In fact, since Roger (the owner) had opted to step back from those decisions, choosing instead to be a silent partner, Dessie was going to be the name and face of the new Monroe's.

And she was killing it.

But she'd been working crazy hours to get there.

None of which made any since as to why was Bailey being so fucking weird about the Three Musketeers getting together for a long overdue visit.

There.

Done.

Mission accomplished. We were at her place, ready for wine and snacks.

"Hey bitches!" Dessie called, striding into the room, moving to Bailey, and hugging her tight. Then to me. Hugging *me* tight.

Something I sank in to.

Until I saw what was happening behind her shoulder.

Until I saw that the front door hadn't closed...because Axel was talking to someone else outside it.

Someone who was walking up the concrete path, up the stairs, up—

Ah, *Christ*.

I understood why Bailey was acting so weird.

Because...Axel stepped back, tugged the door wide, and Joel strolled right into the house.

———

"See?" I said as we walked out of the room, having just barely made it out—mostly because the wine had worn off with about fifteen minutes left on the timer. "You so *totally* needed kick-ass-and-take-no-names-Billie Rose."

Bailey wrinkled her nose.

"Admit it," I pressed.

That nose wrinkled further, and damn, my niece was cute.

She was also stubborn.

Just like Dessie, who shook her head, ordered, "Do *not* admit that, Bailey. She'll be insufferable for the rest of the day if you do. And we still have dinner to get through."

Get through was right.

I'd been conducting extreme evasive maneuvers, making certain I'd never gotten too close to Joel.

To the man who'd held me and given me washi tape and—

Nope.

Not going there.

I shrugged, focused on my friends instead of the men who were walking ahead of us out of the room—acting like *they'd* been the ones who put the pieces of the puzzles together, *hmph* —and grinned at Bailey. "She's right. I *will* be insufferable."

Dessie snorted.

Bailey laughed.

And then, because Bailey was Bailey, she grinned at me and said, "There was no freaking way that we would have escaped on time without Kick Ass Billie Rose." A nudge of my shoulder. "Thank God the wine wore off."

Dessie dropped her head back and groaned. "*No.* Why would you do that?"

"What?" Bailey asked, nudging *her* shoulder. "Admit the truth?"

"Yes," Dessie muttered. "*That.*"

"Just saying"—Bailey grinned—"We would have never made it past that puzzle on the door if not for Billie realizing that the scratches on the wall went with the directional lock."

She was right.

I didn't verbally agree—there was ego, *cocky,* and there was confident. I liked to think I was the latter. Which was why I buffed my knuckles on my shoulder, nodded smartly, and said, "Thank you."

Also, spoken smartly.

Also spoken...a bit smugly.

But I figured my dash of smug was well-earned. Mostly because the group would have still been working on all those puzzles—including the door one—if not for me.

I was Billie Rose, mayor of a small town, master spread-sheeter, collector of washi tape and stickers alike...and escape room extraordinaire.

Okay, so maybe now I was inching toward cocky.

But it was easier to throw myself into escaping the Pirate's Den than to think about Joel.

About what I'd shared and how he'd held me and...

What I'd told him.

And the fact that he was *here,* close enough for me to smell the spice of his cologne.

Bailey grinned. "You're welcome, o goddess of the escape room."

"Come *on,* Bay, don't feed the ego," Dessie said, though she softened the words by looping her arm through mine and drawing me to her side. "I'm already going to hear it for the next however many months about not trying the code backward."

I nudged her. "Just saying—"

Dessie's finger across my lips. "No, Billie boo, please don't *just say*."

My eyes narrowed. "Next time I leave you in the room."

Dessie kissed my cheek, and turned sweet, probably because she knew that I'd do exactly that. "And there I would stay, trapped for eternity, waiting for the band of swarmy pirates to come and rescue me."

My lips twitched. "Hopefully they'd be romance cover worthy."

A waggle of her brows. "*Of course,* they'd be romance cover worthy."

We both giggled, and she squeezed me again.

Then Bailey bumped her shoulder against mine, taking my other arm, sandwiching me between my best friends. "Definitely romance cover worthy," she agreed, and God, I loved these bitches, especially when Bailey's grin softened into a smile, and she dropped her head onto my shoulder. "Pirates aside, honey, I'm glad we got to do this. I've missed you guys."

"Me too," I whispered.

"Me three," Dessie whispered.

We fell quiet then and walked for a bit, arm-in-arm through the crowded San Francisco streets before the sidewalks narrowed and they were both forced to let me go.

Axel swept an arm back, scooped up his woman, and drew her to his side.

Dessie and I dodged and weaved, the path made easier by Axel and him shielding Bailey with his big, broody hockey player body. People gave him a bit of a wide berth—though they didn't do exactly the same for Dessie and I, even with Joel and Ryan in front of us, lending their hockey bodies to fighting the crowd.

But Dessie and I were small, so they just swarmed back in, bumping into us left and right.

"Ugh," Dessie muttered, "I hate the city."

Even as those words crossed her lips, Ryan was turning back, tossing an arm around her shoulders and shielding her in a way that made me look twice—if only for a second. Because the difference between him and Dessie and Axel and Bailey was night and day.

Friends.

Lovers.

Distance and *none.*

I processed that, silently wondered if I should put some effort into that pair—after all, I'd found that my calling as a matchmaking mayor and was batting one for one on happy endings (that being Axel and Bailey). Dessie and Ryan might work—especially since I'd heard through the town gossip channels that Ryan, the one chronically monogamous player on the Rush, was now single.

But...

I didn't see it.

Ryan was too...

Quiet, maybe.

I couldn't pinpoint exactly why he and Dessie wouldn't work. I just knew in my matchmaking belly that they wouldn't.

Dessie needed someone else.

My mouth turned up.

And I had an inkling who would be perfect for her.

That was when I had an arm around *my* shoulders, and there was absolutely not one inch of body between the side of my body and the side of Joel's. He held me close and tight, automatically shielding me from the crowds, surrounding me with his heat and his scent and...

Just him.

More at home than I'd ever been.

That was the feeling he gave me every moment I spent close to him like this.

Holding me. Not sniping at me. Not calling me harpy or bitching about my overworking tendencies.

Just getting close…and talking softly.

Like he did right then, leaning in, murmuring in my ear, his hot breath making me shiver. "Why are you smiling, baby?"

I went still, my smile fading.

"What are you talking about?"

A finger tracing one side of my mouth. Then the other. "You were smiling."

"I was happy about the escape room and spending time with Bailey and Dessie."

His arm tightened.

And I ruined it by adding, "That's all."

Because it was defiant and made it seem like I was hiding something.

Joel knew it, too. He wrapped that arm even more tightly around me, tugged me somehow closer. "That's not it," he said, still in my ear, bent over so far to reach it that he couldn't possibly be comfortable. He didn't let on to that, though. Didn't straighten. Instead, he just kept talking. "But I'm not going to push, sweetheart. Not today." He straightened, tugged one of my curls. "I'm just happy you're smiling."

"Why?"

It was a question that just flew right out of my mouth, but, also, it was a whispered inquiry. One he shouldn't be able to hear, especially with the noise surrounding us on the sidewalk.

He stroked a finger over my cheek, answered. Because, of course, he'd heard. "Last time you weren't."

Okaaay. I didn't know what to do with that.

"And," he whispered, something I shouldn't have been able to hear, and yet I did. "Baby, you've got a great one."

Okaaay again. I still didn't know what the hell to do with that.

His thumb pressed lightly against my bottom lip.

Then he turned and walked away.

It took me several minutes to recover, and thankfully I did it climbing in the back of a Lyft that Joel had led me to, shielded me to, and spent the drive sandwiched again by Dessie and Bailey.

And when I *did* recover, I realized he hadn't let me go until the crowd had thinned out.

Twenty-Five

Joel

I'd left her looking rocked to her core, walking away from her for a change.

But no less intrigued.

No less drawn to her.

I'd bailed on the dinner we were all supposed to go to. Quitting while I was ahead, while I had that soft.

Not wanting to piss her off and cause her to retreat and—

Just basically quitting while I was still ahead.

Plus, I'd had to get on the bus early the next morning, had to drive to a game, the first in a series of them on a road trip that was finally ending tonight.

And...I wanted to stay ahead.

I needed to continue staying ahead.

But I'd left her with that for a week, I was heading home, and now I figured I'd better pull out the big guns...or at least, to up my texting game.

Which was why I'd typed out about a dozen texts to Billie Rose.

None of which were right.

Which was why I'd also deleted about a dozen texts to Billie Rose.

And was currently staring at my phone like it held the keys to the universe—or, at least, like it was going to gain self-awareness and help a man out, help me write something that was amazing and would make Billie magically appear in my bed when I got home, begging me to fuck her.

"Shit," I muttered, dropping my hand—and my cell—to my thigh, and closing my eyes, lulled by the rumble of the bus's engine, by the swaying motion as we drove along the dark highways. No fancy, chartered flights for our team. We spent long hours on the road. Close together—sometimes *too* close together.

Case in point?

Fox snagging my phone from my hand, taking advantage of my closed eyes.

And reading my unlocked screen.

Or the lack of messages on my unlocked screen.

"Wow."

My eyes had already snapped open at the loss of my cell, seeing the smirk on Fox's face. But I really didn't need this.

Not right then.

It was late.

We'd lost three in a row.

My hip hurt like a motherfucker.

And Fox, sitting across from me, expression snarky and all-knowing, sent a surge of adrenaline through me.

My fist would look excellent slamming into his face.

Would be excellent at wiping that dumbass smirk off his face.

I sucked in a breath. Fought for control.

We were on a bus.

There wasn't a lot of personal space.

I was one of the older guys, had been around long enough

that I got one of the double seats toward the back—slightly more space, slightly more privacy (minus Fox's intrusion).

But there were unwritten rules.

Don't be too loud.

Don't be too much of an asshole (here, again, I narrowed my eyes in Fox's direction).

Don't start fistfights when we had several more hours to go.

I released the breath I'd taken in, letting it out between my teeth, and extended my hand, "Give me my cell."

"You sure about that?" Fox said, holding it up, displaying the blank screen.

With Billie's name across the top.

Jesus fucking Christ.

I gritted my teeth. Most of the guys were lost in their phones, listening to music or podcasts or catching up on TV shows. But with the scene Fox seemed to be determined to make, that was sure to end.

"Yes," I muttered, twitching my fingers.

"You *sure?*" he repeated—or sort of repeated, anyway.

My answer was still the same. *"Yes."*

"I mean," he said, still not handing me the damned phone, "I'd ask again, because clearly you're striking out, but worse, this blank screen means you haven't even stepped up to the plate."

I hadn't.

I'd been fucking around. Staying ahead. Biding my time.

But I knew I needed to act.

That was why I was trying to figure out what to text her. How to continue peeling the layers back, how to keep the progress we'd made, how to make absolutely certain that we weren't going to go backward.

Hence me pondering text version number thirteen.

"Phone," I said, twitching my fingers again.

His bushy beard twitched. "You're sure, *sure?*"

Fuck it. I was going to start a fistfight on the bus.

I didn't give a damn.

But before I could launch myself at Fox and introduce my fist to that pretty boy face of his, Ryan popped out an earbud. "Fox."

Spoken quietly.

But with authority. Confident in his ability as the most stable of all of us to get us to behave.

It worked.

Fox made a face, but he silently passed my cell over.

"I'm just saying—" he began.

"Christ almighty," I muttered, digging my head into the seat back, hating my life right then.

Especially when Ryan said, "You sure you want to do this on your own?"

My head shot up. "Seriously?"

"You told me about her weeks ago and you're still"—a nod at my cell, currently safely clutched in my hand—"you're shooting blanks."

Fox cackled.

Ry rolled his eyes. "You know he's the text guru." A shrug. "You might take him up on the offer of help."

Fucking motherfucker.

"Not you too," I gritted.

Ryan shrugged, lips turning up into a smirk. The fucker was quiet, but he had a sly sense of humor. We all had to watch him, or he'd pull one over on us. And do it quietly.

And do it with relish—like right then, the asshole.

"You're shitting on the sidelines, man," he said. "And this means something to you."

I inhaled, ground my teeth, forced myself to hold his eyes. "Yeah."

The amusement bled out of his face, and I knew then he got exactly where I was. Billie Rose and I had been circling each other for years now, always taking snarking and snapping and teasing.

Even knowing we'd fucked, he wouldn't understand that it had changed for me (and hopefully for her as well).

Not until right then, until he understood exactly why I'd struggled for way too long to send a damned text.

To his credit, Ryan did what he always did—he was a good teammate, and more importantly, he was a good friend. "Right then," he said, tone completely neutral. "So, I'm thinking that *you've* been thinking about that text to the mayor for about a hundred miles and you're clearly not getting anywhere."

Another nod to my cell, gripped so tightly in my lap I was surprised the screen hadn't shattered. Well, if it did, I couldn't use it, and then I could stop thinking about this fucking text I needed to send.

Bonus.

"And *I'm* thinking that Fox is charming, and he's made Billie Rose laugh more than once," he said quietly. "Which is why I'm also thinking that you should let him take a crack."

I clenched my hand tighter, grit my teeth together, and stared at Ry.

I knew he'd back off if I asked—verbally, with my eyes, with my fists.

But...something needed to change.

I held the cell back out at Fox.

Who looked at me with uncharacteristic solemnity. "On a scale of one to five, how important is this to you?"

I forced my fingers to unlock, to let him have the device, communicating with my eyes the answer to that question.

"Right," he muttered. "About seven hundred and fifty million."

Then he bent his head, stared at the screen for long moments.

Then—because he was Fox and the fucker couldn't let one

interaction pass without cracking a joke—he kept his bent, but lifted his eyes so they'd connected with mine, and they were sparkling with humor.

Fucker.

"So, just to confirm, you're saying this is important."

"Give it back to me," I snapped, reaching for my phone, but Fox, for as big as he was, as strong and bulky, he was also quick, skirting around my hand and sliding into the seat behind and diagonal to me—close enough to continue to give me shit, but far enough away that I couldn't reach him without making a scene.

I repeat, *fucker*.

"Just making sure I understand the parameters," he drawled.

Murder. Death. Kill.

I raised my brows at Ryan, added dismemberment and castration to my nonverbal threats.

Ry just reclined back against the window, smirking at me from across the row, glancing between the gap in the seats and watching Fox.

Which was when I fully processed everything.

Fox had my cell.

Fox was going to text Billie.

Fuck it. I needed to see this.

I slid across the aisle, bouncing and weaving as the bus continued in motion, avoiding glancing toward the front and seeing if we'd gathered any attention—either from Coach or from our driver, Ronnie, and finding we hadn't.

Not yet anyway.

But with Fox...one never knew.

"What's something you like about her?" Fox asked, fingers moving on the screen, as though he'd always known I was going to end up here—pressed thigh to thigh with him.

And *that*—the whole thigh-to-thigh pressing situation—

sounded like something that Billie Rose and Bailey and Dessie would read for their "book club."

I'd heard enough about their books to know that they read some freaky shit—not that I was complaining about the way that Billie implemented what she'd learned from those books in the bedroom.

But that wasn't something I was going to share with the kids.

With Fox.

"She's smart," I said when Fox did that head bent toward the screen, but eyes on mine thing again.

He sighed, shook his head.

"What?"

"If you're trying to get in this bitch's pants—"

One second, I was thinking of smexy books and the next, my temper snapped. I flashed out a hand, gripped his throat. "Don't call her a bitch."

Low, quiet...deadly words.

Fox just grinned. "I'm just saying you're not going to want to compliment her brain and still have a chance to fuck her."

This wasn't going to work.

They didn't know her.

They didn't *get* her.

But *I* did.

Or at least, I was starting to. I'd begun to peel back the layers.

That thought had me letting Fox go—and not apologizing because, fuck him. I snatched my phone, typed out a text, not caring that he was looking over my shoulder the entire time.

Not caring that he repeated it to Ryan, and they exchanged a look.

That told me everything and nothing.

They didn't get it.

But she would.

And that was enough.

(Even if they looked at me in pity as the hours went by and she didn't reply).

My woman was stubborn.

She'd reply. But she'd do it on her own damned time.

Which was the only thing that kept me calm as the bus continued to move, kept me confident as we disembarked hours later back in River's Bend, kept me certain as I said my goodbyes and headed for my car.

Billie Rose would come to me.

But it would be on her own terms.

TWENTY-SIX

BILLIE ROSE

Washi tape for your thoughts. Six-ring versus disc system?

I'd gotten that text four hours before and I was still periodically picking up my phone and staring at the screen, reading the words.

Trying to decipher the hidden meaning.

This after having to search up the number in my database, thus confirming what I already knew low in my belly.

The number belonged to Joel.

Joel was texting me.

About planners.

"What. The. Fuck?" I whispered, dropping the cell on my desk and frowning at the wall.

Why the wall?

Because I was deliberately avoiding looking at the couch.

The material no longer smelled of Joel, but it had for long

enough that I'd slept heavy and deep and peaceful until the scent had faded.

Then it had been right back to this.

Passing out for a few hours before the nightmares hit. Trying to go back to sleep for a while. Giving up and shuffling to my desk, to my computer, trying to catch up on a stack of work that never seemed to get any smaller.

And worse, next month was the mayoral election.

There wasn't anyone running against me, but there were a multitude of procedures and extra meetings that I had to navigate on top of my normal workload.

Which had always been intense, heavy, almost too much to shoulder.

But I was an achiever, a problem solver.

I *lived* for that.

For my work.

I loved it. Really. I did.

But—I sighed—that night in the city, doing the escape room with Bailey and Dessie and the men, going back to their house after dinner and hanging while Axel served us all—including Veronica, who was definitely growing on me—seemed very far away.

Even though it had only been a week.

And now Joel was texting me.

He'd *never* texted.

I'd never texted, or at least my phone told me I hadn't. I'd apparently delivered all of my instructions in person.

And now Joel was texting me about *planners*.

My brain couldn't process that.

My heart...thudded against my ribcage each and every time I'd thought about it.

And I'd thought about it a lot since it had come in hours before.

But I hadn't replied.

First, because I hadn't known who it was.

Then because I *had* known.

Now it was the middle of the night, and my inbox was empty for one rare instance. I'd planned to excess, planned until I couldn't plan any longer. No meetings to attend. No people to go see and check in on at three in the morning. Nothing to do except to sit in the dark in my desk chair, staring at that message on my phone, my thumbs wanting to move.

I *wanted* to text back.

But it was terrifying, like stepping off a platform for a bungee jump, trying to look off into the distance because if I looked down, the terror would overwhelm me. It was too late, though. I'd glanced below my feet, had seen the gorge, the rocks and water and knew—just *knew*—that the collision was imminent, and it was all going to be terrible...and over.

So...my thumbs wanted to move.

They couldn't, though. Because I was paralyzed.

Sighing, I chucked my cell onto my desk and pushed away, grabbed the basket I kept in the bottom left drawer, and stepped out of my office, moving down the hall, pushing out into the night air.

Then...I did something stupid.

Well, I'd done it from the moment I grabbed the basket.

From the moment I'd kept the keys.

But I'd had them for a long time because I showered here, something the owners had offered up right after the fire. Had offered before the trailers were set up in the parking with more permanent bathrooms—though not showers...which was why I was *still* showering here while everyone had moved onto their temporary housing and their own bathrooms.

So, the showers *here* weren't being used with regularity—except by the hockey players.

And by me.

Because I hadn't relocated from the trailer.

Because I'd kept the keys to the rink.

Because...I'd needed to keep close to a certain hockey player, to be in his space, even without him knowing that I was. Being here had given me some of the peace I'd found in his arms, in his bed, wrapped in his scent on my couch.

I carded in through the player's door, winding my way through the corridors with the confidence of having done it dozens and dozens of times before. I could navigate by the faint light of the occasional recessed exit sign, the dotting of fluorescents that never turned off. But I could have navigated my way without even the least bit of light.

It was muscle memory now.

It was *easy*.

Taking a path I knew the players did, past offices and conference rooms and a large weight room stocked with exercise bikes and free weights and yoga mats, beyond which was another long room where the athletic trainers worked on the guys and the myriad of injuries they received being in the line of fire of pucks and sticks and skates and big ass hockey player bodies.

But I wasn't going to work out—no fucking way.

I got my exercise by hoofing it from one end of River's Bend to the other, tearing washi tape with my bare hands (okay, fine, it was designed to tear easily, but sometimes those glitter rolls were *difficult*). I could also tolerate the occasional hike.

But I couldn't get behind lifting dumbbells or riding one of those fancy bikes or, even worse, running on a treadmill.

It was an awful idea.

Whoever invented it should have all their planners taken away and burned.

Anyway, I hustled past the gym, the training suite, and kept moving.

To the locker room.

There were double swinging doors there, ones that were

locked, and ones I had the keys to as well. A brief pause, making quick work of the lock, pushing into the space.

It had changed when the season had started. More equipment coming in, nameplates suddenly appearing in the little holders screwed into the wood that framed each spot where the players sat to get dressed.

But my eyes only went to one spot.

Joel's name.

Mounted above the center station on the far wall.

"Dumb," I whispered. "*Dumb.*"

I still crossed to it, studying the mostly empty space—there was a small, thin black box up on the shelf that wasn't normally there. I wanted to open it, but I exerted a modicum of self-control and didn't—just stroked my fingertips over the smooth cardboard. Then, because I knew I was already overstepping, just by being in this room, I traced the letters of Joel's name and forced myself to step away. Perhaps if I'd thought this through, I would have had a note to leave him. Some pithy response to his text and an addition to the allure of Billie Rose, mayor of River's Bend.

How does she do that?

Magic, y'all.

Damn right. I had a reputation to uphold.

Maybe instead of the note, I should have brought a planner to leave him—spiral bound, just to make things interesting.

But instead, I'd cut and run.

Like usual.

You've gotta follow through on your responsibilities, BR.

Yup. To make matters even better, I was hearing my dad in full lecture mode.

Because I knew he wouldn't approve of me taking four hours to reply to a text.

Sighing, I moved to the showers, yanked at the silver handle, turning on the stream of water, knowing from experience that it took a few minutes for the temperature to warm. I always chose one right in the middle of the others, the one framed by the open doorway.

Because *I* would be framed in the open doorway.

My naked body, slick with water, breasts tipping up as I arched back to wash my hair.

Imagining Joel watching that water sluice down my skin, his eyes hot and his body hard. He would coax me out of the shower with promises of his mouth on my cunt, and he'd make me come that way before he bent me over one of the benches and fucked me.

Or I would fuck *him* on that bench, sitting astride his hips, his thick cock even thicker in that position, grinding down him until I lost it, and he lost patience, thrusting up into me.

Or Joel would get naked and join me under the stream, would spin me around, pin my front against the wall and wash my hair for me. *Then* he'd fuck me.

Or Joel would get naked and slip into in the stream of water, pinning me against the cold tiles while he stroked his hands over my naked body, massaging my ass, jerking my hips back and angling them so he could finger fuck me before he fucked me with his tongue.

Or Joel would get naked and slip into the stream of water, pinning me against those tiles, angling my hips, and fucking my ass. But not messing around and fumbling, worried about hurting me. He'd do it right—thrusting into me slowly, giving me steady strokes that were a little rough, but perfectly deep. And he wouldn't forget my clit.

My favorite fantasy, though—and clearly, I'd taken enough showers in here to have a litany of them—was when he would see me and without delay, he'd drop his bag, his keys and wallet on the carpet. He'd see me and stride right through the opening of the showers, walk fully clothed into the stream of water.

He'd drop to his knees.

My back would hit the cool tiles on the wall.

His big hand would wrap around my thigh before he lifted my leg up and over his shoulder.

And his mouth—his beautiful, glorious mouth—would devour me.

The water all around us, splattering against the material of his clothes, darkening the fabric as it clung to his skin, plastering his hair to his skull.

A huge, shattering orgasm would barrel down on me with absolutely no quarter.

Glorious.

Perfect.

I shuddered, just the fantasies leaving my legs feeling shaky, my pussy soaking.

So...I gave in.

I stripped down, left my folded clothes on the bench—on *Joel's* portion of the bench—pulled my towel from my caddy, and hung it on one of the hooks near the entrance to the showers. Already, steam was filling the space, clinging to my skin, and I set the plastic container with my body wash and hair products within arm's reach before I stepped into the water, pretending the warm rivulets running over me were Joel's fingers tracing patterns on my skin.

But that was all it was.

Pretend.

TWENTY-SEVEN

JOEL

I sat in the parking lot, watching my teammates drive away, ready to sleep in their own beds for the first time in a week.

I was ready too.

Exhaustion pulled at my body, a body that ached after the four games that week. Four nights of collisions and working my ass off. Sandwiched by four nights being crammed into that bus, being bumped around while trying to make my big, dumb body fit into a seat that wasn't designed for a big, dumb body.

But Billie's car was in the parking lot.

And I could see a light on in her office.

And...she hadn't texted back.

So, I was debating between going to the trailer, seeing if the door was unlocked, and if it wasn't, either banging on it until she answered or picking the lock and letting myself in.

"Step one," I muttered, popping open my car door and moving to the trailer. "See if it's unlocked."

I tugged at the handle. It opened.

Opened...in the middle of the night.

Opened when she might be sleeping and vulnerable, just down the hall.

My temper spiked. I should lock it, close it, turn around and walk away. But she'd left it open in the middle of the night when she might be sleeping and vulnerable, just down the hall.

"Fuck," I muttered, knowing that even if I pretended otherwise for a minute, I was *always* going to go into that trailer.

Always.

I walked down the hall, straight to her office, eyes on the band of light shining out through her open door.

"Harpy, you'd better not be work—"

I walked in and froze.

Because her office was empty.

Her monitors were on, not even sleeping yet.

Her chair was pushed back.

Worry immediately coiled in my belly and I studied the empty space like it would give me answers. And it did, I supposed. Blanket crumpled on the couch, as though she'd tossed it back and got up.

Probably to work on the computer—one of whose screens was showing a spreadsheet.

Chair pushed against the file boxes on the back wall. Bottom desk drawer pulled open.

So awake. Working.

Not a surprise.

But her cell—screen open to my message—was.

One, how she could function without a cell that automatically locked its screen and didn't butt dial constantly was unbelievable.

Two, that she was looking at my message.

Not just swiping up and ignoring it.

But reading it in the middle of the night.

Yeah, I liked that.

Except...leaving her safe space in the middle of the night.

That I didn't like. Especially if she'd left to go and process the fact that I was texting her and maybe that she didn't know how to feel about it. Doing that somewhere out there, in the dark, in the middle of the night.

I *didn't* like that.

So much that I immediately spun on my heel and stormed out of the trailer.

I was going to find her, and I was going to tan her ass—

Okay, I'd make it clear exactly how dumb it was to be wandering alone in the dark, and then, if she was up to it, I'd see about the spanking.

I needed to see that lush ass of hers reddened from my palm.

Right.

Priorities.

Finding her and making sure she was safe.

So, I set about that.

———

I looked.

But I didn't find her.

Not in her little SUV.

Not in the open space behind the trailer.

Not back *in* the trailer, both of us somehow missing each other.

And now it was really late, and I still hadn't come across Billie Rose. And the urge to turn that ass red had grown.

But I'd come to peace with the fact that I wasn't going to find her.

So, I'd tabled the red ass and wanting to find her and kiss her senseless and coax her into telling me what her reply to my text would be.

I'd have to do that tomorrow.

Sighing, I headed back to my car, but then I remembered the

box I'd left in my stall. The one I'd meant to leave at the trailer before the road trip or to slip into Billie Rose's purse when she wasn't looking at the escape room.

The problem was that Billie Rose never looked away.

She was always taking everything in—and she put a fair amount of effort into keeping her distance from me.

Until she didn't.

Hence me wanting to give her that red ass.

So even though I was still worried about the stubborn woman, I retrieved my badge from the center console of my car and knew that if her reaction to the washi tape was any interaction, then she was going to really like the contents of that little leather box.

Maybe enough that I could use it to smooth over the spanking my little harpy had coming.

That had my lips turning up, despite the worry, and I headed for the rink, unlocking the door, and moving determinedly down the hall to the locker room.

There was noise coming from that direction, but it was a familiar noise, so I didn't really process it, didn't really think probably because, I realized later, that I'd heard it so often.

At any rate, I was thinking about that box and Billie's red ass, so I didn't immediately realize the locker room had been unlocked when I pushed through the door, didn't realize the lights were on. Not until I saw what was illuminated within those four walls.

Then I realized the door had been unlocked.

Then I realized the lights were all on.

And what they revealed was...

An encapsulation of every fantasy I'd ever had, every bit of porn I'd ever watched.

Billie Rose was standing in the showers, eyes closed, arms up, her naked body completely on display.

Water had turned her skin into a glistening temptation. With her arms overhead, hands in her hair, her lush breasts were hung in a way that meant I was immediately hard and desperate to get my mouth on those taut pink nipples. My gaze slid lower, down over the rounded curve of her belly, the narrow line of her waist, her hips that demanded to be held—no, to be gripped tightly, yanked back roughly as I thrust my cock deep.

Lower still.

To the thin strip of curls camouflaging that slick cunt.

Her gasp drew my gaze back up.

Away from that pussy, up over those curves, pausing at her breasts—because how *couldn't* I pause there? But then I made it back to that beautiful face of hers, saw that her eyes were open.

And they were locked on me.

Cobalt.

I could tell even from here.

I stopped thinking.

My keycard hit the floor, my cell and keys following suit.

Then I was walking into the shower, water splattering over my shoes, soaking into my sweats, my shirt.

"Joel," she whispered, lifting a hand, touching my chest as though she were uncertain I was really there. But the moment her fingers touched me, she gasped again. "*Joel.*"

I dropped to my knees, hands going to the inside of her thighs, pushing them apart. "Hush," I muttered, nudging her back against the wall. "And hold on."

Her leg over my shoulder.

My tongue sliding lazily through her wet folds.

She shuddered.

"Fuck, you're pretty," I muttered.

She shuddered again.

Then I leaned in, and I ate her like it was my fucking job.

And maybe it was.

I wanted it to be. Forever.

But I'd settle for it to be my job right then, water flowing over her body, over mine, soaking through my clothes. Giving her what her body needed.

Her juices on my tongue, my chin, in my beard.

I didn't give a fuck, not when my name was rolling off her tongue. Not when her hips were bucking against my mouth. Not when she was throwing her head back, hitting the wall with a *crack* that almost pulled me off her.

Probably would have if not for the fact that she was coming.

On my face.

Calling out my name.

Melting in my arms.

And I was really, really glad that she hadn't texted me back.

Twenty-Eight

Billie Rose

I was still half-convinced that I'd passed out, hit my head on the tile, and lost consciousness.

That this was all a dream.

But I wouldn't be cold in a dream, right?

It would all be rainbows and sunshine and orgasms.

Not goose bumps prickling on my arms.

Not my breath whooshing out of me as Joel scooped me up, carrying me out of the showers, only pausing where my towel was hanging to yank it off the hook.

A moment later, I was on the bench, the cotton wrapped tightly around me, Joel in dripping clothes kneeling in front of me. His eyes were...on fire. Blazing for me. Blazing *through* me even as a puddle formed around him on the black skate mats.

His hands moved brusquely, rubbing the cotton over my skin, drying me, warming me, making those goose bumps disappear.

As he bent close, taking care of me, I could see behind him, see the open doors to the locker room.

See the trail of belongings that led to the showers.

His phone.

His keys.

His wallet.

My fantasy played out in real life.

Something sharp and painful pulsed deep inside me.

This couldn't be.

It *wouldn't* be.

But then Joel was tugging on my shirt, dragging it over my head, pulling it down my body. My sweats joined the party next, tugged over my feet, up my thighs, settling over my waist.

"Joel—"

He dropped the towel on my head, rubbed briskly at my curls (briskly enough that they would definitely be crazy in the morning—my curls required gentle drying, scrunch and release and repeat). But I couldn't bring myself to be upset about looking like I'd jabbed my finger into a light socket hours from then.

Not when Joel was kneeling in front of me, his clothes dripping (my *pussy* dripping), after he'd unknowingly fulfilled one of my biggest fantasies.

Without hesitation.

And then was dressing me and drying my hair.

Also, without hesitation.

"Joel," I tried again. "Honey, I—"

He tugged the towel off my hair, set about putting on my socks, my shoes, my hoodie. I didn't miss the fact that he shoved my panties in his pocket. Either he was displaying more of that filthy streak I liked so much, or he wanted a souvenir.

The fucked-up part of me wanted it to be both.

The rest of me wasn't certain it *couldn't* be both.

"Joel—"

He stood, yanked off his shirt, sending it to the floor with a heavy *plop*.

I blinked, momentarily distracted because he was shirtless and some of my favorite parts of him were on display. Strong forearms, thick biceps. Shoulders I knew I could hold tight to... because I *had* held tight to them, multiple times now. His pecs were squeezable and covered with a light dusting of hair—enough to say man, but not so much as to say gross seventies porn star. A flat stomach that had a faint etching of abs.

Perfect.

A big, sexy man.

But not one who would make you feel like shit standing naked next to him.

Beautiful because he was strong and capable.

Just not model perfect.

A man.

One I wanted to have in my life—

Thwump.

His pants and underwear hit the floor.

And...holy hell, if *that* wasn't model perfect, I didn't know what was. Yes, Joel's body was beautiful because he was all man in a way that was absolutely intoxicating. But his dick was... chef's kiss. Thick and not too veiny. A well-shaped head. Balls I wanted smacking my ass as he fucked me from behind. Balls that were covered as he wrapped the towel around his middle and strode out of the room.

My brows lifted, eyes going wide. "Umm," I whispered, trying to process what in the fuck was going on.

The man had just fulfilled one of my biggest fantasies and he was striding right out of the locker room.

Without a word.

Wearing nothing but a towel.

That was...awkward.

But I'd only just begun to realize it *was* awkward, had just begun to feel uncomfortable when he walked back in, his arms full of navy blue.

"Umm," I whispered again as he strode over to me, brushing his knuckles over my cheek.

"I'm sorry," he murmured.

"Umm." Clearly orgasms highlighted a blatant need for me to expand my vocabulary. "What?"

He set his burden onto the bench next to me. "I'm sorry, sweetheart. I just came in and"—hell, if his cheeks didn't go a little pink—"*ate* you, baby. I didn't even ask—"

My words came back. "Thank fuck."

He reared back slightly, blinking once. Twice. "What?"

I sat up, touched his forearm, and the words kept coming. "You just fulfilled one of my biggest fantasies, honey. I'm not going to complain."

His brows lifted.

I gave him more. "You walking in on me in that shower," I murmured. "Seeing me. Not being able to resist the vision of me naked and wet—"

He jerked, a groan bubbling up in his throat.

My eyes—I couldn't help it, okay?—slid down, saw that he was sporting serious tent-age.

So, I kept going.

"You seeing me and dropping everything, coming straight to me, not able to resist, not thinking, not stopping, coming in with your clothes on and just...going down on me?" My lips curved when his eyes heated further. "Yeah, honey. I've thought of that pretty much every time I've showered here. Wanted you to come in and see me and—"

Before I could blink, he was in front of me again, on his knees, palms scorching through the material of my sweats. "What else have you thought about?"

"So, so much." I inhaled, but only after I processed that the words hadn't just existed in my head.

"Tell me."

A command.

I shivered.

And I gave him the rest.

"You'd see me, want me, but I wouldn't come." I shot him a smile. "So, you'd coax me out of the warm water with all sorts of naughty promises. But"—I lowered my voice to a whisper—"I wouldn't come out until you promised to lick me and then"—I nodded to the bench where I was sitting—"you'd bend me over and fuck me from behind."

His fingers convulsed.

"Or sometimes I would give into your coaxing, and you lick me and then I'd climb on top, take you inside, and grind you until you lost patience and took over."

Nostrils flaring on an inhale, he rasped out. "*Baby.*"

"Or maybe you'd strip down and join me under the stream, spin me around, hold me against the wall and tease me by just washing my hair." My lips turned up. "Of course, that would be followed by you licking me and then fucking me."

"Billie Rose."

"*Or* you'd get naked and walk into in the water, holding me in place, ordering me to keep still as you touched me everywhere, before you fucked me with your fingers and tongue."

His dick twitched beneath that thin strip of cotton.

I saw it. My mouth watered for it.

"Or," I whispered, "you'd get naked and come into the water and you'd flip me around, pinning my front against the wall. I'd feel the cold, but only for a few seconds before you tugged my hips back, angling me so you could fuck my ass."

Those fingers on my thighs convulsed so fiercely that it hurt.

But in a good way, that perfect mix of rough and not that had me going wet all over again.

"Baby," he murmured. "You're killing me."

Desire in his voice. His eyes. His touch.

I smoothed my fingers over his jaw, feeling the bristles of his beard on my skin, shivering again when I remembered the feel of that hair rubbing between my thighs. "You like it."

"Yes."

I bit my lip, heart pounding. "You want to do all those things to me."

Another breath in, his shoulders lifting, lungs expanding, abs contracting. "Yes."

His text. The washi tape. How he'd held me and been so gentle when I'd freaked out. How he'd wiped my tears away when I'd cried.

Not to mention the orgasms.

Fulfilling my fantasy.

Wanting me now.

I just...well, the wicked in me took over.

I reached forward, nudged at the tuck in his towel, the little strip of fabric holding it in place.

It puddled on the floor.

His cock sprang up.

"Dealer's choice, honey." A beat, his body going really, really still. "You pick which one you're going to do to me."

Twenty-Nine

JOEL

I wanted to do all of what she'd described.

Wanted to unleash some fantasies of my own—now spinning through my mind, a picture book of fucking I wanted to write, had been plotting for months, for years.

I'd never dreamed about fucking her here.

Now I knew I'd never be in this room without remembering her in the shower, naked and wet and slick on my tongue.

She wrapped her fingers around my cock, stroked, sending me dangerously close to the edge while at the same time reaching for the waistband of her sweats, tugging them partway down her thighs and giving me a glimpse of the curve of her ass.

"Bench," I muttered.

"What?" she whispered.

"*Bench,*" I repeated.

Then I suited words to actions, tugging her hand off my cock, yanking her up from the bench and making quick work of removing her sweats, her shirt.

"Joel," she murmured.

"*Bench,*" I said again, flipping her around, pushing between her shoulder blades and coaxing her down so that lush ass was up in the air. I ran a finger down her spine, dipped it between the cleft of her cheeks, pressed lightly against the taut circle of muscle.

She inhaled sharply.

"Not today, baby." I bent, nipped at one cheek and then the other. "Soon, but not today."

Then I slid that finger forward.

Dripping.

Fuck.

My eyes hazed over, my vision went red at the edges, and my brain...it stopped working. I just reached around her, pinched her nipples, and then flexed my hips.

Hot. Wet. Tight.

Hot. *Wet.* Tight.

"Fuck," I whispered, the fog clearing. I needed to pull out. But I didn't want to slip from the tight clasp, from the slick heat of her.

Only...I didn't have a condom.

I was inside her and I didn't have a condom because I hadn't replaced it after the last time I'd used it.

I was inside her and I didn't know if she was on the pill or the shot or whatever.

I was inside her and I didn't know if I could protect her.

"Fuck," I whispered again.

"Yes." She arched back against me, hips moving on me, pussy clamping down, moaning, "Please fuck me, honey."

My groan bubbled up in my throat.

Pleasure and desire warring with the need to protect her.

Fuck.

I couldn't.

I gave myself one more stroke and then pulled out.

Her head shot up, curls bouncing, gaze hitting mine, mouth shaped into an O, a mewl of protest in the air.

I slid two fingers inside her, knowing it wasn't the same as my cock, but not willing to put her at risk.

Even if my dick was ready to explode.

She bucked against me, pussy flexing. "Why did you stop?"

I pressed a kiss to the base of her spine, flicked out my tongue to taste her skin, to delve into the cleft between her cheeks. A soft moan, one that cut off when I said, "No condom, baby."

She spun around again, the disappointment on her face almost comical.

"I'll take care of you, baby," I told her, flicking her tongue out again. "I just don't have a condom."

Her hips pushed against me, against my fingers. "I have an IUD, honey. Just...stop thinking and fuck me." A beat. "Please just fuck me."

I hesitated.

But only for a minute.

Because Billie Rose was asking me for something.

Asking *me* for something.

And it was something I really wanted to give her...

So, maybe it wasn't the right thing or the admirable thing or even the moral thing. But we were two consenting adults, and we both wanted this. I was clean, and I knew her well enough to understand that she wouldn't ask me to give her this if she wasn't the same.

So...I pushed back in.

And knowing that I was fucking her without any barriers, feeling that wet clamp with nothing between us heightened every sensation.

Hot. *Wet*. Tight.

Mine.

I fucked her hard and fast and deep.

I fucked her hard and fast and deep…until she came apart on my cock.

I fucked her hard and fast and deep until I toppled over right after her.

"Fuck," I whispered when I could speak without passing out. "I'm never going to be able to look at this bench the same way again."

Her head jerked, and she glanced back at me, curls flowing over her shoulders, the pink tip of one breast just visible.

Her eyes were wide, cheeks were flushed.

But the best part was that she was smiling.

Then she shifted, popping off my cock, and leaned up to kiss me, arms wrapping tightly around my shoulders, body coming flush to mine again. A wink, her fingers pressing into my scalp, tongue flicking over my lips.

"Me neither."

———

"I can't believe you," she muttered a half hour later.

Mostly because I'd bustled her into my car and driven her to my apartment.

She glared up at me, kept muttering. "You got me cock drunk and took me home."

I froze in the process of yanking back the blankets on my bed, grinned down at her. "Really?"

A shrug, but I didn't miss that she stood at the side of the mattress instead of climbing into the stretch of bed I'd revealed. "What?"

An innocent question and one that I didn't buy for a fucking *second*.

I raised my brows, fixed her with a look. "Cock drunk?"

That innocent question turned into a not-so-innocent smile. "I stand by what I said."

"Hmm."

One brow arched. "Hmm?"

"Yup." I rounded the bed, placed my hand in the middle of her chest, and pushed.

"I—*eek!*"

"Yup," I said again, smiling down at the sight of her sprawled out on my bed. "Pretty woman," I murmured, brushing my fingers over her mouth, her throat, between her breasts. "*Beautiful* woman."

She inhaled sharply. "I should go home."

"No." And because I had her where I wanted her, I just slipped in next to her, wrapped her in my arms, tugged the blankets up. "You should stay with me."

"Joel—" She was stiff as a board. "*Really,* I should go. I have to get up early."

"So?"

A pause. "So, I don't want to wake you up. It's late. You've been on a bus and—"

"Go to sleep, baby."

"*Joel.*"

"Rosie girl."

Another inhale, but her body didn't soften.

So, I did—or my tone, anyway. "I'll be okay," I told her. "I'll drive you back to the trailer in the morning, but I want you to be comfortable, baby. And this bed and my arms are better than that damned couch."

A beat. "The couch is fine."

"The *couch* is shit."

She pushed at my chest. "I should—"

"*You* should stop talking," I muttered, "close your eyes, and go the fuck to sleep."

"But—"

"Okay, harpy," I muttered, irritation beginning to burn low in my belly as I flipped us, rolling on top of her and pressing her back into the mattress. "E-fucking-*nough*." I cupped her cheek, forced her to look at me. "I want you here. I need to know that you're sleeping in a safe place. A comfortable place. I need to know that you're okay."

She bit her bottom lip again, teeth bright white against the pale pink.

Making *me* want to bite.

Her mouth. Her nipples. Her cunt.

My dick twitched.

Fuck.

Not the time. It was late. We were both tired. I needed her to be safe and we both needed to get some rest.

God knew she didn't get enough of it.

So, I only gave into the urge to nip her bottom lip.

A sigh, but I saw the acquiescence in her eyes.

"You'll stay?"

She exhaled again, those blue irises glimmering with some emotion I couldn't read. "Yeah."

I kissed her cheek, her nose, her mouth. "Thank you, baby."

A long blip of quiet. "Of course." Then she pushed lightly at my chest, rolling me off her. I would have protested, except she curled right up to my side, pressed her lips to my jaw. "Sleep now, honey."

I wrapped my arms around her, one hand buried in her curls, the other on that ass. "Okay, sweetheart."

I closed my eyes, and exhaustion flooding through me, I let sleep come.

What I didn't know—not until the morning—was that Billie Rose waited until I was asleep.

And then she somehow slipped from my hold and snuck out of my bed.

My apartment.

My life.

THIRTY

BILLIE ROSE

Two weeks after I'd left Joel's bed in the middle of the night, feeling like shit and desperate to put some distance between us, I was sneaking up onto a porch of a newly repaired home, on a street of newly repaired houses.

The first neighborhood to be completely back to normal—houses, landscaping, streets, lights, even the fucking stop signs were new.

But not all of my people were doing well.

Some had been stretched to the breaking point with the effort and cost of rebuilding.

So...I came bearing gifts.

Quietly, I set the basket on Thelma's porch, not wanting the older woman to have the chance to reject the offering.

Thelma was stubborn.

She was also not eating enough.

How did I know this?

River's Bend had one grocery store and a handful of restaurants that were in good repair.

And I'd heard from Frank—the owner—that her grocery purchases weren't coming frequently enough or in big enough quantities to sustain an adult woman.

Even one with a small appetite.

So...River's Bend would look after her.

But I knew Thelma wouldn't accept the basket of food and toiletries. I knew that if there was an opportunity to reject it, she'd shove it right back in my hands.

That was okay.

I could be sneaky.

I'd done it regularly, had perfected my sneaky skills in avoiding Joel.

A trait that went perfectly with knowing all—like when practice was and when the Rush games were and when Joel's car was in the parking lot because he was trying to track me down.

I'd left his apartment in the middle of the night.

He wasn't an asshole. He'd come calling multiple times when he hadn't been traveling with the team.

But...harpy. After the shower. After giving me my fantasy. After...

I'd hoped.

He'd called me that name again, in that irritated tone, and I knew that even though he'd given me the locker room, given me the gentle and sweet, in the end, *harpy* would be all he'd give me.

I'd needed to stop things. Stop before I let that hope take me over.

Stop before I let him in further.

Better to cut ties, crush the hope, and move on.

Now finally, weeks later...he'd stopped showing up in the parking lot, stopped forcing me to put my sneaky skills to work.

That hurt.

I couldn't lie.

But it wasn't unexpected...and it was what I'd wanted.

Right?

I inhaled. Exhaled. "Right," I whispered.

Now I got to focus on Thelma, on my town, on what was needed.

Not on the man who could fuck me, could make all my fantasies come to fruition while also breaking my heart.

"Enough," I whispered, deliberately putting Joel from my mind as I sank into a bit of mischief making. I pressed Thelma's doorbell and then dashed down off the porch, along the grass, dodging the sensor for the automatic flood light (see? I really *did* know all) that was mounted near Thelma's garage. Triggered, it would illuminate the entire front yard and blow my cover.

But I was well-practiced in the art of ding dong ditch.

Or had been as a twelve-year-old, anyway.

Though, I supposed those skills never really left a woman.

Case in point?

Moments later, I was safely behind a tree, watching Thelma —now with the door open—look around, sigh, and eventually bring the basket inside.

Mission accomplished.

Mentally, I high-fived myself, then walked down the quiet sidewalk, heading back to my car. I'd parked it around the corner to help with my sneakiness, but I didn't mind the trek. Not when the night sky was clear, and the air was cool on my cheeks, and I was taking care of my people.

My town was slowly putting itself back together.

But it would never be exactly what it had been before.

I was finally at the point where that was okay.

Change was good—*ha*.

I could barely *think* that, let alone internalize it.

Personally, I needed to be in control. I needed things (and people) to stay in place in the carefully thought-out buckets I'd created. Change—like fucking a certain sexy hockey player— could derail that.

Especially when I wasn't the driving force of said change.

Especially when I couldn't control all...and with Joel, I was nowhere near being in charge.

Something my friends and family would be shocked to hear.

But it was something I knew.

I might be pushy and confident and demanding and know what I wanted, but I knew myself, too. I knew my limits, knew that I had to give in on *some* things.

Joel made me give.

"Dangerous," I whispered on a sigh, turning the corner, forcing myself to enjoy that cool, clean night air. My tennis shoes were soundless on the sidewalk and I was mentally going through my checklist. I needed to stop by the construction site that was City Hall before heading back to the trailer. Then I had a boatload of work to finish up. My inbox was full. My spreadsheets needed to be reviewed. My planner needed to be set up for the next day. And...even though it was still late fall, the winter festival needed to be planned.

Construction should be mostly complete by then, everyone should be home, and it would be the first large-scale event we put on since the fire.

It needed to be *perfect*.

Which meant...the work of the mayor was never done.

Something that Joel would give me shit about.

I froze, my grin fading.

Belly churning.

God, I always, *always* wanted him.

Which was annoying. Because, initially, he filled me with irritation. Something that was even more *irritating* than the man himself had been. Because I was supposed to be untouchable.

Unable to be irritated.

But Joel *always* got under my skin.

Because the irritation had turned to wanting...and now after all that avoidance, it had become longing.

To be in his arms, to have his mouth on mine, his hands on

my body, his cock thrusting inside as he gave me the rest of the fantasies I'd described to him.

More.

He'd give me more.

I knew he could get creative.

But right now, I wish he was less creative and less persistent and less...*Joel.*

Because he was leaning back against my little SUV, his arms crossed, his lips curved up into a smile that I wanted to wipe off his face. Either with my fist or some pithy, snarky comment...or with my lips, tasting that smile, tucking it close to my soul and—

Preferably my fist.

Lie.

I was desperate for it to be with my lips.

Except he was tall, so his lips would be hard to reach without his help, without the unconscious way he bent for me.

Ugh. Annoying man.

And yes, I was trying to turn my focus away from my pounding pulse, my pussy that had immediately gone wet when I'd seen him, smelled him.

I needed to stay sane, to keep my distance.

Joel didn't give me that.

He stepped closer, the annoying, *sexy* hockey player making it impossible for me to retreat. "Whatcha doing, harpy?"

I flinched.

I didn't mean to.

It just...came out of nowhere.

It had been two weeks since I'd seen him, two weeks since I'd heard the nickname that used to make my blood boil but had long since cut deep.

I wasn't prepared.

I wasn't able to hide it.

And...he saw.

He *fucking* saw.

And...I knew, one look at the way his expression changed, that he got it.

Knew he finally got how much I hated it. How much it hurt.

Because he was immediately there, pressed to me, arms banding around my middle, my body flush against him. "Baby," he began.

I turned my head away. Wouldn't meet his gaze no matter how gentle his voice, how much he crouched and tried to make it so our eyes connected.

A soft curse.

"Baby," he said again, palm sliding up my spine, fingers dipping into my hair, pressing lightly to my scalp. Tucking me against him when I wouldn't look at him, holding me close so I couldn't back away. "I'm sorry. I didn't get it."

I wouldn't respond.

I couldn't.

Because I might cry.

His voice was even more gentle. "I thought you thought it was funny."

"No." I might be desperately trying to keep my distance (something that was going *really* well considering that I was standing in the circle of his arms), but I still had a spine. "It wasn't funny."

Fingers sliding from my hair, along my jaw. "No," he agreed, "it wasn't. I'm sorry."

I sucked in a breath.

He kept stroking that finger along my skin. "I thought you liked bickering, liked when I teased you and you could dish it back. I wouldn't have used it if I knew."

I leaned back, releasing that breath, and glared up at him. "You honestly thought that someone—a woman in particular— would enjoy being called a harpy?"

A wince.

"No," I muttered, fighting his hold. "You just thought *I* would. Because I'm so fucking terrible."

His brows dragged together. "Billie, baby—"

"Let me go," I whispered.

He kept his arms around me. "That's not what I meant."

"*Let me go*," I repeated.

He tightened his hold, didn't shift, didn't move away from me, and—this was something that would surprise people as well —I was tired.

I. Was. Tired.

That wasn't the Billie Rose everyone knew, the Billie Rose everyone expected, the Billie Rose my parents wanted me to be.

And certainly not the Billie Rose this annoying man knew.

But it was the truth.

And I might be a lot of things, but I always at least tried to be honest with myself.

I knew where I stood.

I got what I brought to the table.

I understood *exactly* what my shortcomings were.

"Rosie?"

The soft, husky voice had me blinking, realizing that my eyes were stinging, that I was dangerously close to crying. With this man close.

Again.

Stupid.

God, I was *so* damned stupid.

"Rosie, baby—"

I shoved him away, and the movement must have been a surprise because I managed to get free from his hold, managed to yank my car door open, nearly smacking him in the chest with it.

Freedom was near, and my seat was within reach, and—

His hand gripped my arm again, and he tugged me back out of the opening, spinning me toward him.

"Let me—"

His hand came to my cheek.

And his thumb brushed the underside of each eye.

I saw the glint of my tears perched on that rough finger and cringed. I was Billie Rose, mayor of River's Bend and badass extraordinaire. I didn't cry...

Except in front of this man.

And he had the evidence right there on his thumb. "I don't think you're terrible," he said so fucking gently that it *hurt*. "I think you're—"

Fuck.

I needed to go before he finished that thought, gave me something that couldn't be and—

His palm came to my face. "Rosie," he said again, and *God*, I loved when he called me that, when he held me so gently. Loved when his lips parted, and his mouth came close enough for me to feel the hot dampness of his breath on my skin. When his fingers flexed on my cheek, tilted my head up so he could stare into my eyes.

And...

I wanted.

And...

I couldn't.

So...that was when I used my last avenue of escape.

My fingers slid into my pocket, felt for the rounded plastic of my key fob.

And I didn't care that I'd just played doorbell ditch, and this could very well get me caught, especially in the quiet evening.

I just...pressed the panic button on my key fob.

THIRTY-ONE

JOEL

R ight.

It was time to get to the bottom of this shit.

Make it clear where I stood.

Figure out exactly what kind of fucked up nonsense was putting that look on her face.

That *I'd* put on her face.

With *harpy*.

Fuck.

I couldn't believe I hadn't put the pieces together until then —the little changes in her face, the way her body had gone still. But I couldn't ignore that the hurt was deep.

And *I'd* done that.

So...I was going to make it right.

But this was more than an idiotic nickname.

This was the walking away, the sneaking out while I was asleep. This was the way she kept everyone at a distance with her work.

This was...her father's lecture in the parking lot. Hiding her feelings about the washi tape.

The fear and embarrassment and shame that had come from losing it after the fire, crying about a brother who hadn't lived long enough.

This was...using her body and all the beautiful things she could do with it, all the things *we* could do with it, to keep me at a distance, in a carefully contained box.

Because otherwise I might see this.

Revelations were colliding in my mind as the puzzle pieces slid together.

But it was after nine and her car alarm was still going off.

Prioritize.

Right.

I grabbed her hands, realized they were empty, so set about the pleasurable experience of searching her pockets for her keys. Not in the back ones. Not in the front right. But there in the front left, were her keys.

I plucked them out, hit unlock, and the alarm cut off.

Then I pocketed the keys.

No sneaking away this time.

The quiet was somehow louder than the alarm, and I knew it was because of all the words—unspoken and not—swirling between us. I also knew that this wasn't the time or the place. That this conversation shouldn't be happening in the dark, on the street.

But...I couldn't let this continue.

Couldn't let her run and hurt any longer.

"I like you."

She jumped, and I closed the door, wrapped her in my arms again.

She was still. So damned still.

"Right," she whispered, and it was clearly lip service, clearly part of that bullshit shield to keep me at a distance.

I shifted us, pinning her back against her SUV, cupping her cheeks, forcing those wide eyes to mine. "I like you," I repeated. "And I want to see where this goes with you, sweetheart."

A shrug. More shield. False confidence joining the party. "Sure you do. The sex is out of this world and—"

My fingers tightened. "Don't make it just sex."

The words were a sharp whip of sound when I'd intended to stay soft, to keep working myself through that shield of hers.

"Because"—deliberate gentle now—"it means more. You know it, baby. That's why you're panicked. That's why you keep running away and avoiding me. That's why even now, you're looking for an escape route."

Silence.

Eyes drifting from mine again.

"I can't be in a relationship," she blurted.

Something coiled tight in my belly, prickled along my nape.

"Because you don't feel the same way about me?"

Maybe I'd read this all wrong. Maybe she didn't like me in the same way. Which would fucking suck. Absolutely. I liked her. Bar none. I wanted her. And not just for quick fucks that didn't mean anything.

Because they already meant more.

Because I *wanted* more.

Her face went gentle, and I relaxed, even before her words hit my ears. "I didn't say that."

"Baby," I muttered. "You gotta clue the dumb jock in. What *are* you saying?"

Her throat worked, eyes darting away and back. "You're not dumb." A breath. "I'm just not good at relationships," she said. "I don't bring an equal share. I work too fucking much and there are a million responsibilities on my shoulders—even more now, after the fire."

I held her closer. "And I'm on the road for half the year and busy with practices and training a lot of the time when I'm home." I tugged at a curl. "I love that your job is important to you and that you're good at it. That's sexy as fuck—how capable you are."

Her lips parted on a shaky exhale. "Really?"

"Yeah, baby. *Really*."

"And you're beautiful and sexy and smart and I love that you can hold your own in any situation." I ran my thumb along her bottom lip. "So, I'd be an idiot to *not* want to explore things with you. Something I've been trying to communicate with you for weeks now."

Guilt on that pretty face. "Really?"

"Yeah, baby," I said again. "*Really.*"

"But"—teeth pressing into her bottom lip—"what about when it goes wrong?"

Not if.

But *when*.

My fingers on her jaw, drifting to her chin, drawing her face up, knowing whatever words I gave her wouldn't be enough to make the uncertainty in her eyes go away. I'd have to show her. I'd have to work at it, to dig it out. Something I'd be more successful at if I could get her to stop running from me. "I like you, Rosie. A lot," I added. "That's not bullshit, and it's not a line to get in your pants. *I* like *you* as you are."

Her shoulders rose and fell on a breath and when she said, "I like you, too," I felt like I was Thor (pre Asgard being destroyed and losing everyone important to him).

But the disquiet in her eyes didn't disappear. Not completely.

Time. Trust took time.

I ran my thumb over her jaw. "We'll be okay, baby. I promise. No matter what happens, we'll figure it out."

A breath.

I gave her more. I had to. "I promise to handle you with care, sweetheart." Another brush over her skin, my lips turning up at the corners, trying for light, hoping it would erase the insecurities in her eyes. "But that would be a whole lot easier if I weren't having to chase you down for weeks at a time."

Eyes on mine, the uncertainty shifting to chagrin. "Right," she whispered.

"Right," I whispered back and held her close, held her until she, eventually—after long moments—relaxed against me.

Then she gave me some Billie Rose flair. Some of that confidence and kicking ass and taking names by looking at me with narrowed eyes and saying, "I guess we're seeing where this goes." A beat. "But know that just because we're doing this, it doesn't mean you can make trouble in my town."

My chuckle was rough. "Reading that loud and clear." A momentary hesitation, because normally I would have inserted *harpy* there. But that wouldn't be happening. Not ever again. "Baby," I finished.

Her face softened and I knew she knew what I'd been thinking, registered the deliberate change I'd made (and would keep making). "I need to watch out for my town," she whispered.

"Yeah," I whispered back. "And I'm going to watch out for you."

Her exhale was shaky, but after a long blip of quiet, she nodded. "Okay."

"Okay." I kissed the tip of her nose. "The first step of this is that you're going to go on a date with me." I crouched a little to meet her eyes. "A *real* date where I pick you up and we go to dinner and a movie or somewhere where there are other people. We spend time together. In public. And then I take you back to that fucking trailer, that goddamned couch, kiss you on the doorstep, and tell you good night."

Uncertainty creeping back into her eyes. "What if I don't want the night to end there?"

"Too bad." I tugged a curl. "But I won't wait the requisite three days to text you. I'll text you when I get home, and in the morning, to tell you I'm thinking about you." A grin. A kiss to her nose. "Because it seems like all I do is think about you, Rosie girl."

A sucked-in breath.

I stroked a finger along her jaw. "Then because I'll need to see you, I'll coax you into breakfast. And you'll come"—I shot her a look—"because even the busy mayor of River's Bend needs to eat."

She nibbled at that tempting bottom lip. "I usually just eat a protein bar at my desk."

Stubborn, beautiful, *workaholic* woman.

But I didn't comment on that. I just tugged another curl and said, "Then we'll eat protein bars at your desk together."

Her face smoothed out. "Really?"

Another light tug. "Really."

"Okay," she whispered.

"Okay," I whispered back again. "Next Tuesday work?"

Uncertainly being beaten back. Determination creeping in. Another deep, slow breath.

I waited. Held my breath until my lungs burned.

Then she gave me the world.

And it was with a simple, "Okay."

THIRTY-TWO

BILLIE ROSE

I'd given in.

How could I not?

He'd told me he wanted to see where things would go, and he'd been so sweet and earnest and gorgeous.

And he'd been holding me.

And...I'd given in.

We were doing this, and I'd agreed to go on a date, a real date, and to make a real effort.

But I couldn't shake the feeling that I was going to be destroyed in the end.

It was like lining up for a rollercoaster that I knew was going to make me sick and woozy at the end, but the ride was going to be so damned good it would be worth puking up my breakfast.

So...here I was.

It was election day, and I was going to dinner with Joel to await the results of my uncontested mayoral election.

I was going on a *date* with Joel.

With Joel.

Clearly, I was much more worried about that than results of an election where no one was running against me.

Because a date was real.

A date wasn't fucking in the dark of night and doing the walk of shame before the sun came up.

A date meant giving into the hope I'd carefully shoved down, hadn't allowed myself to really feel, hadn't allowed to blossom into wanting Joel for more than he could give me.

A date was the beginning of something.

It was potential.

And it was something that had the potential to go wrong.

So, so wrong.

And with this date, with the town's gossip tree still firmly in place, everyone would know when it went wrong.

And they'd know it was because of me.

Because as much as Joel said he liked my spreadsheets and mind for meetings and living for my work, that would grow old. He'd want more than I was capable of giving, or he'd see all that I was, and it wouldn't be enough and—

"Why aren't you out on the streets?"

I blinked.

The weather was gorgeous—the cool glint of November in the air, tightening the skin of my cheeks, making me glad for my scarf. But the sun was still shining, and it felt good on my hair and my clothes, sinking slowly into my skin.

I'd been going all day. All week. All month.

Going in a way that meant exhaustion was clinging to my body—meetings and talking to people in town, walking through the new neighborhoods, making certain there weren't any concerns I was unaware of. The previous weekend had been slammed too. Friday morning, Joel and I had gotten breakfast (he'd brought protein bars and we'd eaten at my desk) before he'd met up with the team to get on the bus and hit the road, and as of Friday evening, our downtown was officially open and

—thank God—it was hopping. I'd made the rounds several times over, pleased to see long lines and plenty of people strolling through the mini Fall Festival I'd organized. A Grand River's Bend Re-opening with some of our smaller local vendors—Kelly's Cakes, The Carvery (wood and stone carvings), Elegant Essentials (clothes and jewelry), and more—set up on the sidewalks with booths.

I'd browsed with everyone else inside the shops and out on the street.

I'd bought a pair of earrings I didn't need.

And signed up for another fucking knitting class I didn't want to take.

Had picked up a half-dozen books I would definitely stay up way too late to read.

Saturday afternoon I'd even cut the ribbon at Monroe's with Dessie, amongst the first to go in and drink a fucking beer (blegh) at the new sleek granite and metal bar top. The Rush game had played on TV, followed by the Gold game, and the mood had been jovial.

River's Bend was officially back.

Then, on Sunday, Joel had called.

And we'd had a conversation on the phone.

Like two normal people.

It had felt...weird.

And good and...weird.

Yesterday, he'd played again, and I'd worked, but he'd texted, and I'd texted back and then, when I'd just begun to lie down on my couch, snuggled beneath my cozy blanket, he'd called me again.

Normal.

Weird.

And tonight, he was coming to pick me up. We were going to grab Italian at Luna's downtown and then head over to Monroe's to receive the official election results.

An election I'd campaigned hard for despite not having an opponent.

Because my people deserved the effort. Because my father wouldn't expect anything less.

But, for the first time, I kind of *wished* I'd had an opponent.

Because maybe...I didn't want to do this—be mayor —forever.

Which was something I shouldn't even allow to cross my mind, let alone on a day like today.

Election day.

And it was a thought that had me feeling even guiltier when I glanced up at my father.

The former mayor.

Son of the former, *former* mayor.

It was all in the family, and the Donovans took their civic responsibilities seriously. It would *not* do to have my dad catching wind of my thoughts at leaving the office.

Anyway, it was just that. A thought.

I loved being mayor.

I was glad I'd been the one to see my town through this crisis. I enjoyed knowing everyone and seeing that they were safe and taken care of and thriving.

But sometimes...the weight was heavy.

And sometimes...I wondered what I might do if I wasn't doing *this*.

"*BR*."

Warning and brusqueness from my father.

Distance and disconnection from my mother.

One hyper-involved to the point that I'd known exactly which step I was expected to take.

The other running on constant autopilot.

I had the homemade dinners and the parent-teacher confer-ences. The dates shopping for prom dresses and now weekly coffee dates with my mom. I had the fresh-baked cookies and the yearly Christmas cards.

But the distance was always there.

Sometimes I understood why Jeff, my much older half-brother (and Bailey's father) got the fuck out the moment he could, why his relationship with River's Bend was filled with so much pull and retreat, so much upheaval that had scarred Bailey deep.

It was *this.*

The brusque and the disconnect.

The love, but almost as an afterthought.

I wasn't complaining.

At least I *had* love, had care, had safety and security.

I just wished...that things could be different. That they could have given me more.

Selfish much?

I swallowed that down, focused on my father before he lost his shit. "I was out all day, Dad," I said, supplying him with the information. "I'm just here to change and meet up with Joel and then we're going out for dinner before the results come in."

"Dinner?"

I bit back a sigh. "Yeah, Dad. I need to eat, and Joel and I have a date scheduled."

My mom blinked, chose that moment to tune in. "A date? You?"

That hurt. I couldn't lie. "Yes, Mom. Surprisingly enough, even someone like *me* will occasionally go on dates."

"Oh." She blinked again, a flash of emotion crossing over her familiar blue eyes. "I didn't mean it like that, baby. I just—" Here she faltered. Because she *didn't* mean it like that, wasn't trying to be mean.

She was just doing Parent Speak.

And *my* parents' Parent Speak edged toward critical.

Always.

"You're just so busy," she finished.

"Yeah," I agreed. Not pushing it further, not engaging further. Down that path led disappointment.

"Who's Joel?" my dad asked, eyes narrowing.

"Me."

I jerked slightly when the man in question came close to me, wrapping an arm around my middle and tugging me back against his chest. A kiss to my temple. Soft words in my ear. "Hi, baby."

He sounded tired.

I glanced up, saw the dark circles beneath his eyes.

He *looked* tired too.

Long hours on the bus. Hundreds of miles and a physically demanding job.

But he was here—I glanced surreptitiously toward my watch—five minutes early. In a nice shirt and nice jeans *and* nice shoes, his hair a little damp and wavy, like he'd just run his fingers through it.

Tempting *me* to run my fingers through it.

"And who're you?" My dad narrowed his eyes. "Not one of those troublemaking hockey players."

The *or else* was unspoken.

"He plays on the Rush," I told my dad and firmed up my tone. "He's been instrumental in helping me get River's Bend back on track."

A silent survey.

Then my dad nodded, extended his hand. "Joel." A beat. "John." Shaking of hands commenced before my dad stepped back. "You make sure that BR here doesn't slack off."

Joel went very still behind me.

"Dad," I said. "You know—"

My dad wasn't listening, and he just kept...being my dad. "She'll take the easy way out. *Every* time. You"—a finger jabbed in Joel's direction—"make sure she stays until every vote has been tallied and everyone has their business taken care of."

That...hurt.

A lot.

But I couldn't focus on that.

"Did I just hear you?"

My dad's eyes narrowed at Joel's voice. It was frosty as hell and he'd gone statue stiff behind me. I glanced up—and yup—the anger I felt pulsing against my spine was written all over Joel's face.

Pissed.

Seriously pissed.

Something expanded in my belly—hope, need, something else, something more, something...deeper.

Because Joel was pissed.

For *me.*

"I—" my dad began.

I turned my back on my dad, on my parents, took Joel's hand and squeezed tightly. "It's okay," I whispered, pleading with him when it looked as though he would say something else. "It's *okay.* Let's just go have our date and not worry about—"

His jaw tightened, and he studied me closely for several long moments.

"It's not okay."

No. It wasn't.

I just...this was how it was with them.

Joel sighed, cupped my jaw, then glanced up at my parents. "Billie and I have plans."

I followed his glance, saw my dad's jaw flexing. "BR—"

Joel slid an arm around my shoulders, tugged me close. "Nice to meet you both," he said firmly, cutting off the conversation. "We'll talk soon."

"Yes, we will," my mom agreed eyes fixing us in place. But only for a moment. Because then I saw her transform in front of me, shifting back to absentminded, her smile small, her tone light and easy. Affecting a role. Saying the right thing. Even if, inside, she was a million miles away. "You two have fun."

"We will," Joel told her, taking us back a step.

"BR," my dad ordered before we'd completed it. "Make sure you—"

If I'd been alone with them, I would have mentally closed my eyes and tried to summon up my well of patience. I would have stayed there and listened and tried—somehow—not to absorb the pain that always trailed his harsh words.

But I wasn't alone.

Joel was next to me. Was *with* me.

So, he spun us away, marched us off, calling back over his shoulder, "Have a nice night."

And then...he took me to dinner.

No lectures.

No snark or fighting.

Just me and Joel...and *normal.*

It was *awesome.*

Thirty-Three

JOEL

My woman had won her election.

Not that it was a surprise.

My woman was a badass—and a great mayor.

Her parents, though...they were shit. I'd known that from witnessing one lecture weeks before—though I'd been holding back a bit of hope that her mom wouldn't be awful.

She wasn't. I guessed.

She just wasn't *there* either.

Another layer peeled back, seeing Billie's face up close as her father's brusque words rolled through the air, scouring my skin, and making me want to lay into the fucker, as her mom tuned into the conversation before drifting right back out of it again.

And Billie—*my* badass Billie Rose—had taken it.

Like she'd taken *harpy*.

Rolling with it, acting like it was no big deal, even as it cut her deep.

Like she drank the celebratory beers a handful of people

bought her that night—at least until I'd started sneaking them away from her and downing them in big gulps.

Now we were back at the trailer, sitting on the steps, and I was pondering the puzzle that was Billie Rose—a woman I always thought took no shit, had a spine of steel. I wasn't saying that wasn't true...

But she had a vulnerable underbelly.

One that seemed to get wounded regularly—wounds she hid or buried or pretended didn't exist.

I didn't like this.

For obvious reasons.

But I *really* didn't like this when it came to her family.

I knew that her brother—and Bailey's dad—was an ass, but I'd always heard that her parents were great. Involved members of the community. Her dad a former mayor and her mom rabid volunteer. Together, they'd spawned all that was Billie Rose.

River's Bend's youngest mayor.

One who'd turned the town from small and isolated to small and thriving.

One who'd made it a point that no one was left behind in that process.

One who'd turned a band of fucked-up hockey players into upstanding members of society.

Yet...that didn't seem to be enough for them.

Or for her dad, anyway. Her mom...I didn't get yet. There was love there—in both, I supposed. I could tell that both of her parents felt love, but it was masked with brusqueness from her dad and that odd sort of distance from her mom.

There was more to unpack there.

Another layer.

One I knew would take time to get to the bottom of, but I also knew it was a layer that was really important.

That wasn't for tonight, though.

But I *did* need to know one thing.

"Why do you drink beer if you don't like it, sweetheart?"

Billie had been staring up at the sky, but my question had her gaze flying down, darting to mine and away. "What do you mean?"

"Beer, baby. You don't like it, but you drink it."

Silence.

For long enough that I thought I'd stepped firmly into the realm of topics that shouldn't be touched on Date One.

But then she turned to me, brows drawn together. "How do you know I don't like beer?"

"Baby," I murmured, tugging at a curl. "I pay attention."

"I—" An inhale, exhale. "*Oh.*"

I watched her, waited for her to say something else, and when she didn't, I asked again. "Why, Rosie girl?"

"I don't know," she whispered. "I just...do."

I wanted to delve into that. I wanted to *know*.

But Date One.

It was too soon to press, especially when I was finally getting somewhere with her. Except...fuck that. Dancing around and sitting back hadn't done shit to move us forward.

I leaned closer. "That's bullshit, baby."

Her shoulders stiffened, jaw going tight.

I cupped that jaw, ran a finger over the taut muscle. "It's bullshit and if we're going to make something of this, of *us,* then we can't sit on this stuff. We just *can't.*" It would eat us alive from the inside out. It would undo all the progress we'd made to date.

And *fuck*, it had been a haul to get us to this point.

To Date One.

"My dad," she whispered.

I blinked.

Held my breath because I knew, *knew* that I wasn't going to like this. But if she was going to share, I had to lock it down.

"You know about Billy," she whispered. "But you don't know that I'm the one they've never wanted."

"Who?" I asked, even though I had a sneaking suspicion that I knew.

And, yup, her face told me that no fucking way was I going to like this.

"My parents." Her voice was barely audible. "They lost Billy, and they got me instead, and I'm not the same. He was...sweet and quiet and their *son*. I'm me and—"

She broke off.

So I took the moment to say gently, "They have another son."

A beat. "You know how it is with Jeff, and he's not my dad's. Not really. And *my* dad, my parents...they've always been like this. Intense. Focused on themselves. Or at least, that's what I remember." A breath. "Jeff was older when they lost Billy and I think he took it hard. Or maybe they were harder on him than me because he was there first, and it was so hard for my mom to get pregnant with Billy."

It shifted my view on Bailey's dad, Jeff. Slightly.

Not that I forgave him for the shit he'd pulled in Bailey's life, namely getting a fucking gold star in being an asshole father who perfected the art looking after himself first, his wife second, and his daughter a distant third.

But having born witness to just two lectures from the Donovan patriarch to his offspring, and I could see the appeal of distance.

I just couldn't see it at the expense of missing out on Bailey's life.

Right. Layer peeled.

Information gathered.

Billie's parents.

Not a fan.

"They love me," she murmured. "I've never doubted that.

It's just...a love that has high expectations and—" A sigh. "A love that isn't tender."

"Baby," I whispered, wrapping an arm around her shoulders, and tugging her closer.

"I'm lucky," she went on, still soft. "Really. I've had more than most, and—"

"*Baby.*"

She kept going. "And they've pushed me to the best version of myself and the town and—"

I tugged her closer. "I didn't exactly love the way he talked to you, Rosie baby. Nor the way your mom just stood there and let him tear into you."

Teeth in her bottom lip. "Tear—"

I tucked a curl behind her ear. "I didn't like it the first time either."

She sucked in a breath. "Honey—"

"So, get ready."

A blink. "Get ready for what?"

I held her eyes. "Be prepared that I'm not going to stand by and allow that to happen again."

"Um..." She bit her lip again. "What?"

Stroking a hand up and down her arm. "I've got your back, and I'm not going to allow you to stand there and be a punching bag."

"Okay," she murmured, disbelief firmly in each of those four letters

Just like everything else, it would take time for her to come around, for her to believe, for her to understand where I was coming from. But I wasn't going to stop. "And I've got your back in more than just that, baby."

"Okay," she whispered again.

I tabled my frustration.

Time. It would take time. But even as I was thinking that, my cell rang. I moved to silence it, but Billie shook her head, nodding at my pocket. "Answer it. I need to grab my blanket from inside anyway."

I waggled my brows. "How about I cuddle you instead?"

"I didn't think that first dates ended with cuddling," she teased. "Especially since cuddling is likely to lead to fucking." She lifted her brows, giving me that sexy, confident Billie Rose smile that had me waking up hard every single morning. A mask in a way. Completely Billie Rose in another.

More layers.

More puzzle pieces of this woman. Of *my* woman.

"I can control myself."

A snort—one that was completely warranted—before she hopped to her feet and tugged at the flat black handle on the door, letting herself into the trailer.

I watched her ass for a moment too long before my phone buzzed again, and I remembered I was supposed to be answering the call. I tugged my cell from my pocket, answered, "Hello?"

"How's my baby boy?"

My lips immediately turned up into a smile.

The door creaked open behind me, Billie Rose pushing out with a blue Rush fleece blanket gathered in her arms.

"Hey, Mom."

My woman's expression went concerned on the heels of my greeting and she grabbed at the handle, like she was going to escape back inside.

Yeah, no.

I snagged her hand, tugged her down into my lap, and hit speaker phone, just as my mom said, "You didn't answer my question—how's my baby boy?"

Billie went very still in my lap.

"I'm good, Mom. I'm actually on a date with a wonderful woman."

Billie choked.

Stunned silence then, "You picked up *your phone* while on a date with a *wonderful woman?*"

I chuckled. "Yup. Her name is Billie Rose. She's smart and capable and beautiful and she's sitting in my lap staring at me like I've grown horns."

"Lost your brain is more like it," my mom muttered. "Or heart."

Billie's eyes went wide.

Fishing. My mom was fishing. But I didn't make her work for it. Just chuckled again, spread the blanket over my Rosie's lap, and laid it out for them both. "Pretty much."

"Well, then," my mom said after a moment, "I guess Dad and I are going to have to make a trip to see you."

Rosie's eyes somehow even went wider.

I kept laying it out. "Probably better bring the sisters too."

More choking. More wide blue eyes.

Laughter in my mom's voice. "And you, my baby boy, probably need crawl yourself out of the hole you just dug."

Considering the look on Billie's face, that *probably* wasn't probably.

"On it, Mom."

We exchanged goodbyes, I hung up, and I tipped up Billie's face.

I tabled the digging for later and just asked,

"Want to meet my family, Rosie girl?"

Thirty-Four

BILLIE ROSE

I was not a woman who took surprises well.

So, Joel springing his family on me—on Date Freaking One no less—shouldn't have been something that made me happy.

But...there was something soft about the way his mom spoke to him through the phone, the gentle admonishment about taking a call on a date, the love clearly shining through her voice that felt...right.

I was glad Joel had that.

I was also...terrified.

And really freaking thankful that I was going to *not* think about it like I had over the last couple of days—for a few hours at least.

Because Bailey was having her girls over.

Dessie. Me. And...Veronica.

For a game and wine night.

I really wanted a wine and *wine* night. And a wine and more wine night.

Mostly because tomorrow I was meeting Joel at his house to see the progress on his rebuild, and then—unless there was some crisis that I was able to conjure up in River's Bend so that I could escape—I was meeting his family.

I couldn't believe that the phone call had developed in an actual meeting so quickly.

Not that it should be a surprise.

It was Joel, after all.

What he wanted, he got—no matter how hard I tried to put distance between us.

Which, seriously, was becoming a problem with him.

We were dating. Not fucking. Just exchanging chaste kisses and cuddling on my trailer's steps. And he was steadily winning my heart by bringing me more washi tape and stickers and, last night, a hairbrush specifically designed for curls.

Winding himself tightly into my life.

In my heart.

And...I liked it.

A lot.

So much so that I was kicking myself for not having a hand up, for not fending him off. Because...I was attached and I wanted more and I really, *really* liked how his mom talked to him and called him her *baby boy*.

As much as I liked the softness that entered his tone when he responded to her.

And the gentle way he'd talked about his three younger sisters—Kira, Avery, and Delilah—after he'd hung up with his mom, and over the days since. Telling me about them, introducing me to his family in a way I knew was deliberate and trying to get me comfortable with the fact that I was going to meet his family and have dinner with them and *interact* with them after they'd flown across the state to make a special trip to do so.

When we hadn't done the same with mine.

Even though my parents lived in the same town.

I didn't want to sit down with my parents and Joel and share a meal. I didn't want to sit with him and endure the lectures and distance. I knew it was coming, that it was unavoidable. Knew I'd need to make arrangements before Joel's family came to avoid further strife.

I just...didn't want to.

I still hit the button on my steering well, yelled out their contact name into the speaker of my SUV (technology, some-times, was a pain in the ass), and waited for their home line to ring.

Yup.

Their *home* number.

They'd moved in last week.

One more check on my never-ending list of tasks.

"Hello?"

"Dad," I said.

"What's up, BR?" he asked, and I heard him immediately perk up, ready for action. "Whatcha need?"

That right there.

That made the rest of it fade away. The demands. The brusqueness. The pit that was never completely filled in the base of my stomach reminding me I couldn't be what he needed.

Because there was never any question that my dad would step in and help.

Mayor once. Mayor always.

"I'm meeting Joel's parents and sisters tomorrow," I told him, executing the offramp for Bailey's place. "He'd like to meet you guys too—in an official capacity."

Silence.

For once, I'd apparently stymied him.

He'd probably already been prepping his to do list for what-ever I was going to ask of him. "The hockey player?"

"Yeah, Dad."

"The *hockey* player?"

"Yes, Dad."

A pause. "I thought you hated hockey players."

That was an insightful thing for my dad to say, so insightful that if someone had asked me if he could deduce that about me, I would have told them absolutely not. Half the time, I wasn't sure he really knew *anything* about me. Then again, I *had* complained about hockey players—and in particular about certain Rush hockey players—many, *many* times over the last years.

So...it had absorbed somewhere.

Something that settled in the vicinity of him always stepping in and helping without question.

More good.

A *small* good.

But it was something, and it was something that reminded me it wasn't all bad with my parents. They were far from perfect, but they were the only parents I had and—

Joel's growly voice slid through my mind.

I've got your back, and I'm not going to allow you to stand there and be a punching bag.

"BR?"

I blinked, turned into Bailey's neighborhood. "They've grown on me."

"And," my dad said, a bit dryly, "especially that one with the beard."

A note of inquisition. And another blip of insight—though, not surprising considering I'd introduced him to Joel before our date. But the thread of protectiveness was...confusing.

My dad wasn't protective of me.

He was all for pushing me out of the nest and making certain I was standing on my own two feet.

Me being independent was the best thing I could be—except at work.

Because work trumped all.

My mom...well, I still didn't get her, but because of her, I'd secured all those gold stars in independence, was standing on my own feet. I didn't really *need* to get her. Not when I was out and about, living my own life.

"Joel," I reminded him. "He's a good man. He's helped the town a lot the last few months."

"And you."

That struck hard.

Because it was the truth—and one I hadn't seen before. Or accepted. Or—

"BR?"

I blinked. Damn. I need to get it together. "Yeah, Dad. He's helped me out, too."

"Right." A beat. "Good."

More blinking. This time for so long, I almost missed Bailey's driveway.

"That all?" my dad asked, brusque making a comeback.

I threw the engine into park, took a breath, confusion settling in my belly. I didn't know what was happening, just that I didn't understand the angle. I didn't have time to understand it, not right then anyway. "Yeah, Dad," I whispered. "That's all."

"Good," he clipped out. "Give me some dates and I'll let you know what works with Mom's and my schedule."

"Okay."

"Right. I got things to do," he said.

Now *that* was normal.

So was the next.

"And don't let the fact that you have this new man in your life mean that you shirk your responsibilities."

"I won't," I promised.

"See that you don't."

I didn't get the chance to make any further promises because my dad hung up (something that was also normal). I sat back in my seat as the click of the call disconnecting echoed through my speakers and processed.

Then knew I couldn't process.

I needed wine. And more wine.

Sighing, I cut the engine and because my dad was my dad (and I was me, with my planning tendencies) I immediately pulled up the calendar app on my phone, cross-referenced it to the Rush schedule I'd bookmarked for emergencies (namely, first for avoiding Joel, and now liking to know when he was playing), and picked a few dates to offer up as tribute.

Then I grabbed my purse, pocketed my phone, and headed up to Bailey's house.

Wine. Board games. More wine. Ignoring the fact that my life was changing.

Ignoring the fact that in a short amount of time, I'd accepted a *hockey player* in my life. As my boyfriend. And I was going to have dinner with his family.

And we were going to have dinner with *my* family because my dad had chosen a date by the time I'd made it up to the door —something I now needed to tell Joel that I'd arranged.

Dinner with my *parents*.

Sweet baby Jesus. What was I thinking?

I paused, sucked in a breath, let it out, and whispered. "Going for it."

That was what I was thinking. I was going for it. I was doing this.

It was going to be interesting.

it was going to be *insane*.

Because I just had the sinking suspicion that it was all going to go wrong.

Thirty-Five

Joel

S he was late.
Late.
Billie Rose was never late.

She had those planners and her life programmed down to the minute, and even despite the various pulls on her time, she wasn't late.

Not *ever.*

Except today.

When my family was here. Waiting for her.

Which was something that I was trying not to take personally.

But...fuck...

How could I not?

I blew out a breath, smothered my frustration—just like I smothered that thought. This wasn't personal. This was a crisis coming up and Billie Rose having copious amounts of people needing her. She'd be here.

She always showed up.

She always—

Gravel crunched, and I spun on the job site, seeing her SUV tear down the road in typical Billie Rose fashion, screeching to a halt and throwing her door open.

"I'm sorry," she called, clicking up to me in a pair of heels that I rarely saw her in. Usually, she swapped those out as soon as possible. But today she was in full mayor mode—those heels, tight black skirt, narrow scarf wrapped around the collar of her white silk button down blouse. Fucking pearls hanging around her neck.

Sexy in a school librarian way.

I wanted to undo those buttons and get at her breasts.

I wanted to wrap my hand around those pearls and tug her down to her knees, undo the zipper of my jeans and slip my dick between those red-slicked lips.

I wanted...to tug up that skirt and—

Fuck her.

Yup.

I wanted to fuck her.

But when I got a glimpse of her face—the worry and the nerves and the anxiety rippling through her bright blue eyes—I wanted to hold her.

"Hi, hi," she said quickly, bussing my cheek with a kiss that barely connected and turning toward my parents. "I'm so sorry I'm late. I had an interview that ran long and then a cow got out of its pasture—a cow!" She laughed and it wasn't Billie's laugh, not the one I knew was hers now. It was the mayor's, something I would have expected to hear from her mouth months ago, and it ran like sandpaper down my spine. "I know we're a small town." She grinned, almost maniacally. "But a cow running down Main Street is a new one, even for me."

All of that was said in a flurry.

Literally a *flurry*. Of sound. Of movements. Of handshakes and hugs and kisses on the cheeks.

"You must be Joel's mother, Janette. I'm Billie Rose, his girl-friend. Wow." A laugh. "It feels weird to say that out loud." She tossed a smile my way. "Especially since we haven't really talked about titles. Oh, wow." Another laugh that was more mayor than woman and it seemed to refocus her—or at least to focus her concern on my parents and sister. "Ignore me. I want to know all about you. How was your trip to town? Were your flights okay? Oh my God, it's so late. *I'm* so late"—more flurry, more words spoken so rapidly that they were barely discernible—"and you're probably hungry. Especially since you've been waiting on me and I'm late and—"

Right.

I'd had enough.

"Mom, Dad," I murmured, stepping close to Billie, and tugging her back against my chest, "excuse us for a moment."

"Oh no," Billie said. "I couldn't possibly inconvenience you any furth—"

I steered her toward the open frame of the back door. "We'll be right back."

My sisters shot me a look when I led Billie away, before I guided her through that opening and to the dirt-filled back yard.

It would need to be landscaped again, but that was a problem for when the rest of the project was finished.

Today, it was level enough—even in those heels—for me to figure out what in the fuck all was happening with my woman.

"We're late," Billie said, the moment they'd reached the dirt ground. "No. *I'm* late," she added, still fully in that flurry, "and I'm so sorry for this. But keeping your parents waiting even longer is unaccept—"

I cupped her cheeks and kissed her.

Deep and long.

Deep and long enough that she stopped trying to push me away and started kissing me back and finally—when I was just beginning to forget that my family was standing thirty feet away in my incomplete house—she relaxed against me.

I felt the press of that pearl necklace, wanted her in nothing but that.

Even *with* my family standing thirty feet away.

Focus.

"Honey," she whispered when I pulled back, her hands in my hair, her body plastered to mine.

"I don't give a fuck that you're late," I whispered, hating that she immediately stiffened, but knowing that I had to get this out, had to make sure she knew this wasn't important. "*They* don't care you're late."

A statue had appeared in my arms, and she tried to pull away.

I held fast. "They *don't* care, baby," I told her, leaning back enough to hold her gaze. "I promise. Though," I said, running my knuckles over her cheek, "I think you can just dial back the mayor. Just be you, baby, and they'll love you."

Like I do.

But I managed to not say the last, even though it was blasting through my mind with the force of a rocket ship tearing through space.

"I'm late," she whispered. "I'm late and I didn't get to change, and a fucking cow was running through Main Street, and—"

"They won't care."

Her eyes were a little wild. "I'm *late.*"

"Baby." I brushed my lips over her forehead. "You let them see you, let them *know* you, and they won't *care.*"

She bit her lip. "I'm wearing dumbass heels and a pearl necklace at a job site."

"They don't care."

"I had a meltdown."

I huffed out a chuckle. "My dad and I grew up with four

women—we've had plenty of experience with meltdowns, sweetheart. And let me tell you, that little *scene* in there can hardly qualify as a meltdown."

"Yeah," she grumbled. "But only because you pulled me outside."

Now my chuckle became full blown laughter.

Because this woman was fucking wonderful.

"Rosie girl," I said, brushing back her hair, "if you think I don't know how to contain my woman, then you've lost your head in your box of washi tape."

She inhaled, exhaled. "Joel."

"Not going to deny it?" I kissed her nose. "Or fight it? Or give me shit about it?"

"No," she whispered. "I just...you haven't been mine very long—"

I lifted my brows. "Haven't I?"

Another of those sharp inhales. Another shaking exhale.

I pushed on. "Just because you're only seeing it now, baby, doesn't mean that's not where I've been for a long time."

Her lips parted. "I—"

My mouth on hers, stealing another kiss, taking advantage of her befuddlement.

"I—" she began again.

Still befuddled, only this time, she'd softened, relaxed against me, warmth filling her eyes. "Deep breaths, sweetheart," I whispered. "Stop worrying about the cow and being late and wearing heels and a pearl necklace I want to fuck you in—"

Heat creeping into her blue eyes. "Wh-what?"

"Yeah, baby," I said, turning her and tucking her into my side, leaning down to finish the sentiment in her ear. "Those heels are hot. But that necklace makes me want to fuck your mouth until I come down your throat."

She gasped, nails digging into my side. "*Joel.*"

"Think about that and not the fucking cow, yeah?"

More nail digging—and for me, more dick twitching. But the hellion didn't answer my question.

"Baby, yeah?"

Her cheeks went pink. "How am I supposed to think about that *and* focus on your family?"

I grinned at her chastising tone, leaned down, and kissed the tip of her nose. "You're the badass mayor of River's Bend, baby. I know you can multitask."

Then I held her a little closer.

And I led her back inside.

THIRTY-SIX

BILLIE ROSE

Despite the horrible start, it wasn't going all that badly.

I was multitasking—focusing on Joel's hand in mine, on the way his thigh was pressed to mine in a booth at Luna's. A basket of garlic bread had been settled between us and normally I'd be diving right in there, throwing a few elbows to make sure I got my fair of the sourdough deliciousness.

But...multitasking.

As in, Joel's hand on mine, his thigh pressed to mine, garlic in my nose, three sisters, two parents, curious waitstaff, and nosy as fuck townspeople focused on me.

Some of whom were probably waiting for me to lose it again.

Which wasn't fair.

After Joel had led me back into the half-built house, his arm holding me close, he'd introduced me all around—to Kira, Avery, and Delilah. All of whom were sweet and nice and didn't comment on my flustering about and being late and acting like an insane person. Neither did Janette nor Rob, Joel's parents.

Both of whom had shaken my hand and asked me about the cow.

A peace offering.

Something that had broken the tension and calmed me down.

Allowed me to multitask, as a girlfriend, not a mayor.

And trying *not* to think about being naked in heels and a pearl necklace, Joel shoving his cock between my lips, pressing it deep, making my eyes water as he gripped my curls and fucked me hard and fast. Until he lost control, pulling out, and fucked my pussy, doing it just as hard and fast and not stopping until both of us were in the throes of orgasms that—

"Garlic bread, Rosie?"

I inhaled, blinked, and my fantasy cut off so quickly it was almost whiplash.

But...Rosie.

I glanced up, saw that Kira had lifted the basket in my direction, offering me buttery, garlicky carbs.

Nice.

They were *all* nice.

Not fighting me for carbs, like Dessie and Bailey would have done. Picking up on Joel's nickname and getting on board, using it in a soft, gentle way that wrapped me in warm velvet.

"Yeah, thanks," I said, scooping up a piece that was practically coated in garlic.

Probably not conducive for Joel's plans later, but meh. I took a huge bite...because it was garlic bread from Luna's.

Joel's thigh shifted on mine as he leaned forward and grabbed his own piece.

Ah, well, double the garlic, double the fun.

"Your hair is fabulous."

I looked from my bread to Delilah, who was a hairstylist with obviously fabulous hair (and chunky blonde highlights), expecting her to be looking at someone else—Kira, for example, who had gorgeous shining brown locks, or Janette, whose gray hair was gorgeous and sleek and fell to her shoulders, or Avery, who rocked a platinum pixie cut in a way I never could, or even Rob, whose salt and pepper close-cropped hair showed off the rugged lines of his face.

But Delilah was looking at me.

At *my* hair.

Something I'd cursed on a regular basis my entire life because it was way too much fucking work. Though, recently, it was also something that was looking damned good. Mostly because of the new brush Joel had bought me, along with some sort of cream I put in before I blow-dried it.

Yup.

The man had bought me a brush and curl cream and now looking at Lila (see? I was on the nickname kick, too), I realized that thoughtfulness was probably genetic.

A Marshall family trait.

Reinforced by Janette murmuring, "It really is," as she scooped up her own piece of bread. "I've always wanted curls, but this"—she tugged at a strand of her hair—"always goes limp."

"Well," I admitted. "They've been a bear to deal with my whole life. Though"—I glanced up at Joel through my lashes—"it's gotten a little easier since this one hooked me up with a new brush and cream."

Lila grinned. "*That's* why you called me and asked about curly hair?"

A shrug, Joel's cheeks going a little pink. "You had knowledge. I needed it."

And I'd complained about my hair. I remembered doing it after the shower we took together a few nights before, lamenting how much of a pain it was to deal with. Then the next time I'd grabbed my shower caddy there was a new brush and the curl cream tucked inside.

Joel.

Washi tape.

Curl cream.

A special brush.

And he'd gone to his sister for the information.

My heart squeezed, and I lifted my hand, cupping it over his jaw, the bristles of his beard tickling my palm, whispered, "Thank you."

Joel glanced down at me, turning his head so that his lips pressed to my palm instead, kissing me lightly there. "Anything for you, sweetheart."

I inhaled.

And...I thought he meant it.

I thought he believed it.

And...I...*God*, I was falling for this man.

For the hope of him and the reality and the way he looked at me and his thoughtfulness and...Joel. The man he'd shown me he was. The one, who with his mouth curved, his eyes warm, was completely nonplussed with the fact that I'd just told his family that he'd bought me a brush and curls and that we were sharing a moment.

A *moment* after my flurry of chaos and me being late.

There weren't any snide comments.

There wasn't any anger or resentment that I hadn't been there on time, that I'd been a mess who certainly hadn't lived up to their expectations of the person they wanted to be with their son.

Instead, they'd been kind and nice and like...*Joel*.

And I found, because of that, I could relax.

Could settle into a meal that wasn't tense, didn't leave me on edge. A meal during which I could just sit next to Joel and *relax*.

And listen to them tease each other.

Over pasta and garlic bread.

"Here I thought," Rob said, eyes twinkling, "that Joel was working on taming his curls with all those Brazilian blowouts."

My mouth dropped open, and I glanced up at Joel. "Um, what?"

Annoyance in deep green eyes. "Don't ask."

"I mean"—I fought a smile—"I *have* to ask."

He dropped his chin, amusement now glimmering, even as he shook his head. "Three younger sisters means I was a doll for them to practice on." A beat. "Even for Lila's Brazilian blowouts."

"Well," I said, a giggle bubbling up in the back of my throat, "it *did* make your hair silky and smooth."

His lips twitched.

"*And*, bonus, it hid the bald spot at the back of his head," Avery teased.

"Hey!" Joel rubbed a self-conscious hand over his scalp. "I'm not balding."

"Yeah?" I leaned up, pretending to study the back of his head scrupulously, running my fingers through his thick, ridiculously soft hair. "Are you sure that right there isn't a—"

He captured my hand, tugged me against his chest. "I'm sure."

I lost hold on my giggles.

A nip to the top of my ear, his tongue flicking out against the shell, voice quiet and hot when he muttered, "Behave or no naked time later."

I leaned back, brows lifting. "Really? *That's* what you're going with?"

"Yup." He kissed the tipped of my nose.

I rolled my eyes, ignored the curious eyes across from us, and reached for another piece of garlic bread.

"Men," Janette muttered, making my lips turn up.

"Exactly," Kira agreed. "We can't live with them—"

"So says your husband," Rob chimed in.

A toss of that shining hair as she ignored the interruption and finished, "And we can't live without them." A pout, but then her lips were turning up, and she gave me wide eyes, her irises so similar to Joel's, especially with the mirth in those deep green depths. She winked at me. "And so says my husband."

"Tell me about him," I semi-ordered. "And I want to hear about school"—to Avery—"and the salon you just opened"—Lila—"and I want to hear about the cruise Joel told me you guys"—Janette and Rob—"are taking for your anniversary."

I wanted to learn all about them.

To expand on the small details I'd come to know about them so far, details Joel had shared willingly.

Details that freaked me the fuck out because my family wasn't like this.

My family *couldn't* be like this.

But...maybe *I* could be like this, could fit in and participate in this conversation, this meal. Maybe I could just be with a family that was...normal.

And downed garlic bread and pasta properly—like the delicacies they were.

Lila jumped right in, garlic bread hanging from her fingers and launching into a story about a client who'd apparently committed the cardinal sin of dyeing her hair black and then wanted to go platinum...and had tried.

At home.

The descriptions had me laughing as much as I did when I was with Bailey and Dessie, had me relaxing. So did Kyra's softer voice as she spoke about her husband and job, Avery's enthusiasm when she talked about classes, Rob's love blatant on his face as he watched Janette describe the trip up to Alaska and how excited she was to go whale watching.

And Joel.

Smiling down at me at regular intervals, brushing his

knuckles over my cheek, tugging a curl, stroking a hand down my spine.

Making me think maybe I could be a normal woman, in a normal relationship, with a normal man.

Not the mayor of a town who hid behind her responsibilities because she was too scared to have anything else.

Not a woman who was terrified to step out of her box because she wouldn't be enough.

Maybe I could just be me.

And maybe he'd love me for it anyway.

THIRTY-SEVEN

JOEL

"That's it, baby," I murmured, gripping her hips, my dick hard and deep inside her, grinding her down, knowing that she needed the friction, especially when she was in this position.

Ten dates.

Four weeks.

Lots of hockey. Lots of work.

But also, lots of us.

And it had been fucking *great*. We'd found our rhythm, my Rosie girl wasn't fending me off and avoiding me, and...it was fucking great.

Christmas was coming up.

The town was having a Winter Festival and Billie was elbow deep in sugar cookies and Christmas lights and elf costumes.

The Rush's season was going well—we were leading our division.

My season was going well—I'd played a few games up with the Gold and done it well enough to be on the occasional rotation (I liked this for many reasons, including that I got paid more money when I played with the Gold, and I had house to rebuild).

And...I had this woman in my life.

She was stubborn and technically still living in the trailer, but she was staying at my apartment almost every night.

Clothes in my closet.

Toiletries—including that jar of expensive as shit cream that Lila had recommended—in my shower.

And a naked woman in my bed, nearly every night.

And morning.

Like *this* morning.

Me dragging my ass home from the bus just after dawn, looking forward to some sleep before we went to Dessie's for some stupid cookie decorating event (cookies that would be sold at the Winter Festival).

And finding Billie awake in my bed.

In those heels.

In that pearl necklace.

In...black lace.

How she knew exactly when I was going to walk through my bedroom door, I didn't know. Or care. Because I'd come to a halt in the doorway, the vision of her in those heels and pearls and black lace, her long, sleek legs spread wide enough to get me hard in an instant.

I'd dropped my bag, forgotten that I was exhausted, and I'd dove—*dove*—for those legs.

Made her come on my tongue.

Now I was going to make her come on my cock.

Lurching up, I bent and latched onto her nipple, sucking a bit too hard. Because she liked that. Because it always made her pussy clamp around me. Because it had her grinding down even deeper, taking me until her pelvis was flush to mine, until I could press my thumb between her cheeks, fuck her back *and* front—

"Joel!"

"*Fuck*," I groaned, the taste of her on my tongue, her body wrapped around mine, those pearls pressed into my skin.

"Honey," she whispered, hips bucking, back arching.

"Come, baby," I told her, stroking into her front and back, keeping her moving, rocking on my cock. "Come *now*."

She sucked in a breath, kept moving, kept tightening around me, kept grinding.

Too slow. Too good. Too close to the edge without her.

I worked her other breast.

Her head dropped back. "Honey, I—"

I slid another finger into her ass, fucked her slow and steady with it, fucked her until my orgasm was right there, until I was ready to explode.

Fucked her until—

"Joel!"

She shattered around me.

Thank God.

I flipped us, pounded into her, those heels digging into my spine, her pussy still convulsing, her body wrapping tightly around mine, her pearls crushed into my chest.

Tight.

Wet.

Hot.

Mine.

I exploded all of ten seconds later.

And collapsed on top of her a heartbeat after that.

She didn't let me go, though. Just held on tight and took my weight.

Since I didn't want to smother her, I rolled us to the side, held her close, waited until we'd both caught our breath. Then I smoothed her hair back. "Sure I can't convince you to shirk your cookie decorating and just stay in bed all day?"

"Mmm." A lazy sound punctuated by a kiss to my chest. "Tempting. But I have to help Dessie."

I made a face.

Something she apparently felt because she pushed up on one hand and looked down at me, her face gentle in a way I knew not too many others saw.

That gentle was for me.

Only me.

"Why don't you just rest, honey?" she murmured. "You had a late night, and I can handle cookie decorating."

I was tired.

Exhausted, really.

This was one of those crunch times of the season and trying to practice, play, spend time with Billie, and make sure she wasn't working too hard meant I was navigating more than a handful of full-time jobs.

So, yeah, I was tired.

But I wouldn't take the chance of missing out on time with her.

It didn't come often enough.

Plus...there were going to be cookies.

"I'm good, baby," I said, rolling her again and pressing a kiss to the slightly red spot where her pearls had left indentations on her skin, and leaning back enough to reach down and tug off her heels. I'd divested her of the black lace approximately two seconds after I'd seen her on the bed with her legs spread.

"Really," she said, her foot arching when it was free. "It's okay."

A kiss to each toe, and I didn't even have a foot fetish, but I could see getting off on sucking these.

Another time, though.

Today...cookies and quality time with Billie.

"*Really*," I told her, rubbing the sole of her foot, touching my mouth to her ankle. "I'm good. I should stay up anyway, or my sleep cycle will be off."

She froze, narrowed her eyes in my direction. "You just want free cookies."

Yes.

But...

"I'll pay for them," I said. "Consider it my donation to the festival."

Those eyes stayed narrowed. "You were going to make a donation, anyway."

My mouth dropped open and I studied her, feeling amusement curl up in my belly. "And it's not going to just be for cookies, is it?"

A beatific smile. "Nope."

I chuckled, shook my head. "Okay, then," I said. "Free cookies, a donation, and your ass later."

She'd been smiling, nodding in agreement.

Until the last.

The last had her blue eyes going cobalt, her body arching against mine, her lips parting on an exhale.

I flicked my tongue out along her bottom lip. "So that's a yes?"

"For the cookies?" A wicked grin. "And the donation?"

I chuckled, pulled open the drawer and extracted a black box I'd stored there. Not the same one from my locker weeks before. That was still in my closet.

The contents in this one I'd picked up when I'd played a game for the Gold a week back.

She frowned. "What's this?"

"My payment for cookie decorating."

"*Your* payment?" she asked, taking it when I held it out. "I thought that was the free cookies."

A nod to the box. "And that."

"And this," she murmured, tapping a finger on the black cardboard.

"Yup."

Brows lifting, eyes curious, she opened the lid.

Then, lips curving, she glanced back at me. "Your payment?" she asked again. "Or my reward?"

I grinned. "Either." A beat. "Both."

She tugged out the plug—glittery and heavy and something I'd been dreaming about using on her from the moment I saw it in the store, from the moment she'd told me about her fantasy of me fucking her ass in the locker room.

"Yeah," she whispered, finger running over the bulb in a way that had my cock twitching. "It's both."

Cookies.

This woman.

And finding our way back to this bed.

Yeah.

It was definitely both.

Thirty-Eight

BILLIE ROSE

It was late, and I was trying to summon the energy to get out of bed.

Mostly because...

Yeah, Joel knew *exactly* how to fuck me.

With that plug and with his cock and with his fingers and teeth and tongue and lips and—

Well, he'd been inspired in a way that was...*damn.*

In a way that meant I was really, *really* glad I'd taken today off.

Especially because I'd been tempted to work every minute of today.

Tonight...was dinner with my parents.

The date my dad had picked. It had seemed so far off when I'd offered it up, but now that it was here, I was nearly desperate to find some excuse to delay.

I could.

I knew I could create a work crisis—especially with the

Winter Festival coming up—and my dad wouldn't blink at me putting them off.

Hell, he'd probably be glad to have his evening freed up, to have some bonus time to check some shit off his to do list.

But...Joel wouldn't let that slide.

He had tonight off, and he'd blocked the time for me and my parents and—

He wouldn't let me use work as an excuse.

That excuse didn't fly anymore.

And yup, that was me making a pouty face.

Mostly because he'd see right through any delay tactics, same as he'd seen through all of my shields and knew exactly how worried I was about my parents and this meeting. Hence, the orgasm distraction he'd given me, and the gentle way he'd held me, and—

Blegh.

I'd been full-on Band-aid a month ago. Ready to tear it off and deal with whatever blood or pus or platelets came rushing out.

Definitely not the analogy I wanted just before noon after my man had kept me up half the night, fucking me into glorious oblivion.

But...my mind was my mind.

I knew it would be okay.

Joel would be there, drowning out my father's frustrations, my mother's distance (preferably with orgasms). But my parents weren't his family, and I *knew* dinner wouldn't be nearly as nice as it had been with Joel's folks, and—

Warm arms tightening around me. "I can hear the spiraling from here, baby."

He was half sleepy—and half sleepy was far too awake for me and my shields—and all hard. The latter I could use to my advantage...and for my pleasure. Distraction. More orgasms.

Yup.

Scratch *that* onto my to do list.

But before I could climb him like a tree, Joel rolled me to my back and leaned down, pressed his forehead to mine, expression as gentle as his voice. "It'll be okay, sweetheart."

I snaked my palm down, wrapped my fingers around his cock, still stuck on distraction.

And proving this man got me, Joel snagged my hand, tugged it free, and lifted it to his mouth, kissing my palm.

"It'll be *okay,* baby."

He got me.

Too damned much.

I sucked in a breath, forgot his cock for the moment. "They're not like your family."

Fingers in my hair, pressing gently on my scalp. "You know I know that." A light tug on one curl. "And you need to know that the most important thing isn't that they're like my parents." I inhaled. "It's that I care about you and what we're making together and that I know—*know*—that it's good, baby."

He dropped his forehead to mine.

Stared into my eyes.

"It's *good.*"

I exhaled.

"So whatever comes our way, we'll weather it, yeah?"

I bit my lip, wanting to argue, wanting to focus on all the bad shit. But...I couldn't. Not with Joel on top of me, holding me, his green eyes warm on mine.

Because there was so much good.

And it was centered on the man I was falling for.

So, I didn't argue.

I just nodded and agreed. "Yeah, honey."

His mouth curved. "It'll be good," he murmured, kissing my forehead. "I promise."

That was a promise he couldn't keep.

He *couldn't.*

But...in that moment, I believed him.

———

Suffice to say, Luna's garlic bread didn't have the same calming qualities on my parents as it had before.

On me—nor on my parents.

And it wasn't because I'd spent my time in a flurry.

It was because I was off my game.

The moment my ass had hit the leather, my dad had started in on it. On *me*.

He'd heard about my day off.

And...he didn't approve.

I'd managed to distract him with a discussion of the festival and the progress we'd made with the outstanding insurance claims and revisiting his plans for the senior center.

Now...we were waiting to order entrees.

And he was being my dad.

And Joel...well, Joel was riding that razor's edge.

I could feel his fury bubbling beneath the surface and...I was trying to play mediator.

"And I'll tell you one thing," my dad was rambling. "If it's one thing this generation is lacking, it's work ethic."

Oh, for fuck's sake.

I bit back my sigh, studied the wine menu like it was the fucking Rosetta Stone. I'd passed on the waitress's first ask, but I was going to order some.

I needed it to get through this meal.

"And like I always tell BR," my dad rambled on, "she needs to work harder and—"

"No."

I blinked, losing sight of the cabernets for a heartbeat before my lids snapped open and I gaped up at Joel.

Then at my dad, whose brows were lifted, as he repeated, "No?"

"No," Joel said again. "Billie Rose is one of the hardest working people I know. Bar none," he said, slightly louder, talking over my dad when he began to say something.

Or protest.

Or express disbelief.

Or pass along his anger.

Who the fuck knew?

It might be all of them (likely). It might be none of them (less likely).

But Joel didn't give my dad a chance to express any of it. Instead, he pulled out his cell, hit a couple of buttons and then set it on speakerphone.

It rang once, twice—

"Hello, baby boy!"

"Mom," Joel said without preamble. "I've got a question for you."

A pause. Then, "Shoot."

"Rosie. Is she a harder worker?"

Not a pause.

Not at freaking *all*.

Joel barely had the words out before his mom said, "Absolutely."

"Thanks. Talk soon."

He hung up. Repeated the dialing and call on speaker phone sitch.

"Excuse—" my dad began, and he was impatient in the best of times. In *this,* he was bordering on murderous.

"Hey, son," *Joel's* dad answered.

"Billie Rose," Joel clipped. "What's her work ethic like?"

No hesitation again. Just, "One of the hardest workers I've ever come across."

"Right," Joel replied and repeated the goodbye, the hang-up.

And made another call.

My heart, meanwhile, was thudding in my chest.

"Yo, Joel," Axel said. "What's up?"

"You and Bailey there?"

A blip of quiet. "Yeah."

"Speakerphone."

Rustling, then another, "Yeah."

He asked about me again.

And, my heart still thundering, I listened as Bailey and Axel declared I was the hardest working person they knew. Then Dessie. Then Ryan and Fox and even Frank, the sheriff.

This exercise was ridiculous.

I mean...it shouldn't *mean* anything.

It shouldn't matter because I knew in my heart that I *did* work hard.

But it did.

Because the people that Joel was calling were people who mattered to me and they weren't even hesitating in taking my back, without even knowing why the hell that Joel was asking such a random question. About something important to me, critically important because I'd spent so long with my dad in my head and my mom was sitting there totally disengaged from the world around her, it wasn't an easy thing for me to accept.

I always felt the need to do more.

Because maybe then they would see.

Because maybe then I'd be enough for them.

But I was beginning to understand, even with the crumbs of love and acceptance, I would *never* be enough for them. And... maybe I needed to find that place of being enough in myself. Look to Joel and my friends when I wasn't feeling it, wasn't trusting it.

But...maybe I needed to look at myself and...

Be happy.

In inhaled deeply just as Joel asked sharply, his cell clattering to the table, "Do I need to go on?"

My dad bristled even as my mom sat there, not touching her garlic bread, staring at her plate, not seeming to hear the conversations. I waited for implosion as I watched the vein throb in his temple.

"Boy—" he began.

"I stopped being a *boy* a long time ago," Joel said softly. Softly, but firmly, and my heart was still thundering, still pounding against my ribcage. Because Joel was right. Sitting there with his arm around me, his jaw tight, and his tone firm, he was very far from a boy.

He was a man.

A good one.

Who...wasn't going to sit there and let me be a punching bag.

Even if I kept trying to make myself one.

"Kids these days don't respect—"

"Respect is earned."

I felt my mouth drop open.

Because I'd been thinking the same thing.

Only, it hadn't come from my mouth.

Nor from Joel's.

It had come...

From my mother's.

There were four of us at that table, but now three of us had turned to my mom and were staring at her with our mouths dropped open.

For me, it was because I'd never heard that tone from her before.

And I'd never seen her look like that before.

And I'd never watched her face change like that—never witnessed the determination that made my breath catch as it bled across her features.

"Respect is earned, John," she sort of repeated, turning toward my dad, fixing him with a look that made me question every single thing I thought I'd known about their relationship.

It was easy to focus on my dad.

He was loud and brusque, and it wasn't difficult to know exactly what he was thinking.

Because he was saying it.

But my mom wasn't.

I *never* knew where she stood.

This was...

A growl rumbled up in my dad's throat, but it didn't have time to escape because my mom reached over, placed her hand on his, and squeezed lightly. "John."

Joel had fallen quiet next to me, but that movement, my mom warning my dad, had him moving again, tugging me a little closer, his fingers trailing lightly over my arm. "She's right," he said, not looking away from my parents. "Respect is earned, and I know that I'm new in Rosie's life, but I've seen in how you interact with her, how it doesn't make her happy. And it sure as fuck doesn't make *me* happy." A poignant pause. "So, I'm not going to let it happen."

I don't know what I'd expected from him taking my back.

Flipping the table and checking my dad to the ground.

Dishing out a beatdown with those enormous fists.

Getting into a shit-talking match up in the middle of Luna's.

I certainly didn't expect a series of phone calls and quiet but firm words.

A clear declaration.

I'm not going to let it happen.

And my mom was engaged in the conversation? Softly chastising my dad?

That was...just a total mind fuck.

That was...why couldn't I just sit there and take it.

Not like I always did.

I couldn't lock down, buckle in, keep my gaze pointed ahead and move forward, ignoring all the old and new hurts. "I can't keep doing this, dad," I whispered. "I can't keep doing this with *you*."

He'd opened his mouth, eyes flashing, and I braced.

But then my mom's hand flexed on his, cutting him off. "I know, sweetie. I know you can't."

She was looking at me.

Seeing me.

And...I wanted to grab on to that, to pull it close, and delve into that feeling.

But I didn't trust it. I didn't even know how to comprehend it.

Sweetie.

Looking at me.

Looking at me.

"Umm," I whispered.

She glanced away. That bubble in my belly started to pop.

Joel's hand tightened on my waist. "What kind of wine do you want, baby?"

Whiplash.

Again.

My neck was going to hurt tomorrow from all the rapid changes in direction.

"Umm," I whispered again.

His fingers tightened slightly. "What wine do you want, Rosie baby?"

I bit my lip, nodded, knew I'd need time to process this later, and focused on the menu again. "The Napa Valley."

Soft eyes. "Then get the Napa Valley, sweetheart."

"Right," I said, still whispering.

A kiss to my temple. "Right," he whispered back.

"Rosie."

It wasn't a request for my attention, and it wasn't from Joel.

It was shocking as shit...because it was coming from my mom again.

I glanced over at her, saw something fluttering in her eyes, something that was so foreign I couldn't even begin to focus on it. Her face went gentle, and she nodded. "Yes. *Rosie.*"

Then she went back to looking at her menu, to existing in her own world.

Something Joel noticed, too, if his staying close and tense was any indication.

Waiting for my dad to take advantage of my mom checking out again.

But, shocking as shit, he didn't.

He just looked down at his menu too, and when the waitress —Gabi—came by the table, he ordered a beer. I ordered my wine. Joel ordered a beer. My mom stuck with water.

And then...we had dinner.

It was quiet and awkward and not at all like any other family dinner I'd ever had.

It definitely wasn't like dinner with Joel's family.

Not at *all*.

But...it wasn't bad.

And I thought that for me, for us, for this moment, it was better than anything I could have ever hoped for.

THIRTY-NINE

JOEL

"And then we looked at each other and were in perfect kismet."

I rolled my eyes at Fox, who was trying to charm my woman, and standing too damned close to *my* woman, and talking too damned much to *my* woman.

"Kismet?" Billie giggled.

A solemn nod from my annoying teammate.

Who'd just gotten word to pack his bags because he was taking his turn with the Gold.

He'd already had a few stints with the NHL team, and things were looking good for his progress to stay in the big leagues permanently.

It wouldn't be long now.

We might get him back, at least for a few more games.

But it wouldn't be permanent.

He was our team's leading goal-scorer, a pain in the ass on the ice (for our opponents), and he lightened the locker room.

Just like he was lightening *this* situation.

Me. Billie Rose. Ryan. Dessie. Fox. A couple of my teammates.

All sitting in a booth at Monroe's.

The last time I'd been here, Billie Rose's thigh pressed to mine, I hadn't understood what I was feeling.

Now...I was all in.

And I really didn't like that Fox was pressed to her other side, making her laugh and smile and—

"You're gone, man."

Ryan's quiet words had my gaze jerking from Fox and Billie to my teammate, who was smirking at me.

"What are you talking about?"

"The mayor." Ry grinned. "You. Both of you are fucking gone for each other."

"I—" After the texting incident, I didn't love discussing this with my teammates. I wanted more time with Billie, more time to continue building us.

But...it wasn't like my feelings weren't obvious.

Which was why I just lifted my brows, shrugged. "Yeah. What about it?"

Ryan lifted his hands in surrender. "Don't get pissed at the single man. I'm just pointing out the truth."

"That I like, Billie Rose?"

Ryan nodded.

"Congrats, Sherlock," I muttered.

Laughter in his words. "In fairness, I've also deduced that Billie likes you back." A pause. "Despite your lack of text game."

I'd been lifting my beer to take a sip, but that dry insult had me inhaling sharply, nearly snorting up my beer. "Asshole," I grumbled.

He laughed.

But I didn't dump my beer in his lap, or over his head— mostly because that would be a waste of perfectly good beer, but also because the waitress came over right then, another glass of the hoppy stuff in her hand.

She plunked it on the table, smiled proudly. "For the mayor."

Billie had looked up at the sound of the glass on the table, and I watched her smile change when her gaze hit the glass of beer.

Turn *mayor*-like.

Her mask slipped back into place.

"Thanks, Becky," she said. "How's Solomon?"

And just like that, we were all listening to River's Bend's mayor talking to her compatriots, hearing a complaint about the city's preschool, brainstorming a solution to that issue, and making a promise to sort it.

I knew it wasn't an empty one.

Because I knew Billie Rose.

Just like Becky knew her well enough to understand that same fact. Billie Rose would take care of the problem at the preschool. And that was why Becky immediately relaxed and walked away with a smile on her face.

And left the beer.

Fox slid it closer to her. "Your spoils, lady mayor," he said, all gallant idiot.

Right up there with *kismet.*

Billie nodded her thanks but didn't pick up the beer. "Tell me more about this *perfect kismet*," she said instead.

"Well then, your man and I were in *perfect kismet* because we both closed in on that fucker and took him right down—"

I really didn't need to hear Fox relive the hit we'd dished out last night.

It was a good one, and the fucker on the other team deserved it—namely because he'd been trying to fuck with our goalie. But I'd heard this retelling in the locker room and on the bus and the hit got more grandiose with each iteration. I didn't need to hear it again.

I nudged Ryan. "Let me out, yeah?"

Ryan's brows snapped together, but he wasn't a man of many words (when he wasn't giving me shit, anyway), so he slid out of the booth.

I went to the bar.

A few minutes later, I came back to the table, saw Ryan had dragged a chair over, leaving my spot next to Billie vacant, and thus ending (also thank fuck) our thigh-to-thigh connection. I slid the glass of Napa Valley in front of her, dragged the beer over to my spot, and shifted so I could start to scoot in next to her.

Not realizing she'd frozen, eyes wide.

"What's this?"

For a second, I didn't process the question.

"What's that, baby?" I asked, pausing in the booth's opening, my eyes flicking to hers, then down to the glass of wine I'd bought for her. "It's Napa Valley."

She sucked in a breath. "But..."

I leaned close. "No more beer, baby."

Her air whooshed out in a hiss.

Then she was shoving past me, darting out of the booth, slipping through the crowded floor of Monroe's, and dashing out of sight.

What the—

I didn't wait to see if the guys were just as dumbstruck, didn't wait to see if they'd even noticed. I just took off after my woman, bumping into people on the floor, caching a sight of blond curls just as they disappeared through the back door.

I slammed into the metal latch, shoved the wooden panel wide...and paused.

Breathed.

Because she'd stopped near the gazebo, wrapped her arms around it and rested her head on the wood.

Then I moved to her.

"Baby," I whispered, tugging her away from the gazebo, wrapping my arms around her. "What's going on?"

Silence. Long enough for worry to gather at the base of my spine.

Then, "You bought me wine."

I paused again. Because... "Yeah, baby, I did."

"Why?"

Okaaay.

A breath in. An exhale.

Why were we covering this again? I knew her. I wanted to take care of her.

That was what boyfriends did.

"You already know the answer to that," I whispered.

Another breath in. Another exhale, her nails digging into the column. "Do I?"

"Baby." I cupped her cheek. "You know the answer is because you like wine and hate beer."

Earnest blue eyes on mine. "That's why."

A statement. Not a question. And yet...it *was* a question.

"Yes."

Her throat worked, mouth pressing together for a moment before she whispered, "But you looked horrified."

I frowned. "What are you talking about, sweetheart?"

She bit her bottom lip, released it. Then shook her head. "It doesn't matter."

Right. I wasn't falling for that shit.

I cupped her jaw, tilted her head up. "It matters."

"I—"

"It *matters.*"

"Forget me," she said. "I'm just tired and emotional and—" A sharp shake of her head. "Forget me."

I laughed. "Right. Like that's ever going to happen."

Silence. Then, "But you did."

Said so quietly I almost didn't hear it.

But I *did* hear it.

"What?"

A breath, her voice marginally louder. "You forgot me."

What the fuck?

Because...*what the fuck?*

This woman had been on my mind for *years.*

Then, since that was really the only natural response, I repeated it out loud, "What the fuck?"

"That first time we were together," she whispered. "I thought you were awake. Thought you'd remember it was me you were with." A shaking breath. "But you didn't." Another. "You gave me an orgasm that shook me to my core, and then you looked up at me with shock and disgust on your face."

Fuck.

Fuck.

"Baby—"

"It's okay," she said softly. "I've gotten that before. A lot of times, actually." A shrug. "I get it. I'm a woman who men don't like that way—"

"*Bullshit.*"

She kept talking. "I'm a lot to handle and we're in a good place now and I don't want to go backward and mess this up. Just ignore me—"

I gripped her shoulders when she would have turned away, started back for the bar, seeing this for what it was.

Another shield.

Another wall between us.

Another layer to peel back.

I cupped her cheek. "When are you going to see?"

She stared up at me with wide eyes. "See what?"

I stepped closer. "That you can run, but I'm always going to come after you."

"Wh-what?"

"That you can push me away, but I'm still going to always want you."

"Joel," she whispered.

"That I've dreamed of you, wanted you, *liked* you for so damned long I can't think of a moment over the last years where you haven't shaded every thought."

Her mouth dropped open.

"I knew it was you that first morning and I *was* disgusted—"

She flinched, but I powered on.

She had to know, had to understand.

"At *myself*, Rosie baby. Because I'd gotten drunk and couldn't remember everything we'd done and that's not me, not the way I treat women." I brushed my knuckles along her cheek. "And I never wanted to be in a position to make you feel uncomfortable or to hurt you or to make it bad for you or—"

A tear slid from the corner of her eye. "Honey," she whispered.

She had to know.

Had to know.

"You are fucking *perfect*, baby. Perfect for me. Perfect for my life. I couldn't forget you years ago, and I can't forget you now."

"Because you want me," she murmured.

"Yes."

"You like *all* of me."

I nodded. "Yes, baby."

"I..." She bit her lip again. "I'm not sure I believe that right now."

"That's okay," I told her. "We have time."

Her bottom lip trembled, and I watched as what I was saying finally sank in and her face changed, going soft, her body relaxing against mine. She was processing and it wasn't all there yet, but we were making progress and she at least *heard* what I was telling her.

This woman.

Layers upon layers.

I wanted to peel them away, memorize every detail as they were revealed.

I wanted to know everyone who had hurt her, wanted to understand why what I was telling her was so hard for her to believe.

But even if I *could* understand why she didn't believe me, and even if I kept telling her what I felt, she wasn't going to believe it.

Not right then.

Not just with words.

She needed time.

And actions.

And *time.*

So, I held her close, and I told her again, "We have time."

And she held me back.

And...she proved she knew me too.

Because long moments later, she shifted back, fingers gazing my beard as she stared into my eyes, "But you're also going to keep showing me too, aren't you?"

I grinned, pressed my mouth to hers.

And figured that was answer enough.

FORTY

BILLIE ROSE

We were at the trailer.

It was weeks after Joel had made that promise to prove his feelings to me.

And...he was.

He was thoughtful and kind and *Joel*. And we were us. And...that never seemed to change.

No matter how cranky I was or how many hours I worked or how many boxes of washi tape he discovered in my office.

He didn't care if people needed my time.

He'd survived another dinner with my parents (and so had I, especially since my dad had been well behaved for the most part).

He did his job. I did mine.

We went on dates. We fucked and slept together afterward.

We were progressing.

We were boyfriend and girlfriend...and it was good. *Really* good.

Now—today—Joel's game was starting in just over an hour and we'd been holed up in my office for a while now.

Mostly because when I'd been getting ready to meet him at the rink, to catch up and grab some food before he had to play that evening, my assistant had popped her head into my office and requested I review a few contracts and sign off on some documents before I left. Which meant my workday hadn't been over. Instead, I'd needed to sit down at my computer and focus. Luckily, I was learned that Joel was flexible and patient. He'd come over and chilled in my space, relaxing on the couch until he needed to walk back across the lot to play some hockey.

I'd gotten Greek food delivered. We'd eaten on my lumpy couch.

It wasn't quite the same as an actual date.

But it was good—the food *and* the time together.

Because it was us, and Joel didn't seem to care that I was working while he hung out.

Then again, he never did. He was never annoyed or frustrated or put out or mean. I didn't need to walk on eggshells or pretend to be someone else to make him happy.

I could be me.

And he was just…Joel.

And that was pretty fucking great.

Plus, now I was conveniently close to the rink where I was going to get to watch some hockey.

In my new Rush jersey.

Something he'd appreciated me showing him that morning if him snagging my wrist and tugging me into bed after I'd walked out of the closet in it—and only *it*—was any indication.

It had ended up in a puddle on the floor.

But—good news—I'd been naked beneath that jersey. And being naked had meant that I'd reaped some serious benefits.

And—more good news—hockey jerseys didn't really wrinkle, so when I'd put it on after Joel had rocked my world in bed, it hadn't looked any worse for wear.

I'd just been a hockey fan living in a town that had begun to live and breathe for its team.

Just a hockey fan who was dating one of the sexiest players on the team.

Smiling, I saved the documents I'd been working on, made certain they were sent off to the proper recipients and then pushed back from my desk to see Joel sitting on my couch, looking through my planner—something that was nearly as terrifying as him looking through my underwear drawer.

Lie.

It was significantly *more* terrifying than him looking through my underwear.

Looking through my underwear would most likely lead to fucking.

And fucking was great. It was awesome. It wasn't scary at all.

My planning, on the other hand, was light and unimportant, but it also...wasn't.

It was my *life* he was casually flipping through—every single day of my existence, every insignificant—and boring to him, but critical to me—detail.

"What are you doing?" I asked softly.

He glanced up, lips curving. "Checking in on my woman."

I narrowed my eyes, worry gnawing at my belly, and rose from my chair, rounding the desk, but when I would have nudged his feet aside and sat in my visitor chair, he set the planner on the couch next to him, captured my hand, and tugged me down onto his lap.

"Mmm," he murmured, burying his face in my throat.

Frisky time in my office.

Okay, now *that* was something I could get behind.

As in, he could get behind me.

Heh.

Because it had been far too long since we'd fucked. Hours even.

Also, *heh.*

But also...curiosity was bubbling up in my belly and the man had fucked me well enough that morning that I could temper my need for him (for the moment...and also because he had to play hockey and do it well in less than an hour). So, instead of jumping him, I asked, "Why are you checking up on me?"

A shrug. His lips pressing to my skin. His tongue flicking out to taste me.

My fingers slid into his hair, tightened.

But just as things were getting good, his head popped up, and he smiled at me, brushing back a few unruly curls from my face. "Because you work too hard."

My brows lifted at that, but where, once, that might have made me insecure, might have sent me spiraling, today I just smiled and said, "You *like* me working hard, remember?"

His arms tightened around me, and his mouth took mine in a way that was intentionally distracting (though I didn't care). Not even when he pulled back, said, "I do. I *do*, baby."

Also, something that I didn't really care about—mostly because I *knew* it was true and because I was less concerned with his words and more focused on how to fuck him while saving his energy so he could play hockey in a less than an hour.

Especially when he kissed me *again*, not breaking away until we were both breathing heavy.

I could definitely fuck him. I'd do all the work and he could relax back and enjoy the process. Or if he took over—as was likely — I'd just...call it a pregame warmup. Yup. Good plan. *Good* pl—

"I've just decided that sometimes I need to take evasive maneuvers to make sure I get my time, too."

"Evasive?" I frowned, blinking a few times, mostly because my mind was in sexual fantasy land before his words processed.

Evasive maneuvers.

Evasive.

With...my planner.

My *planner.*

Eek!

I lurched for my precious baby. "What did you do?"

His hands slid up—traveling along several (well, *two*) very nice places—but I wasn't going to be distracted from the matter at hand.

Not even when he brushed my nipples, rolled them gently between thumb and forefinger.

My planner!

The man had done something to my planner, and that was sacrilegious in the most dangerous of ways.

Focusing—*somehow*—I knocked his hands away and snagged my precious, prepared to go full-on Mayor-in-a-Rant Mode if he'd ruined my glorious, *glorious* plans.

But...then I saw it.

I'd noticed him carrying in a small black box earlier—thinner and flatter than the box he'd given me with the plug a while back. I'd even noticed that he'd set the lid on my desk, leaving the box itself open for me to see the contents inside.

But I'd been distracted by contracts.

And then my man.

And then...my planner.

I'd missed that *inside* the thin, black box was a stack of sticker sheets.

Now I'd seen them, and I leaned closer, and I...sucked in a breath.

Because those stickers...

Hell, if they didn't have me falling in love with Joel.

Right there and then.

I'd been sliding that way, teetering on the precipice, wanting to believe in us, in the feeling in my heart, but also worried it would all change and go wrong and unwilling to let that last bit of resistance go. Because if I put myself out there and his feelings changed...

Devastating.

But one look at the contents of that box and I dropped head-first into the feeling, accepted my love for this man as it fused itself directly to my soul.

I *loved* this man.

Because of who he was.

Because of how he treated me.

Because of what was *in* the box.

One sticker was missing from the top sheet, and it was missing—I saw now—because he'd stuck it in my planner, placed it on my schedule of events for that day. He'd positioned it right in the time slot I'd blocked for the game, then had used my pen to draw an arrow down through midnight, blocking off our time together like I normally would.

But it wasn't the arrow he'd drawn (in proper matching ink), or even the placement of the sticker that sent me tumbling head-first into love with Joel.

It was what was *on* the stickers that got me.

A little cartoon image of a hockey player holding a woman.

A hockey player that looked like Joel. A woman who looked like me.

"My sister sent me a listing on Etsy for something she wanted for her birthday and the stickers happened to come up," he said like it was no big deal. "I thought you'd like them for your planning stuff, so I had the artist put something together."

I inhaled again. Sharply.

And my exhale was shaky.

Mostly because the little drawing sent my heart thudding, made my lungs work hard, made it so I felt like I couldn't get enough air.

Because...

Goddamn.

This was *such* a small thing—for him to get some stickers made for me. But also...it was such a thoughtful thing. Mostly because it showed exactly how well he knew me.

The small things.

The day-to-day stuff.

That was the most important.

I felt that realization deep in my soul, knew he'd shown me *I* was important time and time again.

Important to *him*.

He showed he paid attention to me.

He showed he never found me lacking or annoying or someone he wanted to avoid—even if his pregame plans were shifted around because I needed to look at contracts.

"Joel," I whispered.

He touched my cheek, gave me those deep green eyes. "Yeah, Rosie baby?"

"I—"

Rosie baby.

My words stoppered up in my throat even as I wanted to bare it all, as I wanted to tell him exactly what he meant to me, exactly what I'd realized and how safe he'd made me.

But...I also wanted to sit in this moment, to *feel* what he'd made me feel.

To *bask* in it.

To let it curl up in my heart, expand in my middle, to wrap me up in its warmth.

To love him, all by myself, just for a little bit.

He brushed his knuckles over my cheek. "What were you gonna say, baby?"

I loved him.

That felt...great.

Perfect.

And because of that, I needed to find a perfect way to tell him.

So, I held in the urge to blurt out my feelings to him, smoothed my hand over the bristles of his beard, and teased, "You had to block yourself *all* the way to midnight?"

His mouth curved, green eyes dancing. "Not going to just eleven-thirty, Rosie baby."

"No"—I brushed my mouth over his—"I guess you wouldn't."

That brush turned into more.

Into something that distracted me from planners and stickers and fancy declarations.

Into something that distracted us both from anything except getting naked...at least until Fox came to the trailer and pounded on my office door and Joel had to scramble to get dressed and rush over to the rink.

I was in less of a hurry—mostly because I was practically boneless with pleasure.

Luckily, Joel hadn't been.

He hadn't...well...he gotten to that point yet.

But he'd had his pregame warmup.

He just...also had plenty of pent-up energy to work off on the ice.

Bonus?

Heh.

I'd make it up to my poor, abused hockey player boyfriend later.

FORTY-ONE

JOEL

Billie Rose sighed, rolled over in my arms, the hem of the Rush jersey riding high on her thighs, giving me a glimpse of the lush curves of her ass, and yeah, this was exactly where I wanted to be.

Her body pressed to mine.

My hands on her naked skin.

Luckily, she seemed to feel the same.

How did I know this? Because she was in my bed without any underwear on, that jersey with my last name and number clinging to the curves of her body.

I'd seen it that morning.

But tonight's repeat performance?

Chef's kiss.

I was a genius asking her to put it back on. Totally.

I grinned at the ceiling, knowing I was an idiot, but not giving a fuck because we were happy.

And we were here in this place.

And it was great.

"Joel?" she murmured, burying her face in my throat.

"Yeah, baby?"

"Thanks for a good night," she whispered on a yawn, pressing a kiss to my jaw.

Yeah. *This* was exactly where I wanted to be.

"Anytime." I smoothed one hand over her curls, sat in the silence for a moment before asking, "Rosie?"

"Mmm?" A lazy question.

"How was the rest of your night before the game?" I asked softly, stroking through those silky curls.

"*Mmm.*" She burrowed closer.

I grinned, taking that answer for what it was, and kept my hand on her ass, but used my other to tug the blankets up and over us. She didn't move, probably because she was mellow and quiet and sated.

I was sated...sort of. I was here with her and that was great. That was perfect.

But *she'd* gotten off before the game. *I* hadn't before Fox had barged into the trailer and reminded me of the time and I'd had to get dressed, only a handful of strokes away from coming in Billie's tight pussy. And while I appreciated the reminder—since I sure as shit hadn't been thinking about hockey right then—I hadn't enjoyed spending the game in a state of chub.

Now it was after the game and I'd just fucked my woman and she was in my arms, her breathing relaxed, slowing, her mind heading for sleep. I was relaxed, too, but only semi-sated, mostly because I was still riding that post-game high.

In fact, I was ready for another round, eager to expend the rest of my energy, but when I swept my fingers between her thighs, brushed her clit, my Rosie baby sharply smacked my arm.

"I will cut off your fingers if you try that, buster."

Grinning, I held her closer. "Buster?"

More nuzzling. Her lips hitting my throat. "Shut up."

"I will." A beat. "But *buster?*"

A huffed out laugh before she snuggled closer, slinging her arm over my belly. "Mmm-hmm. *Buster.*"

I grinned again, allowed my body to relax, my thoughts to start wandering. They took their cue and set to drifting, set to wondering, and because I was relaxed and in my happy place, my woman curled up to me, I ended up blurting out a question I'd been thinking for weeks, "When are we going to move the rest of your stuff in, baby?"

Stiff.

All that sated, relaxed woman gone.

"What?" she whispered, pressing a palm to my chest, and pushing up, looking down at me with wide eyes. "What are you talking about?"

"I'm talking about you living here," I said. "With me," I added, just in case her swirling mind wasn't clear on that.

Wide, wide eyes. "Um..."

"We're good together," I told her. "And you're here every night, anyway." And I wanted her off that couch. And here. *Every* night. And in my house after it was rebuilt, which should be in just a few more months.

"I—" She bit her lip. "What are you saying exactly, honey?"

"Baby." I smothered a laugh. "I want you to move into my apartment with me."

The surprise didn't fade. "I—" A breath. "*Really?*"

Now I couldn't smother the laugh. "Really, baby."

She didn't join me in that, just asked, "What if you get tired of me?"

Christ.

"Baby," I began.

"Or what if you need your space?"

"*Baby.*"

"Or what if you want to, I don't know," she whispered, "have the guys over or jerk off or get drunk or—"

I rolled us, pinned her lower body with mine, and cupped

her cheek, getting those pretty blue eyes focused on mine. "If I want the guys over, I'll invite them—though I'll tell you, I see their dumb faces five or six times a week, so it's unlikely I'll want to see them even more often." She bit her lip again. "And if they *do* come over, you can hang with us or go meet up with Dessie or, if you want to be here by yourself, the boys and I can go somewhere else." I dropped my forehead to hers, freed that lip. "And baby, I like a beer, but I'm not big on getting drunk. Not anymore, anyway. But if I'm in a mood to get blitzed, I'm gonna do it with you. Because"—I nipped her reddened bottom lip— "if the sex is this good when we're sober, then imagine what it'll be like when we're drunk."

Her exhale was shaky.

"Also, my Rosie baby, I think I've made it clear that I'd much rather have your hand on my cock than my own."

"Joel," she whispered.

"*And* I don't want space. I want *more* time. I want every spare second of the day you'll give me."

A long, long silence.

"Oh." A beat. "Really?"

I laughed again. "Yeah, baby. *Really.*"

Silence. For long enough that I felt nerves begin to prickle along my spine.

Maybe she wasn't ready for this yet.

Maybe I was pushing too fast, and this was too big of a step.

"I—" Her arm collapsed, and she dropped against my chest, burrowing her face into me, holding me close and tight. "*Joel.*"

The tension slid away, and I wrapped my arms around her, held her just as tightly back. "Is that a yes, baby?"

Silence.

But not long for the nerves to creep back in this time.

Mostly because her head popped up, and she met my stare. "It's a yes." She bit her lip again, released it. "I mean, it's a yes and I'm freaking out a bit and I'm still not a hundred percent sure that you really want this, but...it's an excited, wholehearted *yes*," she whispered. Then her eyes sparkled. "Mostly because we're already doing it."

I brushed back her curls. "Yes, baby, we are." I grinned. "Wondered when you'd realize that."

A breath, her nose wrinkling. "Yeah, yeah. Take advantage of the workaholic who doesn't recognize the machinations of her man."

"You like when I take advantage of you."

"I..." A grin. "I do, honey." A breath, her expression growing serious. "And I like you and I really like what we're building... even if it still freaks me out sometimes."

"Billie."

"I'm good."

I touched her cheek. "If it's too soon—"

"It's not." And then before I could say anything else, my woman—my strong, smart, capable woman shook off her worry and fell back onto what we both knew. Snark and sarcasm and love. "Also, note that my agreement mostly comes because your mattress is a hell of a lot better than my couch."

I chuckled. "That much is true."

She settled back down on my chest, holding me close, her fingers drifting in random patterns on my skin.

We settled.

In this bed.

In each other.

Then again, we'd been doing that for a while, hadn't we?

Drifting toward friendship, toward companionship. Now toward *more*.

Thank fuck.

I needed this woman in my life.

Forever.

Relaxing back into the mattress, I let my eyes slide closed, let sleep approach.

"Does this mean you'll clear out space for my washi tape?"

My lids flew open.

And...forget sleep.

We needed to celebrate this.

Laughter bubbled up in my chest, boiled over. "Yeah, baby," I said, rolling us, tugging up the hem of the jersey, yanking it over her head.

It ended up on the floor.

But I was too busy to worry about its final destination.

Not when I was welcoming my woman home.

And for the record, I made room for her stickers and planners too.

Forty-Two

BILLIE ROSE

I tugged at the handle of Joel's—now *our*—front door, my planner pack tucked under one arm, my phone with my calendar app open held tight in my hand.

A roll of washi tape on my thumb.

My foot needing to join in on the action of opening Joel's front door.

I had a meeting coming up in a few minutes, but I was going to take it in my office—yup, *my* office.

Joel had cleared out the den of his—*our*—apartment, and he'd dedicated that space as my office.

It was just a room, and a small one at that. The entire apartment was just a temporary space to take residence in until his house was finished being built. But he'd made the room beautiful for me. A sleek wooden bookcase painted a pale lilac and taking up one wall. A large desk to hold my computer. Another huge desk placed with a few feet behind it so I could just turn from my computer and access the other one, use the huge flat top to really spread out and do my planning.

I'd just finished placing all my knickknacks perfectly on the bookshelf and tucking a cozy reading chair in one corner of the room.

It was...perfect and mine and the most peaceful space I'd ever had.

Even before I'd lived in one room in a trailer, back when I'd had my own apartment, I'd never had a space like this.

Home.

But then again...anything with Joel was home.

We had a system and a schedule and every moment I spent with him was better than the last.

I had a boyfriend.

And he hadn't run screaming.

He'd doubled down, and I'd moved in a week ago and we were doing *this*.

And...I was happy.

With my office and my boyfriend and my copious amounts of washi tape.

Grinning to myself, I nudged the door wide enough to finish opening it with my hip, revealing a beautiful blonde woman, her hair pulled back into an effortless ponytail, her makeup absolutely flawless—perfect contour, perfect highlights, brows on fleek. Tits. Ass. In between.

This woman had it *all*.

But—I smiled to myself—so did I.

A man.

A life that was filled with work and planning and washi.

More peace than I'd had. Ever.

Finally, *finally*, I wasn't measuring myself against anyone else, wasn't thinking about how I was going to fuck things up. Wasn't thinking that Joel was going to look at me, see things he didn't like, and toss me aside.

Find me lacking.

I was me and I was great and—

That was enough.

Even in the face of this woman and her beauty and all that flawless hair and makeup and her gorgeous clothes.

"Can I help you?" I asked, catching the door with my hip so it didn't shut on her.

"I—" She'd been smiling, but one look at me had her grin fading, her expression changing from excited to worried. "Umm..."

Concern immediately took over, my mayor instincts prickling.

"Are you okay?" I asked, shifting my burden, and reaching a hand out toward her.

She immediately scooted back a step. "I'm—" A shake of her head. "Does Joel live here?"

Suddenly there was a snake coiling in my belly, and it was ready to strike.

"Um, yeah," I whispered, tempering that, containing it. "Joel lives here."

"Is he...home?"

No. He wasn't home.

He was at practice.

The only reason *I* was at home at a two o'clock on a weekday afternoon was because I had this home office. Well, that and because the Civic Center was complete, and I'd let the trailer go.

And I had the home office.

I had my *home*...with a beautiful woman standing at the front door.

"He's not here right now," I said softly.

"Oh." A long, *long* pause. "Do you..." She glanced over her shoulder like Joel was going to appear behind her. "Um...do you know when he'll be back?"

Okay, this was weird.

That snack flexed in my belly.

"Not for a couple of hours," I told her. "Did you want to, um, leave him a note or something?"

She bit her lip but didn't answer.

Off. My spidey senses were prickling because this was *off* and wrong and...that snake in my belly was slowly tightening, tensing, readying itself to strike.

But I was the mayor of a small town.

I was friendly by default.

"I'm Billie Rose," I said, extending my mostly free hand again, the roll of washi still dangling around my thumb.

That plump bottom lip was released, and she stepped forward, shook my hand. "Willow."

Her skin was like *silk*.

And she smelled nice.

And, just a pace away, she was even more beautiful.

Did the woman even have pores?

She looked like one of those Facebook ad videos for a fancy foundation.

"Nice to meet you," I said, ignoring that and falling back onto my manners.

An awkward pause. "Nice to meet you, too."

Silence fell between us again.

Then manners took over again.

And later...I'd really—*really*—wish they hadn't.

Later, I wished I'd slammed the door, gone back to my brand-new office, blew off my meeting, and got lost in my planner stuff.

But I had manners, and I was the mayor of River's Bend. So, I let them loose.

"How do you know Joel?"

That this was fine.

Everything was fine.

Until I heard the beautiful woman's answer.

"I'm Joel's wife."

———

EEK! I hope you love Joel and Billie Rose as much as I do! The next book in their Rush Hockey trilogy is ALL'S FAIR IN PUCKS AND WAR. **I'd wanted her from the first moment I'd seen her. But now...she hated me.**

CLICK HERE TO READ ALL'S FAIR IN PUCKS AND WAR NOW>

And if you enjoyed LOVE, PUCKS, AND OTHER STORIES, you'll love the sexy, sweet, and close-knit Breakers Hockey crew. The first book in the series, BROKEN, is now live!

It is sexy, hot, adorable and such a fun read. You will not be able to put this down!" —Amazon Reviewer

———

I so appreciate your help in spreading the word about my books, including sharing with friends! Please leave a review on your favorite book site!

You can also join my Facebook group, the Fabinators, for exclusive giveaways and sneak peeks of future books.

SIGN UP FOR ELISE FABER'S NEWSLETTER HERE:
https://www.elisefaber.com/newsletter

Hate missing Elise's new releases? Love contests, exclusive excerpts and giveaways?

Then signup for Elise's newsletter here!

www.elisefaber.com/newsletter

And join Elise's fan group, the Fabinators (https://www.facebook.com/groups/fabinators) for insider information, sneak peaks at new releases, and fun freebies! Hope to see you there!

Rush Hockey

Big Puck Energy
Filthy Puckboy
So Pucking Over It
Love, Pucks, and Other Stories
All's Fair in Pucks and War

ALSO BY ELISE FABER

Breakout

Checked

Coasting

Centered

Charging

Caged

Crashed

A Gold Christmas

Cycled

Caught

Cap

Covered

Breakers Hockey (all stand alone)

<u>Broken</u>

<u>Boldly</u>

<u>Breathless</u>

<u>Ballsy</u>

Rush Hockey

Big Puck Energy

Filthy Puckboy

So Pucking Over It

Love, Pucks, and Other Stories

Love, Action, Camera (all stand alone)

Dotted Line

Action Shot

Close-Up

End Scene

Meet Cute

Love After Midnight (all stand alone)

Rum And Notes

Virgin Daiquiri

On The Rocks

Sex On The Seats

Life Sucks Series (all stand alone)

Train Wreck

Hot Mess

Dumpster Fire

Clusterf*@k

FUBAR

Roosevelt Ranch Series (all stand alone, series complete)

Disaster at Roosevelt Ranch

Heartbreak at Roosevelt Ranch

Collision at Roosevelt Ranch

Regret at Roosevelt Ranch

Desire at Roosevelt Ranch

Phoenix Series (read in order)

Phoenix Rising

Dark Phoenix

Phoenix Freed

Phoenix: LexTal Chronicles **(rereleasing soon, stand alone, Phoenix world)**

From Ashes

In Flames

To Smoke

KTS Series (all stand alone, series complete)

Riding The Edge

Crossing The Line

Leveling The Field

Scorching The Earth

Cocky Heroes World

Tattooed Troublemaker

ABOUT THE AUTHOR

USA Today bestselling author, Elise Faber, loves chocolate, Star Wars, Harry Potter, and hockey (the order depending on the day and how well her team -- the Sharks! -- are playing). She and her husband also play as much hockey as they can squeeze into their schedules, so much so that their typical date night is spent on the ice. Elise is the mom to two exuberant boys and lives in Northern California. Connect with her in her Facebook group, the Fabinators or find more information about her books at www.elisefaber.com.

f facebook.com/elisefaberauthor

a amazon.com/author/elisefaber

BB bookbub.com/profile/elise-faber

O instagram.com/elisefaber

d tiktok.com/@elisefaberauthor

g goodreads.com/elisefaber